HiTCHERS

WiLL McINTOSh

NIGHT SHADE BOOKS
SAN FRANCISCO

First Edition

ISBN: 978-1-59780-335-9

Night Shade Books
http://www.nightshadebooks.com

For my grandparents:

Francis C. McIntosh (1899–1977)

Mildred M. McIntosh (1903–1979)

Thomas McNally (1908–1991)

Blanche McNally (1907–2001)

PROLOGUE

Only thirty minutes separated my grandfather's death from Lorena's. I didn't find out Grandpa was dead until the next day, but I knew he was dying, so it wasn't exactly a surprise. I figured the selfish old bastard would live a few more months, at least. His lungs had seemed fine when we'd argued that morning.

About the time dear old Grandpa was dying I was pulling a dripping oar into a canoe on the Chattahoochee River, thinking it would be nice to drift with the current for a while. The morning had been one long relentless paddle upstream (metaphorically speaking) and I felt I deserved a break.

"You don't think she'll get fired, do you?" Lorena had asked drowsily as we drifted. "I didn't mean to get her in trouble, even though she was incredibly rude to me." She was still ruminating about the argument she'd had with our waitress at the Blue Boy Diner. I was ruminating about the argument I'd had with my grandfather that morning, which had far greater implications for our future.

What I didn't know at the time was that we had no future. We had about twenty-five minutes.

1

"I'd feel terrible if she got fired," Lorena added.

"I doubt they'll fire her," I said, not sure if that was true. The truth was, I thought Lorena had overreacted a little. If it had been my pancakes I would have let it go. But I'd never tell Lorena that now. What would be the point, except to make Lorena feel bad?

It had been one of those loud, public confrontations that made me cringe inside, even when it was taking place at someone else's table, and as I said, I'd already had one extremely traumatic argument that day. Lorena had asked nicely for the waitress to take the pancakes back, and I distinctly remember her telling the waitress to hold the butter. Of course she had—she's lactose intolerant. She always does.

When the pancakes arrived and Lorena pointed out the butter, the waitress suggested Lorena move it into the cup that held the little cream containers. She'd been frazzled, slightly huffy, her dark bangs pasted to her forehead by sweat. She was about our age— late twenties—and had long tattoos of assault rifles morphing into flowers trailing up each of her forearms. The tattoos suggested she was an easygoing neo-hippy sort of woman, but her eyes suggested much of that peace, love, and good times listening to Phish had been blunted by double-shifts at the Blue Boy.

Faces had lifted from grilled chicken sandwich platters to watch Lorena and the waitress go at it.

I said I'll take it back.

I heard what you said. It's the tone and the eye roll I didn't appreciate.

The waitress had backpedaled from her huffiness as soon as Lorena reacted, but it was too late. Lorena looked like such a sweetheart that people sometimes made the mistake of thinking they could push her around, but Lorena was a sweetheart who would bite if poked.

"Look at the bright side—we got our meal for free," I said.

"Not that I could eat after that. My lunch is still in my throat," Lorena said.

I'd dropped a ten dollar tip on our table when Lorena wasn't looking. Somehow I sensed that the waitress had been having a bad day, just like us.

The scenery unrolled along the Chattahoochee River, shifting from dense forest to cozy cabins to grassy hills. I can still see it. Dense clouds formed a low ceiling just above the treetops. Everything was crisp and clear.

Eyes closed, Lorena stretched languidly, her wrists bent, her Latin-with-a-touch-of-Asian face turned toward the sky. "This is so beautiful. We should do this more often, when we're not feeling so depressed." She reached out and massaged my neck. I remember feeling that familiar jolt of pleasure and surprise that this incredible woman had married me. It was a sensation I'd felt almost hourly during the first few months of our marriage. In all of our wedding photos I look stunned.

"Can I say something that's sneaky and makes me seem like a bad person?" Lorena asked, kneading the knots in my neck.

"You? You're incapable of sneaky. You'd bleed out your ears if you tried to be sneaky."

"Oh, that's a lovely image," Lorena laughed. "It would be sneaky, though."

We paused to admire a dilapidated shack leaning out over the river, clearly abandoned. On another day we might have paddled over to take a peek inside. We both had a weird fascination with abandoned places.

I turned in the canoe, sat with my hands between my knees. "So what's your sneaky idea?" I had no way of knowing how profoundly her words would affect my life. Not her life, of course. Just mine.

Lorena waited a beat, as if deliberating on whether she should say it.

"Do you think your grandfather set it up legally so you can't continue the comic strip after he dies? Maybe he just told your grandma that's the way he wanted it."

"I don't know. I could see him doing either." We passed out of thick woods into open fields; I noticed a line of black clouds dividing the sky. I pointed at them. "We may get rained on."

Lorena looked up, shrugged. "Oh, well. We'll survive."

"Grandma would never go against his wishes," I said. I was pretty sure my grandmother hated my grandfather, but they had faced the outside world as a grim, unassailable wall for sixty years, and I didn't see that changing just because he was dead.

It was so hard to grasp that he was dying. This morning as he sat hooked to an IV bag, telling me in no uncertain terms that I would not be succeeding him as the artist of his comic strip, Toy Shop, he seemed ready to roll himself to the summit of Bear Mountain in the wheelchair he'd occupied for the past fifty years.

"How much is he leaving her again?" Lorena asked. She knew it was almost nothing. Grandpa had never made huge money, and he lost most of what he'd made bankrolling Toy Shop Village, my father's lunatic idea for a themed amusement center (and, unbeknownst to me at that moment, soon to become my home). Grandma would get the house and some merchandising and royalty money, but after the strip was discontinued the merchandising would dry up. When was the last time anyone manufactured a Nancy and Sluggo t-shirt, or a Dick Tracy toy radio watch? When a strip dies (unless it's an iconic strip that's become part of the fabric of our culture. Like, oh, I don't know…Peanuts?), people tend to forget it.

An icy rain began to fall. I looked at the clouds, heavy and dark, bunched like fists. "Maybe you're right, maybe she would be willing to cut a deal after he's gone," I mused. "She's a child of the Depression, not one to put sentimentality above the practicalities of paying the bills." I considered for a moment, then shook my head. "Nah. I couldn't do it even if she was willing."

"I feel slimy even bringing it up," Lorena said, shrugging.

"There's no harm in looking at all the options." Lorena had nothing to feel slimy about. She'd been nothing but kind to my grandfather in the face of his thinly veiled contempt. Grandpa was certain all Latinos would be cleaning ladies and lawn mowers if not for that "affirmative action crap."

My phone rang. It was my mom (calling, I would learn much later, to tell me Grandpa was dead), but I stashed the phone in my pocket as the rain turned into a pelting downpour, soaking my thin t-shirt.

Lorena shrieked with delight and held a sweatshirt over her head. In a moment the sweatshirt was soaked and she tossed it aside. We grabbed our paddles and got moving.

"We're probably half an hour from the pickup area if we go hard," I said, shouting to be heard over the splashing. The rain formed a lovely dappled pattern on the surface of the water. I still remember that so vividly.

"That's okay. I love it," Lorena shouted back.

As I paddled I thought about Lorena's suggestion. From Grandma's perspective, it sucked that Grandpa was putting his pride of ownership in the strip ahead of her financial well-being. Maybe as time passed I would change my mind, especially if reviving the strip meant Grandma could live more comfortably.

The sound of the rain took on a hard edge. Laughing, Lorena grabbed a little red and white cooler that had held our lunch and tried to shield her head from hailstones. They thunked off the steel canoe, ricocheting madly. I hunched my shoulders and paddled, laughing too. The little chunks almost, but didn't quite, hurt, like a too-vigorous massage.

"This is so weird," Lorena shouted over the din. "It was sunny two seconds ago!"

A long, growling rumble erupted all around us.

I stopped laughing. We were in a metal canoe, on a river. "Shit." I paddled harder. "We need to get off the water." I looked at both banks: they were steep, but we could use the waist-high weeds to pull ourselves up.

A tremendous bolt of lightning tore across the sky, thick as a tree trunk. I turned toward shore.

"What are you doing?" Lorena asked.

"We have to get off the water!" I paddled like mad, splashing water everywhere.

"Not over there," Lorena said, "there could be snakes!"

"Not in the rain," I said, not sure if snakes took shelter from rain or not, but with no time to argue. Lorena was terrified of snakes—the word "phobia" didn't begin to cover it.

I wasn't making any progress. I glanced back: Lorena was paddling against me, away from shore.

"What are you doing? We have to get off the water!" I paddled harder, but got nowhere. I stopped, looked down the river for another place to get off, one that wasn't as weedy, but there was nothing.

Another boom of thunder, like dynamite going off. I cringed, expecting to feel the jolt of a million volts rip through me. We were going to die if we didn't get off the river, and we were moving away from the shore as Lorena continued to paddle. She said something about going further downstream. We might have time to do that, but it was stupid to take the chance.

Seeing no other option I stood up, gathered my balance, and jumped into the river, one hand outstretched to grab the canoe. I sunk chest deep before feeling the sandy bottom under my sneakers, the water warm compared to the hail and chill wind above.

I dragged the canoe toward shore, ignoring Lorena's squeals and panicked paddling.

I pulled the nose of the canoe onto shore. "Come on," I shouted, scrambling to the top of the bank to show her there was nothing to fear in the weeds. I waved her on frantically. She shrieked incoherently, shaking her head, still in the canoe.

"I'll carry you," I offered. I clutched a tall jimson weed and stepped down the bank, seeking firm footing in the runny mess.

A blinding golden zigzag of lightning struck the far shore, accompanied by a deafening electric sizzle that sprang across the surface of the water.

Lorena jerked like a marionette as the water danced with a sideways current that looked like nothing so much as a thousand slithering snakes.

I don't remember screaming. I imagine I did as I leapt down the bank and caught Lorena as she crumpled, expecting to feel the current race through me. Her head flopped sideways across my shoulder.

Her clothes were smoldering. The soles of her boots were gone. So were the soles of her feet. I was saying something over and over, but I couldn't make out my own words as I laid her on the grass above the bank and pressed her chest. Air hissed between her lips like it was leaking from a flat tire. I shouted her name, told her she needed to wake up now, needed to breathe, needed to fight, as the hail pelted us and thunder cracked, farther away now, heedless of what it had done. In between my exhortations I shouted for help, shouted so hard it felt like someone was raking my throat and lungs.

When do you give up pushing on your true love's chest, breathing into your true love's lips, when you know that when you stop, her life is over? You push forever, or at least for what feels like forever as you watch her lifeless eyes, afraid to look at her ruined feet.

CHAPTER 1

TWO YEARS LATER.

My date looked bored. Her name was Lyndsay. Lyndsay had dark eyes that were a little too close together, long brown hair, and lovely, very prominent collar bones. She was a corporate person; my guess was she wore her hair up at work and didn't take any shit. I'd met her on Match.com.

Lyndsay had immediately taken control of the conversation. Not in an obnoxious way, but in an alarmingly assertive way. She struck me as the sort of woman who went for the alpha male—the confident, square-jawed ex-jock who said bold things on first dates. I was not the alpha male, and Lyndsay was clearly becoming aware of this.

"We're, like, the only people here," Lyndsay said, scanning the desolate restaurant. There were actually two other tables occupied, but it was a big place, forty or fifty tables, a sea of empty white tablecloths.

"Everyone's rattled by the flu outbreak," I said. It had hit Atlanta very suddenly, and hard, and it wasn't breaking out anywhere else. People were dying from it—even healthy people, and the medical community was worried as hell. "People are lying low, waiting to see if it's got an animal in the name—swine flu or bird flu. Maybe this time it'll be duck flu."

She didn't even toss me a perfunctory chuckle. "I almost cancelled on you, but decided I needed to get out of my apartment." She propped her chin lightly on her knuckles. "So, what do you do again?"

"I'm an illustrator." Illustrator sounded less juvenile than cartoonist. It had been in my profile, but evidently she hadn't read the whole thing, or had forgotten.

"What do you illustrate?"

A surge of anticipatory pleasure rushed through me. Here was my chance to crumble Lyndsay's snap judgment that I was a loser who wasn't worth knowing.

"I draw a newspaper comic strip."

In the brief time I'd been back in the dating world, I'd discovered that a lot of women were impressed by even the most marginal fame.

Lyndsay squinted. It was the first facial expression that crossed her face that seemed unplanned, and I couldn't help but enjoy the moment. "Really? Which one?"

"Toy Shop."

Her mouth opened in surprise, then she smiled brightly, her eyes suddenly alive with interest. "No kidding?"

I smiled. The smile felt a little tight. It was a cheap way to prove you were someone worth knowing. "No kidding."

Lyndsay sat up in her chair, flipped her hair back over one shoulder. She paused, looked up at the white ceiling tiles. "Wait a minute." The hair slid off her shoulder and brushed the white tablecloth. "Hasn't Toy Shop been around forever? Since, like, the fifties?"

I'd grown used to explaining this discrepancy, and had honed it down to two efficient sentences. "My grandfather created the strip in 1957. He died in 2008, and I resurrected the strip in 2010." I didn't mention that Grandpa hadn't wanted me to carry on the strip, that I had convinced Grandma to let me resurrect it when Grandpa was only four months in the grave and she was struggling financially. "I gave the strip a new look, though. I created Wolfie." And tripled the strip's revenue, much to Grandma's pleasure.

"That's right, Wolfie is in Toy Shop! I have a Wolfie coffee mug." She looked at me expectantly, eyebrows raised, I guess to convey the kismet inherent in her owning a Wolfie mug.

"That's terrific," I said.

Lyndsay stirred her margarita, forming a little whirlpool. "So why didn't you mention that you draw Toy Shop in your profile?"

I took a swig of Jack and Coke. "I guess I don't want to take a lot of credit for Toy Shop, because I didn't create it."

"You create it new every day," Lyndsay said, her tone overly earnest.

"I guess."

She patted my hand, gave me her best empathetic look. "Sure you do."

It was an incredibly complex issue to me, one that a "Sure you do" didn't begin to resolve. "Well, thanks," I said, hoping that would close out this particular topic.

The strip was more successful than it had ever been, but somehow the better it did, the more I felt like a fraud. My success came by standing on the shoulders of someone I hadn't even liked, who had expressly forbidden me from doing what I did. On his death bed. None of the ideas for a strip I'd tried on my own before taking over Toy Shop had generated the least bit of interest from the syndicates. I hadn't even been able to land an agent until I acquired the rights to Toy Shop.

I pushed back in my chair. "Excuse me. I'll be right back."

I called my friend Annie from the bathroom.

"Help."

"That bad?" Annie asked. "Is she ugly?" Her voice was raspy and drained.

"You don't sound good."

"I have the flu. I feel awful."

"Have you been to the doctor?"

"Duh. Have you been watching the news? Doctors' offices are packed. So's the emergency room. Half the city's got it."

"Yeah, I forgot." I'd been too nervous about my date to pay much attention to the news. All they were covering, even on the big national networks, was the flu outbreak. I was probably an idiot for being out.

"I'll let you get some rest. Why don't I stop by after?" I could surprise her with some soup from Stone Soup Kitchen.

"It's okay. What else am I going to do? Is she ugly?"

A tall guy in cowboy boots came into the bathroom. He nodded a pointless greeting and bellied up to a urinal. "No," I said, talking lower, "she's really good looking—better looking than her photo. She's just…I don't know." I felt self-conscious with the cowboy guy in the room. I also felt strangely emasculated—guys don't stand around in bathrooms talking on the phone. Women probably don't either.

The sound of urine on porcelain filled the small bathroom. "She's kind of slick. I just don't get a good vibe." Cowboy guy stared at the wall.

"Mm. It's always best to trust your gut. Want me to do a phone call rescue?" She coughed harshly. "Sorry."

I considered as cowboy guy brushed past me without washing his hands. Usually I was the one rescuing Annie from bad dates by calling so she could pretend an emergency had come up, because there were far more men than women who were nightmare dates, and somehow the worst of them always found Annie. That was true of Annie's life in general, really.

This wasn't really a nightmare date, though. "No, I'll stick it out. Just needed some emotional support."

"Big hug," Annie said. "Call me as soon as you're done. Hey, what if she offers to sleep with you?"

"She's not going to."

"She might."

"She won't."

"But what if she does? You said she was good looking."

An image of Lyndsay unbuttoning her silk blouse flashed through my mind. I banished it.

"Are you going to kiss her goodnight?" Annie persisted.

"No!"

"Then what are you going to do? Are you going to shake her hand?" Her tone was teasing now.

An old guy pushed open the door, nodded curtly and squeezed past me.

"I'll talk to you later."

"Call me as soon as you leave the restaurant."

I closed my phone, grateful for Annie. It was amazing how close Lorena's death had drawn us. Before, she'd mostly been Lorena's friend.

I needed to pee, but the old guy was standing pushed up to the urinal, clearly finding it difficult to get a flow going with me three feet away. It would be cruel, and awkward, to wait.

Lyndsay had brushed her hair and put on fresh lipstick. She opened her mouth, likely to say something clever she'd been rehearsing while I was in the bathroom, but I jumped in.

"So tell me about the publishing business."

Lyndsay leaned back in her chair, draped her arms over the armrests. "What I was going to say is more interesting." Her smile was brimming with promises that both scared me and made my head spin. It had been more than two years since I'd been with a woman.

Since I'd been with my wife.

I felt a dizzy sinking in my stomach, like I'd just dropped twenty floors in an elevator. This all felt wrong—wrong place, wrong time, wrong woman. I wanted to be home, in front of the TV watching

Lost reruns and drinking decaffeinated Earl Grey tea.

I wasn't sure how to respond to Lyndsay's leading comment. The only appropriate response would be "What were you going to say?" Part of me was curious about what she was going to say, but most of me wanted to go home. Most of me felt like I was cheating on Lorena.

There was a cup of coffee in front of me, so I took a sip in lieu of a reply, and burned my mouth. It was a big sip, so I got caught in that moment where you have something hot in your mouth and you don't know whether to spit it out, which would mean passing it back over the tender parts at the front of your mouth, or roll it around in the back of your mouth and tolerate the pain until it cools. I tolerated the pain until it cooled. It seemed to take a long time.

"I guess I've left you speechless," Lyndsay said, raising an eyebrow.

I set my coffee down. "I'm really sorry. I think I made a mistake. I thought I was ready to date, but I'm not." My tongue felt thick and cottony, maybe from the burn.

Lyndsay regarded me, then fished the strap of her purse from the back of her chair. "If you're not interested in me, just say so." She pulled two twenties from her purse and dropped them on the table. "The least you could do is be honest if you're going to waste my Friday night."

"It's not an excuse, it's the truth," I insisted, although it was only partially true. I wasn't ready to date, but I also was not interested in her.

"Mm hm." She pulled on her coat.

I picked up her twenties, offered them back to her. "I can get this."

She looked at my hand like I was offering her a dead rat. "I'm not sure you're ready."

I dropped the bills back on the table. "Look, my wife died, okay?" Even as I said it, I regretted it. I was using Lorena's death to win an argument. "I left that out of my profile as well. I'm sorry if I wasted your valuable time, but this is hard for me."

Lyndsay froze, her hand buried in her purse. "I'm sorry. Your profile said you were divorced."

"I know." I didn't want her to be sorry; I resented her even knowing.

Lyndsay nodded understanding. "Why don't you go ahead? I'll wait for the bill."

Relieved, I thanked her, pushed two twenties of my own into her hand and rushed for the exit.

The wind dug into me as I opened the door—a wind more appropriate for Detroit than Atlanta. I ducked my head, clamped a fist over my collar and trotted through a haze of snow flurries to my car.

I didn't understand how Lyndsay could be the same woman who wrote the profile I'd responded to. Quirky, easygoing bookworm who loves organic gardening and wandering Little Five Points. I felt guilty about running out; it was clear from Lyndsay's reaction that she had a good heart.

As soon as I was out of the parking lot I called Annie.

"I lost it. Completely melted down. Something made me think of Lorena, and that was it."

"Aw," she said. "I'm sorry." She coughed thickly.

"You sound worse."

"I've never felt so terrible."

"I'm coming over. Is there anything I can get you?" Up ahead, a police officer was diverting traffic. Barricades were set up across Piedmont Avenue.

"That's okay. I'm way out of your way."

"I'm coming," I said. "It'd be nice to see a friendly face right now. What can I bring you?"

I hung a right onto Baker, then tried to go left on Courtland, but it was blocked off as well. Red lights flashed languidly on three or four parked cruisers. I craned my neck as I drove past, peering down the blocked-off street. A dozen police officers and people in blue windbreakers conferred in the middle of the street.

"Wow, something's going on downtown. Everything's blocked off."

Further down I spotted another half-dozen officers. One of them was running—not trotting, running—toward the huddled group.

"There are police everywhere," I added.

"Can you see smoke or anything?" Annie asked.

"No."

I drove on. I despised onlookers who lined up at barricades, nosing to find out what was going on even though it had nothing to do with them, and I didn't want to be one.

Annie was quiet—either waiting for an update or feeling too sick to talk.

Peachtree was blocked as well.

"Damn. It's all blocked off."

An ambulance was parked halfway on the sidewalk. Nearby, a guy was handing out medical masks from a red plastic crate. Some of the police were already wearing them, their mouths and noses hidden under a white swatch.

"You okay?" I asked Annie. She sounded wheezy.

"Yeah."

"I was going to stop and get you soup, but I'm thinking I should come straight there."

"Thanks, I don't feel like soup anyway. You get full credit for the thought, though."

A big, unmarked black truck rumbled past, swerved to a stop at the next corner. The back door flew open and seven or eight men in military uniforms jumped out carrying assault rifles.

"Oh, shit," I said.

A news van pulled up beside the truck.

"What?" Annie asked.

"There are soldiers running around. Is this on the news?"

I clicked on the radio, turned to WSB. They were covering the flu outbreak at the moment—no mention of blocked-off streets and soldiers with guns.

The air was filled with the whine of sirens. I cracked the window: it sounded like a pack of coyotes howling.

"Jesus," I muttered.

"It's on TV," Annie said. I heard a news anchor's voice in the background, waited while Annie listened. "They don't know what's going on. They think it's about the flu outbreak. People are being rushed to hospitals."

The door to an apartment building flew open. Two paramedics rushed out carrying a stretcher. Two more followed close behind with a second stretcher. I pulled over, rolled down my window.

"What's going on?"

One guy looked up at me and shook his head. It might have meant he didn't know, or that he wasn't saying, if it wasn't for the warning in his eyes. He was saying I should get out of there.

The problem was, Annie lived fifteen blocks into that sealed-off area.

I got out of my car. "Excuse me, I need to get to Auburn Avenue. Is there a way around this?" There was a young blonde woman in the stretcher, her eyes glassy and scared. Every strained breath she managed was accompanied by an awful rattling.

"You can't go there," said a big, muscular guy in a surgical mask carrying one end of a stretcher. "Go home now."

"What's going on?" I asked in a tone that made me sound like a lost child. The woman in the stretcher looked more than very sick—she looked like she was dying.

"Go home." He gestured toward my car with his head.

They hurried the stretchers into the ambulance and turned on the red bubble. The big guy rolled his window halfway. His voice was half-drowned by the scream of the siren, his lips hidden by the mask and unreadable, but I was almost certain he shouted "anthrax."

They raced off, giving me no time to ask if I'd heard right, if they were sure, if they were shitting me, if they were high.

Anthrax? Had he said anthrax?

I got in my car, and drove off, afraid to call Annie back. Could she have anthrax? No, she didn't seem nearly as sick as the woman in the stretcher. Unless Annie was just earlier along. I didn't know anything about anthrax, except that it killed people.

I passed two Latina women straining with a big man, trying to push him into the back seat of a sedan. I slowed as I passed, peered through the window at the man. His eyes were open but blank, as if he was in shock. His chest was hitching, spasming.

"Oh God," I whispered. I wanted to get out of there, but it would be cowardly to leave Annie. I called her.

"It's on CNN," Annie said immediately. "They're saying it's the flu epidemic. They're saying it gets much worse after the first forty-eight hours, that people are dying."

"Oh, God." It came out before I could stop it.

"What?"

I didn't want to tell her. Annie was a painfully anxious person; this would terrify her, probably needlessly.

"What?" she repeated. "Tell me."

I couldn't lie to her. "I heard something. From someone on the street."

"What did you hear?" Annie sounded like she wasn't at all sure she wanted to know.

"It was one person, in the street." I didn't add that it was a paramedic. I wanted to water it down if I was going to say it.

"Just tell me." She sounded annoyed.

"Someone said it could be anthrax."

Annie whimpered.

"I shouldn't have said anything. I'm sure it's not true."

A man in a business suit was half-lying on the bottom step of a walk-up. He raised a weak hand to a couple hurrying past. They picked up their pace.

Annie stopped crying; there was silence on the line. "Are you okay?" I asked.

"I'm Googling anthrax," she said.

I waited, listening to the wet hiss of her breathing. It wasn't nearly as bad as the woman on the stretcher.

"Causes muscle aches, fever, sore throat. Often mistaken for the flu. After twenty-four to forty-eight hours, severe breathing problems, shock, meningitis." She sobbed. "Almost always fatal."

"There are a million things that give people flulike symptoms. We don't know that's what it is."

"What are all those sirens? Are they ambulances?"

"Some are." Up ahead the street was blocked off, forcing me to turn left, away from Annie. "I'm coming to get you."

"You said it's blocked off."

"I'll find a way in."

Annie coughed. The next right was blocked off as well, pushing me another block out of my way.

"Don't you dare come," Annie said. "If it's the flu, I don't need you. If it's anthrax, you can't help me. Go home and lock your door."

"I can't leave you there alone. I'm coming," I said. I ran away and left Lorena to die, was what I was thinking. I'm not doing the same to her best friend.

"Finn, there's no point. I don't feel that sick. I probably have the flu; I visited my sister last weekend and my little nephew was sick. I probably caught what he had."

"Should I call 911? Just to be safe?"

"I don't know."

"I'm calling," I said. "I'll call you right back."

I punched 911 and got a recording. All lines were in use. I waited thirty seconds, called again, and got the same recording. I called Annie back.

"How do you feel?"

"About the same, I guess."

I wondered if I could circle around, try to get in on the minor roads coming from the west.

"Listen." Annie's voice got low, to almost a whisper. "I was thinking. If I've got it, it's okay. Living is so hard for me that I wouldn't be that disappointed if it stopped. You know?"

I didn't know what to say. Annie suffered from such terrible anxiety and depression that it seeped from her pores. She was on tremendous doses of SSRIs and other anti-depression meds. Was it really so bad she wanted to die? "I didn't know it was that bad."

"It is. I'm really not afraid to die. I'm just afraid it's going to hurt. You know?"

"Yeah." I choked back tears. "I still don't think you should be alone. If I can get close, I'll cover my face with a sweatshirt."

"Why don't we wait an hour, see if things calm down?" Annie suggested. "Just stay on the phone with me?"

"Okay." That made sense. I could stay on the phone with her the whole time, try again in an hour when things had hopefully calmed down.

"My throat hurts, so you talk, I'll listen."

"What should I talk about?"

"I don't know."

I tried to think of something happy. I heard a gurgling from Annie's end. "Are you okay?"

"I'm just drinking. Drink lots of fluids and get plenty of rest, right?"

"Absolutely."

Annie laughed a little.

"The two of us are going to laugh about this over drinks in a few days, after you're over the flu," I said. "It's the flu. Even if there was an anthrax outbreak, people still get the flu this time of year."

"You're probably right."

I tried to drive with tunnel vision. I didn't want to see what was happening outside. Every block seemed crowded with people trying to get help. A woman wearing a head scarf flagged me from between two parked cars. I didn't stop; I felt like shit, but I didn't want to contract anthrax. Could it get into the car through the vent? I turned off the heat, just in case.

"Would you say your life has been mostly happy up till now?" Annie asked.

I wasn't sure how to answer. "Yes and no. I'm happy when the universe isn't dropping giant shit-bombs on me." I was going for an ironic tone, but it came out dripping with self-pity.

"How old were you when your twin sister died?" Annie asked.

"Twelve." I had a flash of memory: sitting in the Buckhead diner, holding Lorena's hand, Annie sitting across from us in the booth, tears rolling down her cheeks as I told her the story of how Kayleigh drowned.

I made it to the 75/85 interchange. It was crowded, but so far the traffic was moving.

Annie started to say something, but it tripped off a coughing jag. "You still there?"

"I'm here," I said.

"Someone on CNN said anthrax. Maybe terrorist attack. Not confirmed."

"They're probably hearing the same rumor I heard."

I drove in silence, the phone to my ear, digesting Annie's words. Terrorist attack? They were just sensationalizing a bad flu outbreak for ratings. That had to be it.

My chest felt tight, and for a second I wondered if I was infected. Annie had said the breathing difficulties came later. This was just anxiety.

I made it to Collier and got off at the exit. It wasn't mine, but the parkway was bogging with traffic.

I tried to think of something else to say—something that didn't involve terrorists, ambulances that sounded like a pack of wolves. I was flying along Howell Mill Road, with the reservoir on my right. Almost home now—another fifteen minutes. Almost safe. "I'm on Howell Mill Road. Have you ever heard the legend about this road?"

"No," Annie said.

"There's a local legend that this road is haunted, that if you put your car in neutral at a certain spot and let it coast, a ghost will pull you uphill. When I was a senior we would come here all the time. Everyone had a different opinion of where the spot was, and none of them—"

There was a woman kneeling in the middle of the road.

I hit the brake, jerked the steering wheel to avoid her. As my wheels screeched and the car skidded toward the guardrail I wondered what the hell she was doing there, down on her knees like she was praying.

The impact was deafening. I squeezed the wheel, my teeth clenched, as my car flipped over the guardrail.

For a moment my car was airborne and there was silence, except for Annie calling my name, her voice tiny and far away.

Then the car hit, front-end first, and cartwheeled down the embankment. My head slammed into the window and I heard something crack. There was a loud pop; I couldn't see anything, and realized the airbag was in my face.

Something slammed against the roof like a giant fist, and everything stopped.

Then there was Annie's voice again, asking what was wrong, imploring me to answer.

Water surged into the car above my head. For a moment I didn't understand what was happening, then I grasped that the car was upside-down in the reservoir. I reached for the buttons to close the windows, but they were already closed—the water was coming from somewhere else. It didn't matter; I was sinking and I needed to get out. I fumbled with the seat belt, unable to locate the release as freezing water washed over my face. Shocked by the cold, I lifted my face up out of the water, but it followed. A second later my entire head was under.

I panicked. I thrashed in my seat as if I could bust myself out of the seatbelt, realizing too late that I should have taken a deep breath before the water rose over my head. My arms and hands clenched as the numbing water rushed over them.

All I could think was, this shouldn't be so hard. I should be able to get out.

I followed the seatbelt up to my lap and found the release, felt a jolt, then I was floating free. The water had stopped churning—the car was completely filled. I clawed at the door, seeking the latch, and instead found the buttons for the windows.

They didn't work. Or maybe I wasn't pushing them right. My fingers were so numb I couldn't tell if the buttons were moving.

There was a gentle thump: my car had hit bottom. The thought of it horrified me. I was at the bottom, my head inches from the mud.

I pushed feebly at the window. My chest hitched, resisting my lungs' insistence that I breathe. I went back to searching for the door latch.

I finally found it, down lower than I'd thought. I was so disoriented from the cold, the upside-down car. I jammed my fingers into the cavity and pulled the latch, sensed rather than heard the door pop. I pushed with my shoulder; it eased open in slow-motion.

I tugged myself free of the seatbelt, and drifted into the open water.

Swim. I willed myself to move, but my limbs wouldn't work. It was like they'd been disconnected. I managed to wriggle my hands, but my arms wouldn't move, not together in a coordinated way.

The water couldn't be that deep—I only needed to swim a few feet. Or stand. Maybe I only needed to stand. If I could figure out which way was up. I wasn't cold any more, just very, very stiff, as if I were wrapped in a thick layer of gauze.

It occurred to me that I'd just been talking about Kayleigh drowning. I didn't want to drown. I sputtered in fear. Bubbles burst out of my mouth, trailed across my face.

Follow the bubbles. Where had I read that? Was it in a movie? If you don't know which way is up when you're underwater, follow the bubbles, because they're going up, they're escaping the cold, black water into blessed air. I felt the bottom pressing my elbow. I tried to reach out and push off, but I didn't move far.

There was a terrific humming in my ears, like electricity. Electricity always reminded me of Lorena. Rivers and electricity. Canoes. Lorena hadn't drowned, though; she'd been on the edge of the water.

Images flashed in my head, incredibly vivid. Geometrical figures flying past, like futuristic cities, each shape glowing colorfully, creating a kaleidoscope that spun and twisted around me. Outside sensations—the press of water, the sound of my body struggling not to breathe, then, finally, giving in and inhaling—receded. Then my thoughts receded too.

CHAPTER 2

snapped awake.

The TV was on.

"This is not good. This is not good," a woman said. She was crying.

I thought it was the woman I'd swerved to avoid in the road, that she had pulled me out of the water and for some reason taken me to her house. But I was in the same seat as the woman, like she was sitting in my lap, only she wasn't, because she wasn't blocking my view of the TV. I tried to look around, but couldn't.

I leaned forward and retrieved a cigarette from a pack of Camels sitting on the coffee table. Only I didn't. It was as if someone else was moving me. I didn't smoke. I never smoked.

"Oh, Christ," the woman moaned. I looked at my hands as I lit the cigarette with a red plastic lighter, only again, I didn't mean to look at my hands—my eyes just went there. They weren't even my hands—they were a woman's hands, slim and pale, with rings on three fingers. They were trembling. The cigarette came to my mouth and my lips wrapped around it. Not my lips, this woman's lips. I was watching from behind her eyes. She didn't seem to know I was there.

I felt her heart pounding, and that at least felt right, because I was terrified. Her heart was pounding for her own reasons, though, not mine.

We looked toward the TV. A reporter wearing a medical mask stood in front of a hospital, its windows dancing with reflected red lights from emergency vehicles. Behind the reporter people raced around, all of them wearing masks.

The supporting title at the bottom of the screen read: Anthrax Attack in Atlanta.

The reporter was speaking in a breathless voice. "Peter, Emergency personnel are scrambling to find some way to handle the crush of victims in what is now being described as a terrorist attack that may have originated in the MARTA subway system."

I thought of Annie, hoped that somehow, against all odds, she was all right.

I stood, or the woman stood, and went into the kitchen. We grabbed a bottle of red wine by the neck, and, as we turned toward a drawer, I caught a glimpse of the woman reflected in the microwave. It was Lyndsay, my date.

We took a long swig right from the bottle, set it down on the coffee table, then picked up a phone, punched a number, got an "all circuits are busy" recording.

"Shit!" We threw the phone down.

I tried to make sense of what was happening to me. This must be a hallucination. I was dying, and for some reason my brain was creating this vivid, pointless hallucination of what Lyndsay might be doing at this moment as it flickered out.

If that was true I had to snap out of it, move my arms and swim. I didn't want to die at all; I wasn't like Annie.

On the news they showed Fifth Avenue, an impossible tangle of cars and people.

"Authorities are instructing people to stay in their homes, but clearly, Peter, thousands are not heeding these instructions…"

For a second I considered that this whole thing was a hallucination, starting with my phone call to Annie, or even back to the date. I had stayed home, went to sleep, was having an incredibly vivid dream.

My vision broke apart, splintering into a million colorful shards. The shards morphed into geometric shapes again, and I watched them fly by, twisting and stretching out to an unseen horizon.

CHAPTER 3

"**H**is eyes are open again."

A face hovered over me. It wasn't the woman with the cigarette, it was a man with a goatee. He was wet and shaking.

"Can you hear me?" he asked. Droplets of water dribbled off his goatee.

I tried to answer, but my lungs cramped painfully. Water burst from my mouth, briefly creating a fountain rising toward the goateed man. I was seized by a painful coughing fit.

"Get him on his side," the man said. I felt myself being rolled, and my lungs stopped aching a little. I'd never been so cold. And confused. How had I gone from the bottom of the reservoir to Lyndsay's living room to here?

"Here," another man said. I was covered to the neck with a blanket, but it didn't help. "Nine-one-one didn't answer." The man laughed. "Imagine that. You think we should take him to a hospital?"

"Are you kidding me?" the goateed man said. "You want anthrax?"

"I'm going to go to sleep now," I mumbled, drawing my hands up under my chin.

"Whoa, you better not." The goateed guy said, pulling my wrist away from my face. "Come on, let's walk to my truck. We can turn the heater up full blast."

That sounded great. Just the idea of a heater filled me with longing like I'd never experienced before. I struggled to raise myself on one elbow, but couldn't manage it. The two men pulled me to my feet. They half-dragged me toward a truck, which was parked on the shoulder of the highway.

The woman I'd swerved to avoid was still sprawled in the road. She was an old woman, clearly very sick. She was pleading for someone to help her. Two cars had pulled over. A small group was huddled on the shoulder.

My saviors shoved me into the truck. It was a tight fit for the three of us, but I didn't care. Heat blasted from the vents—that's all that mattered. I held my frozen hands in front of the heater, my jaw chattering.

The guy on the passenger side, a big, Italian-looking guy, abruptly leaned away from me. "Hey, you're not sick or anything, are you? It just occurred to me."

I shook my head, feeling my neck muscles creak. "I don't have it."

He relaxed, let his big thigh settle back against mine. "You're one lucky bastard. Five minutes ago you were dead."

"Dead?" I echoed.

"Dead," the driver said. "No pulse, not breathing."

"Toby saved your life," the Italian guy said. "I got it all on my phone." He showed me the phone. "You want to see it?"

I shook my head. I didn't want to see my own dead body.

"He spotted the back of your head in the water and pulled you out." He slapped the dash. "Shit, Toby, you saved a guy's life! Un-fucking-believable."

I looked at Toby, who kept his eyes on the road, smiling, clearly proud.

"Thanks, Toby," I offered. It wasn't nearly enough, but I couldn't find the energy to elaborate.

"No problem." He held out his fist. I bumped the top of it with mine, like we were playing one-potato, two-potato, not sure if that's what he wanted.

"I'm Joe, by the way," the Italian guy said.

"I have to sleep now," I said.

✠

A wriggling in my pants woke me. Joe was fishing around in my pocket.

"Don't worry, I ain't ripping you off," Joe said when he saw I was awake. He withdrew his hand. "I was trying to see if there were phone numbers in your wallet, but your wallet's all wet and it's stuck to your pants. Is there someone I can call? We're not sure what to do with you. We gotta be somewhere."

My first thought was Annie. My second was that I should call my mom to let her know I was all right. She was probably frantic, out in Arizona with no information, calling my phone and getting no answer. Later. Right now I needed someone to come and help me. There was my friend Dave. He had a family to worry about, but if he could, he'd come.

"Call my friend, David Bash."

I couldn't remember the number, and my phone was in my car. Joe looked it up, dialed, and handed me the phone.

All circuits were busy.

I shut the phone, handed it back to Joe. "You can just drop me at my house." I gave Toby directions.

Joe clicked on the radio. The roads out of Atlanta were closed. The National Guard was setting up auxiliary hospitals in armories and schools. The office of Homeland Security had released a statement saying the outbreak had tentatively been traced back to the subway, and was assumed to be a terrorist attack.

"How did you bring me back?" I asked Toby.

"I pushed on your chest. That didn't work, so I punched your chest like they do in the movies."

"You never took CPR?"

Toby made a face. "Hell, no."

We slowed to pass a police cruiser parked half in the road. The police officer was nowhere in sight.

"How long was I in the water?" I asked.

They glanced at each other. "What would you say?" Toby asked Joe.

Joe shrugged. "What? Ten, fifteen minutes?"

"Right in there, yeah," Toby said.

I tried to wrap my mind around it. I'd been dead. Not unconscious, dead. I had that vision, of being Lyndsay watching the news. A lot of people who had near-death experiences reported vivid hallucinations, and now that my head was clearer it seemed likely that that's what happened.

It had been remarkably vivid, though. It hadn't felt like a hallucination at all.

The radio was describing the symptoms of anthrax, but I already knew them from my conversation with Annie.

"Wait a minute," I said aloud without meaning to. Both men looked at me. "Did they say it started in the subways?" I thought I'd heard that, but that couldn't be right, because I'd heard the same thing during my hallucination that I was Lyndsay.

"That's what they're saying," Joe said.

I wrapped my arms around myself and trembled harder. "Jesus," I whimpered.

"What?" Joe asked.

"Nothing." I was so tired.

We pulled through the gates into the remnants of Toy Shop Village, with its empty bumper-boats pool, rusting rides, rotting streamers, and Toby and Joe were sure I was delirious. Who lives in a defunct amusement center? I directed them toward the drive-in theater toward the back of the Village, assuring them I lived there.

I thanked both men from the bottom of my heart. Joe's eyes filled with tears and he nodded; Toby waved me off, insisting it was no big deal. I got Toby's business card, intending to come up with a truly awesome thank you gift to send once I could think straight. Quivering in front of my locked front door, it took me a moment to remember the spare key over the door frame.

As soon as I got inside I tried to call Annie on my land line, but got no answer. I stripped, pulled every blanket and towel out of the linen closet, threw them on my bed, and passed out underneath them.

CHAPTER 4

I woke trembling with cold and utterly disoriented. My fingers and toes felt like they could never possibly be warm again. I wondered if I had frostbite.

There were so many people I needed to call immediately. Mom. Annie. Grandma. Jeez, Grandma lived closer to downtown than I did. She didn't go out much, so hopefully she was all right.

I went for my phone on the night stand, then remembered it was in my car, in the reservoir. To call anyone I would have to get up and reach the land line in the kitchen. I tried to sit up; my back and neck blazed with pain. In fact, every single part of me hurt.

Slowly, painfully, I struggled to a sitting position. The blankets slid off of my torso, exposing me to arctic air. I felt like I was in a meat locker.

"I need a hot shower," I said, tucking my fingers under my armpits.

I slid out of bed. My hip was bruised, and my right knee and ankle hurt, but it didn't seem that I had any serious injuries. I looked longingly at the door to the bathroom before grabbing a bathrobe and limping into the kitchen to call Annie.

There was no answer.

That didn't necessarily mean anything, I told myself. There were a hundred reasons she might not be able to answer. For all I knew she was taking a shower.

I decided to try again in a few minutes, and in the meantime, called my mom. She sobbed with relief while I trembled and ached, and simultaneously assured her I was fine. When I told her about the accident, she flipped. She wanted to hop on the next plane from Phoenix and take care of me, but all flights into the Atlanta area were suspended.

I never quite understood how my mom turned out to be so well-adjusted. When damaged people had children, it seemed to me their children invariably ended up damaged in some way. Somehow Mom had escaped that fate, or compensated for it.

Mom told me that Grandma was fine, but afraid to leave her house in Ansley Park. Smiling, I promised to look in on her as soon as I was able. Grandma could take care of herself, as she'd demonstrated in negotiating terms for giving me the rights to Toy Shop. She didn't need my help or my warm fuzzies.

I asked what was happening with the anthrax.

When all was said and done, the CDC was estimating half a million casualties. Half a million. The city was under martial law. Ten thousand Iraq War vets had been called back into service because they were vaccinated against anthrax, but it was taking time to get them assembled.

"There's a vaccine?" I asked.

"They don't have much," Mom said. "Antibiotics are supposed to work sometimes as well, but in this case they haven't. They're saying that means it's 'weaponized' anthrax—designed to be resistant to antibiotics so it's better at killing people.

Half a million people. I still couldn't get that number out of my head. I needed to try Annie again, and then Dave Bash. Two other local friends came to mind.

"I'm so relieved you're okay," Mom said. "You almost drowning...I can't help thinking of Kayleigh."

It took me a moment to answer. "She was one of my last thoughts, before I—" Drowned. "It seemed so, I don't know, so fateful that both of us would die in the water." Whenever I thought of Kayleigh it wasn't her face I saw, it was the pier she'd jumped from, trying to keep up with her twin brother. I could see every knot in the pier's wood planking, smell the fish guts left by fishermen, every time I thought of her.

"I'm so grateful you didn't. I couldn't lose you. Not both of you. When I get up there I want to meet the man who saved your life and hug him."

"Well, I've got his card, so that can be arranged."

I got off the phone and limped to the bathroom. There was an abrasion on my forehead, probably from the airbag.

It hit me again, as I stood there in front of the mirror. I had died.

I choked up, my throat clenching. It didn't ease up, though—it stayed clenched. It was a strange feeling, as if a finger had wrapped around my vocal cords and was tugging. I gripped my throat, coughed, turned my head from side to side.

Finally, it relaxed.

I parted my hair to examine a cut. It wasn't bad, not deep enough for stitches. Not that I'd be able to get anywhere near a doctor or a hospital right now.

Maybe that's where Annie was—at a hospital or a clinic. Though, wouldn't she have her phone right by the bed? I just couldn't believe she was mortally ill, or worse. Annie was the athlete, always covered with a sheen of sweat, jumping into the shower after a five-mile run when I went over to watch reruns of The Sopranos. Emotionally, she struggled mightily, but physically she was a rock. If only I had her parents' number, to see if they'd heard from her. They lived in New York, so I couldn't count on them to get to her and help her, assuming she needed help.

That's what I'd have to do, I realized. If I couldn't get her on the phone, I had to get to her. I couldn't leave her stranded in her apartment. The first thing I had to do, though, was shower.

As hot water pounded the back of my head I puzzled over my vision of Lyndsay in her apartment. I was sure I heard on her TV that the outbreak began in the subway. Either I had to chalk it up to coincidence, or believe, what, that my soul had left my body and witnessed what was happening?

Maybe as you die your mind unleashes everything it's got, to the point that you can pick up on things around you in an extra-sensory way. When the dust had settled I'd have to check the Internet for any mention of that happening in other people's near-death experiences.

I tried Annie again after my shower. No answer. She'd only been mildly sick when I talked to her last night; was it possible she could be so sick now she couldn't reach the phone? I turned on the news, trying to get more information about how someone might walk through the worst-hit area without getting sick. The emergency personnel were wearing masks, gloves, and clothes that left no exposed skin. I could put together everything but the mask, and one of the shots on the news showed National Guard troops helping themselves to masks from a truly huge pile.

From what the feds had pieced together so far (and were willing to share with the public), the terrorists had used light bulbs filled with "weaponized" anthrax. They'd dropped the bulbs from between moving MARTA cars onto the tracks at the Five Points station, where four separate lines use the same track. As trains flew by, the spores were drawn up into the cars, infecting the passengers. Those passengers got off at malls, bus stations, and the airport and spread the anthrax.

The incubation period was twenty-four to forty-eight hours— time for hundreds of thousands of people to inhale the spores and carry them to other places on their shoes, fingertips, clothes before anyone knew what was happening.

I dragged myself off the couch like an octogenarian and donned heavy flannel sweats and brown leather gloves. The very last thing I wanted to do was march into the eye of the storm, but someone had to help Annie.

#

I was momentarily confused by the absence of my Jetta in the gravel drive, then remembered it was at the bottom of the reservoir. I went back inside to retrieve the key to Lorena's Toyota Avalon. It felt strange to drive Lorena's car, especially while using her old flip cell phone after reactivating it to my number. Suddenly things I'd hidden away because I didn't want to deal with them were useful again.

I called Grandma. I didn't tell her where I was headed, but I gave her a blow-by-blow account of my accident. We agreed this anthrax attack was scary, exchanged a few tidbits of what we'd heard on the news, then I told her I was tired and had to go.

I called Dave and got his voice mail. Cursing, I closed the phone. People who were okay would be answering their phones to let people know they were okay.

I couldn't lose Dave. I couldn't lose Annie. That was all there was to it. I'd suffered my losses. Maybe that was a selfish way to look at it, but I didn't care. I was already too alone; my twin sister and my wife were gone, the core of my inner circle carved away. On top of that, when I lost Lorena a lot of my friends went as well. They'd been her friends, it turned out, or they'd been couple-friends who came as a matching set and preferred their friends come in similar matching sets. After that I'd discovered I was no longer very good at making friends on my own. It had come as a surprise; I wasn't painfully shy, but I was somewhat shy, and I learned that in adulthood that was enough.

My agent Steve called my home phone, checking to see if I was okay. He'd grown worried when I didn't answer my cell. Once again I related the story of my death and recovery. Steve interjected with "Oh my Gods" until I finished, then gave a low whistle.

"Unbelievable. So glad you made it, my friend. Sounds like you've had a rough time."

For an instant the black water was rushing in again. "Do they know who did it yet? I haven't seen anything on the news."

"They haven't figured it out. I'm thinking Al-Qaeda. My wife thinks anti-government right-wingers. I have a client who's an army colonel, and he's saying Russia."

"Russia? Why would he think that?" As soon as I asked I realized I didn't care all that much.

"They're the only ones known to possess weaponized anthrax—enough to kill everyone in the world several times over, in fact. The thing is, their supply was loaded onto tanker cars, covered with bleach, and buried on an island in the Aral Sea in 1988. Gorbachev had just signed a weapons treaty with the U.S., and didn't want us to discover it."

"I just don't see what they have to gain."

"No, it doesn't make any sense. The colonel also thought some of their supply could have been pilfered long ago and sold to some nut."

Some Nut. I'd be willing to put money on Some Nut being involved.

"I'll contact the syndicate and tell them there may be a delay on the strips we're supposed to deliver Friday," Steve said, trying to strike a tone that said the strips were not important in the scheme of things, but sounding panicked nonetheless.

"Okay," I said noncommittally. Right now the thought of working on the strip was like returning to my upside-down car with the water rushing in.

CHAPTER 5

Moving southbound, Route 85 was deserted. I breezed along in the Avalon, my unease growing as I flew past mile upon mile of grinding, bumper-to-bumper traffic heading the other way. I had no idea how I'd get home once I reached Annie.

I cleared a rise; the forest of skyscrapers that comprised the downtown area came into view. Dozens of helicopters, like giant bumblebees, drifted among the skyscrapers. My bowels loosened at the sight. I'd seen that skyline a thousand times, but today it looked foreign, like a battle zone in some war-torn country.

When I reached the roadblocks at Baker Street I turned and drove along the perimeter, scanning the sidewalks, until I spotted a box sitting on a low concrete wall. Masks. I parked, plucked a mask out of the box as I went by, and slipped it on. It fit snugly over the bottom half of my face, made me feel both anonymous and oddly powerful. No anthrax spores could touch me now. I put my head down and walked, watching the frenetic activity out of the corners of my eyes.

People in uniform were everywhere, shouting orders, clomping boots, flashing lights. I spotted a police officer moving to intercept me. I kept my head down, tried to look like I belonged.

"Where you headed?" she asked. She had braided hair and reminded me of Whoopi Goldberg.

"I live on Auburn Avenue." I swallowed, my casual expression falling away for an instant to reveal the scared boy underneath. "My wife is all alone; I was away at a conference and I have to get back to her."

She nodded, took my elbow and propelled me gently. "Get inside once you're home, and stay inside."

"I will. Thank you." I kept moving.

A block further a big canopy had been erected. Medics and doctors in white scrubs were moving among victims in cots. Screams of pain ripped the air; a raised syringe caught the light. I half-closed my eyes, willing myself to walk faster. I wanted to run, but didn't want someone with a gun to mistake me for a looter.

Down the street I spotted white bags piled in a heap. They looked to be trash, but as I got closer I realized they were body bags. I crossed the street to avoid getting too close, but couldn't help staring at them as I passed. It was hard to wrap my mind around it; those were people, dead, in a pile. According to the news they were just the tip of the iceberg.

I desperately wanted to get out of there and climb back into bed. I was so sore, so achy. I'd always thought Atlanta was a striking city, but today I felt like I was walking in an enormous tomb, the buildings blackened by the soot of a billion tailpipes, a million grey gum-smears mottling its sidewalks.

The glass door to a high-rise swung open; a woman in a black coat guided a young girl out.

"Excuse me," the woman called. I kept my head down and hurried on, pretending I didn't hear. I wasn't afraid to catch anthrax—on the news they'd made it clear it wasn't contagious. You picked up or inhaled spores, and they could be anywhere. I just didn't want to get waylaid from reaching Annie.

"Hello? Can you help us?"

I stopped, turned. The young girl was wheezing, her eyes ringed in red and her nose running. She was wearing a pink Dora the Explorer jacket.

"She's sick," the woman said. "On the news I saw big tents with doctors—do you know where I can find one?"

I pointed back down Courtland. "I passed one about three blocks down. You can't miss it."

She thanked me more profusely than my stingy help deserved. I wished her luck and hurried on, watching my sneakers—white blurs flitting in and out of my narrow field of vision.

My damned throat seized again, like it had in the shower, and my first thought—laced with a jolt of fear-induced adrenaline—was that it was the first whispers of an anthrax infection. I hadn't heard anything about throat clenching as an early symptom, though, only a sore throat, and mine wasn't sore.

I spotted Annie's building and quickened my pace, suddenly filled with a sense of urgency.

Annie lived on the third floor of a brown brick walk-up. My muscles screaming, I took the steps three at a time, huffing from the exertion, the scratchy mask pressing against my lips on the in-breath.

Annie didn't answer the door. She could be out getting food, or looking for help. I weighed my options. I didn't relish the thought of sitting in the hall, and if Annie was inside and too sick to answer, I wasn't doing her any good in the hall.

I'd never knocked in a door before. After making sure the hall was empty I tried kicking it. After seven or eight fruitless kicks I tried ramming it with my lowered shoulder. When I hit the door, pain lanced up my neck, but I felt the door rattle. I tried again, and this time heard a splintering crunch. It swung open on my third attempt.

Annie was lying on the couch, curled on her side.

"Annie?" I knew she wouldn't answer. If she hadn't heard me

break in the door, she was beyond answering.

There was an empty bottle of Valium on the coffee table, and a note.

> Finn,
> I know I have it, and it's hurting too much. Love you.
> Tell my family goodbye.
> XX
> Annie

CHAPTER 6

Exhausted from dealing with the police and emergency management, from six hours in the crush of traffic heading out of the city, I stayed in my apartment and watched the news for the next few days. There were people sick in dozens of U.S. cities, plus London, Cape Town, Hong Kong, the list went on.

People in what looked like space suits were spraying the subways, MARTA stations, and the surfaces all around the hardest-hit stations. But the spores had been carried all over the city and beyond, on the wind, tires, the soles of shoes. They couldn't scrub it all.

Footage of army engineers using bulldozers to plow up the big field in Chastain Park played on all the news channels. They were digging mass graves—big enough to bury half a million people.

When the guy in the hazard suit had taken Annie from my arms, while another took down her name and address, they assured me they'd take good care of her. I knew they were lying, but I also knew they weren't going to let me put her in the back seat of my car and drive away.

CHAPTER 7

sipped tea with gobs of honey, my mom's suggestion for relaxing the spasms in my throat. It hadn't worked so far, but it tasted good.

On TV, the Wolfman was strangling a remarkably well-dressed young woman in a fog-laden forest. The hero, waving a silver-tipped walking stick, rushed to save her.

The problem with the original version of The Wolfman was that the Wolfman was too cute. With that blow-dried bouffant hair and puppy nose you wanted to hug him, not flee in terror. Come to think of it, how much of Wolfie was conjured from my memories of The Wolfman? I hadn't done it consciously, but the similarities were hard to miss.

I felt frozen to the couch. No way I could concentrate on work, or on a book, on anything really. I'd be a fool to go out needlessly, but that was all right, because the thought of putting on shoes and a coat and walking outside was more than I could even contemplate.

I turned back to the news.

The dead looked like giant cocooned larvae as they were bull-dozed into the burial pit. One of those bags, or one just like them, held Annie, and Dave, and Dave's wife Karen.

On day three the military had begun setting up food banks, and now, on day seven, everyone in the affected area was getting enough to eat. There was no formal quarantine, because the spores had quickly spread beyond any feasible protection zone, but no one was coming into the city voluntarily. So far I'd kept my mother from driving in from Arizona by calling three or four times a day with updates on how well I was doing.

Now the worst seemed to be over. Anthrax spores were still out there, but the number of deaths had dropped off dramatically in the past forty-eight hours.

I dropped the TV remote on the couch and looked for something to distract me. My photo album lay on the coffee table, open to the page of pics from the rock climbing trip Dave Bash and I had taken after high school graduation. Dave had been my best friend back then, and, though it had been about a month since I last talked to him, he'd still been when he died. Or maybe he and Annie had been tied.

There was a photo of Dave dangling from the safety line, look-ing chagrined after a fall; another of me in my stupid hat with the Velcro flap, about to start a climb. We had such a ball on that trip.

I closed the album. I shouldn't have let a month go by without calling Dave. Now it was too late.

It wasn't fair. I'd already suffered my losses.

I pressed my palm to the photo album, got up and wandered into my studio. The thought of working made me want to scream. Five or six more days and we would be at code red—the syndicate would be out of strips. Typically they liked to have an eight-week cushion; I was trying their patience, to say the least.

When I first got control of the strip Cathy Guisewite warned me that coming up with a strip each and every day was more difficult than I thought. Add to that the prospect of creating something funny while thousands of bodies were being bulldozed into mass graves in Central Park, and you had the perfect storm. Steve said Toy Shop was more popular than ever, that the new look was catching on in a big way. It would be a shame to start printing reruns.

I threw on a coat, went downstairs, through the empty drive-in snack bar, and pushed through the big swinging doors that led outside.

There was a layer of thin snow on the benches surrounding the empty bumper boats lagoon. I swept a spot and sat for a moment, hands in my pockets. Washed-out images of Tina and Little Joe in maritime outfits covered the fence that surrounded the lagoon. A tiny lighthouse sat on a concrete island in the center, the base dented and scratched, evidence that once motorized rubber boats had careened madly off of it.

I'd put my share of dings in that lighthouse during the eighteen months that Toy Shop Village was open. So had Kayleigh. We rode for free, the grandchildren of the owner, wide-eyed eleven-year-olds astonished by their luck. Hard to believe that had only been nineteen years ago—Toy Shop Village looked fifty years old.

What had my grandfather been thinking when he let Dad talk him into this? We couldn't even sell the property now, out in the middle of this industrial purgatory. Anyone who bought it would have to demolish and haul away tons of metal and concrete before it would be usable for anything. How had they thought people would drive all the way out here to play miniature golf? Cheap real estate is cheap for a reason. That hadn't even been their biggest mistake, thinking people would haul their asses out to the middle of this depressing area, across the highway from a junk yard. Their biggest mistake had been their choice of businesses, which was thirty years behind the times.

I tossed a piece of windblown Styrofoam into the concrete pond. Maybe it was time to brave the Wal-Mart. I'd spent the past week living off canned goods from the pantry and forgotten frozen entrees from the back of the freezer, all of the crap that had looked good in the supermarket but sat uneaten year after year.

My butt still felt strange on the Avalon's leather seat. I rolled down the windows, sniffed the cold air as I sped down Johnson Road.

I coughed, tried to relax my aching throat. The twitching just kept getting worse. It felt like there was a gerbil in there.

I hung a quick right on West Marietta and picked up speed. The near-empty roads looked so strange. I'd always hated the congestion of Atlanta, the intersections perpetually clogged with vehicles, but now I missed it. I wanted things to return to normal, or as close to normal as it was likely to get.

There was a lot of talk on TV about the long-term effects the attack would have on Atlanta. The city had literally been decimated, having lost around ten percent of its population. That was the theoretical cutoff point for when irreparable damage is done to the psyche of a community.

There was a tank in the Wal-Mart parking lot. The place was packed; I had to park across the highway in a strip-mall, on the lawn. In the parking lot I passed two people, both wearing white medical masks, who looked at me the way my eighth grade English teacher used to when I forgot my homework. I wasn't wearing a mask, I realized. That was a no-no. Most people didn't seem to grasp that I wasn't endangering them by not wearing a mask, only myself. Anthrax wasn't contagious, you could only inhale the spores if they were around, and they weren't likely to be in the parking lot of a Wal-Mart ten miles from ground zero this late in the game.

At the entrance two National Guard troops stopped me.

"Mask," one of them said, pointing at her face.

"I know, I forgot."

She jerked her thumb at the doorway. "On your left. Put one on right away."

A mountainous display of pale blue medical masks met me just inside the door. I grabbed two boxes, opened one and retrieved a mask. It smelled like rubbing alcohol.

Half of the shelves were empty in the grocery area. Most of the basics were there—milk, water, cereal, ramen noodles—but non-essentials like olives and Snickers bars were pretty much nonexistent. Signs beside each item listed the maximum number you could buy. Mostly that number was one. Troops patrolled the aisles, evidently making sure no one took more than their share.

When I finished grocery shopping I didn't feel like going home. After a week in solitary I wanted to be around people a while longer. I pushed my cart around the store, feeling punchy as I wandered past laundry detergent, between walls of pink girls' toys. My Little Princess. Barbie Snip 'n Style Salon. A dozen big-screen TVs flashed identical Dentyne ads. In the pharmacy area I discovered licorice toothpaste. That was a new one. Or maybe I just hadn't noticed it before. I picked up a tube, then sought out the candy aisle, suddenly craving real licorice.

They had licorice, both black and red. I chose the black, opened it with my teeth and pulled out a fat stick. I felt like a rebel, the way I was opening packages before I'd paid for them.

I hadn't eaten licorice since I was a kid. Kayleigh and I used to each take an end and pull, stretching the stick until it snapped. We'd compare our stretched pieces to see who got the longer.

I'd been thinking about Kayleigh a lot lately, I realized. She was never far from my mind, even now, eighteen years after her death, but usually her presence was just an untethered ache of guilt. Lately I was getting more concrete flashes, like Mom taking the call from Grandma, dropping the phone when Grandma told her Kayleigh had drowned. Or the moment I realized it was my fault. Kayleigh agreed to jump off the thirty-foot pier if I did first, but she hadn't really expected me to do it, and she'd chickened out. Kayleigh didn't like to chicken out—she was the fearless one, the athlete, the doer. I told everyone about my courageous feat, rubbing it in, so she stayed behind when we went out to eat.

And she jumped, and she died.

Kayleigh, who was beautiful and outgoing, who always watched out for me. When she died I escaped into comic strips. Not even comic books—the cool nerds went for Spider-Man and The X-Men, I went for Peanuts and For Better or For Worse.

As I dropped my purchases on the conveyor belt and nodded a greeting to the exhausted-looking cashier, I realized that despite all of the awfulness of the past week, despite the recurring thoughts of Kayleigh, I felt okay. Maybe I was simply feeling grateful to be alive. Everyone around me had lost someone now. Some had lost whole families. In the face of that, my own losses didn't seem as staggering as they used to.

"You look tired. You near the end of your shift?" I asked the cashier.

She shook her head mournfully. "I'm on till four a.m."

I winced in sympathy. "That's got to be rough."

"Mm hm," she nodded, working her gum as she jiggled the licorice across the scanner, trying to get the price to register. It must be maddening to spend eight hours waving packages in front of that scanner, trying to get it to beep so you can move on to the next package.

"I never said I was perfect," I said. The words burst out in a deep, horrible croak that raked my throat.

The cashier looked stunned.

"Sorry," I said, my voice returned to normal. I had no idea why I'd just said that. It had just come out. I rubbed my twitching throat, swallowed.

I got out of there as quickly as I could.

"Jesus Christ," I said as I launched the Avalon out of the lot. "I never said I was perfect"? Why would I say that to a stranger? I felt like an idiot. I closed my hand over my throat, felt my racing pulse through my fingertips. Maybe it was a one-time fluke. Massive fatigue; a post-traumatic hiccup.

CHAPTER 8

Maybe it was my stroll down the toy aisle at Wal-Mart, or maybe it was just getting out of the apartment, but by the time I got home the ideas were flowing. I was hungry, and suddenly had real food (well, real frozen microwavable food), but I was afraid if I stopped to eat I'd lose the mood, so I went straight to my studio.

My throat constricted.

"One thirty-nine for a head of lettuce?"

Just like in the checkout line, the words forced themselves out as if they'd been trapped inside me. It sounded like gas rising from a fetid swamp, and it was something I would never say voluntarily. I was not a complainer about the price of produce. I rarely bought fresh produce, for that matter. I massaged my throat. Something was very wrong with me.

It occurred to me as I cleaned my inking brush that I could be developing Tourette's syndrome. The thought got me panicked.

Turning to my computer I looked up Tourette's on Wikipedia and read frantically, my heart thumping, until I saw that it always developed in childhood. But what else could it be? Some other, rarer, neurological disorder? Or maybe it really was a second-order symptom of anthrax exposure.

I would call my doctor in the morning. There was nothing to do until then, so I tried not to think about it and kept working.

CHAPTER 9

I sprawled on the couch with a carton of Ben and Jerry's and a spoon while Letterman did his monologue against a backdrop of the New York City skyline at night. My throat was especially sore after having a scope on a rope pushed down there by Doctor Purvis earlier in the day, so the ice cream felt good. I relished these mundane moments—they made things feel normal. Things weren't normal, not by a long shot—the city was still crawling with National Guard, many businesses were still shuttered—but things were at least moving in the direction of normal. There were olives and Snickers bars to be had, and Ben and Jerry's ice cream.

My throat twisted up. It was getting easier to identify the telltale signs that I was about to blurt something. I made a concerted effort to stifle it.

"Poor little thing, down in that black water."

I set the ice cream on the coffee table, my appetite for it vanished. The poor little thing was Kayleigh, I knew instantly. Suddenly I felt incredibly isolated in this apartment, in the middle of rusting amusements surrounded by industrial sites.

I didn't have a superstitious bone in my body, but the image of Kayleigh down in the black water, still twelve, gave me the shivers. For years after she died I had nightmares of discovering Kayleigh in unlikely places, her hair and clothes soaked, seaweed clinging to her face. Guilt will do that to you. When you're partly to blame for someone's death, they show up in the most unlikely places.

How could this problem be psychological?

In the meantime let's have you consult with a psychiatrist, just to cover all of our bases, the neurologist had said matter-of-factly.

It seemed like it had to be something physical—a brain injury or something, though I'd dutifully made my appointment with the psychiatrist Doctor Purvis had suggested.

On the other hand I was grateful to the doctor for giving me a dignified medical-sounding term with which to refer to my weird and undignified outbursts. Vocalizations. I should practice using it in a sentence.

Please pardon my vocalizations. My neurologist says they're either myoclonic jerks brought on by a rare neurological disorder, or I'm batshit crazy.

It occurred to me the psychiatrist would probably want to know what sorts of things I was blurting. I wrote down what I'd just said, and some of the others I remembered.

"You all know the comic strip Toy Shop, right?" Letterman asked his audience.

"What?" I looked up at the TV, my heart suddenly pounding.

"Nice old strip, right?" Letterman said. "Cute kids running a toy store." I couldn't believe it. Letterman was talking about my strip.

"Have any of you read Toy Shop recently?" Murmurs rolled through the audience.

"Unbelievable," I whispered.

"Well in case you missed it, Finn Darby, the grandson of the guy who started the strip, has made a few changes. For example he added a talking toy robot werewolf doll to the cast." Letterman paused for laughter. "A talking toy robot werewolf doll." He enunciated each word in that droll mock-incredulous tone. "Word is he'll be making more changes in upcoming strips, including adding another new character: a badger roadkill clown cashier." A symbol crash punctuated the punchline as Letterman swung his arm like a pitcher getting loose.

I dragged a hand through my hair, trying to grasp this. I'd just been mentioned on Letterman.

When I resurrected Toy Shop two years ago, no one noticed. It was like I'd pushed an old, comfortable piece of furniture back into place—people were happy enough to sit in it, but no one had missed it. There'd been a few little features in magazines, a filler feature on NPR. When I overhauled the strip, it had gotten a little more attention. But Letterman? This was unbelievable.

Inspired, I cloistered myself in my studio and worked on another strip. The vocalizations continued to squeeze from my throat. I wrote them down.

That stuck up son of a bitch Schulz. (I sounded like my grandfather. I have nothing but respect for Charles Schulz.)

You're never going to make it with that attitude.

Bend that elbow, Danny. I paid for a whole drink. (I'm not much of a drinker—a glass of wine, maybe one martini after a long day. I don't know any bartenders by name. Again, I sounded like my grandfather, who made a point of knowing every bartender within twenty miles of his house by name.)

As I was putting the finishing touches on my second strip of the night (a blistering pace for me), I was interrupted by a call from my mother.

"Are you watching the news? They found them," Mom said.

"Who?" I asked, then instantly realized it was a stupid question.

"The nuts who carried out the attack. The news people are yammering back and forth without much information to report, but they found the guys—that much is clear."

I hurried into the living room and dug around in the couch cushions for the remote. "When will they know who it was?"

"They're waiting for the police to make a statement."

I located the remote, clicked on the TV to a shot of an empty dais packed with microphones.

"Who the hell do you think you're talking to?" I croaked, startling myself. I would never get used to that horrible sound.

"Oh, Jesus, Finn," Mom said. "It doesn't sound any better. Is the medication making it any better?"

"Not really," I said. The cameras shifted to a figure coming out of police headquarters. "Here he is." A red-eyed chief of police with a bushy mustache stepped in front of the microphones.

I was nervous, as if learning the identity of the killers could somehow make the situation better or worse. Or maybe it was that this felt personal; the killer or killers had taken my two closest friends.

Mom and I stayed on the phone, but stayed silent as the police chief told us who it was. It wasn't Al-Qaeda, or China, the Tea Partiers, or Russia. It was four men, each with a different reason for doing what they did. When the SWAT team burst into the mastermind's apartment they found the four of them dead from barbiturate overdose, each tucked peacefully into a bed, their personal rant/manifesto/diary on the nightstand beside them.

The mastermind was a Russian scientist who'd emigrated to the U.S. in 1988. He'd been part of the team commissioned to bury Russia's secret stockpile of weaponized anthrax, but before doing it he secreted some away. What was his reason for killing six hundred thousand people? He wanted to get back at his wife, who ran off with his protégé. There was also an unemployed college professor, an anti-government nut, a Jehovah's Witness who believed Atlanta was the epicenter of all sin. They'd met at an AA meeting, then going for coffee together after meetings to rant.

When I'd seen enough I said goodbye to my mom and went for a walk. I hit some baseballs in the Toy Shop Village batting cage, where I'd set up life-sized cutouts of Tina and Little Joe to use as targets. They'd originally been mounted in the façade of the penny arcade. I swung hard, so I hit a lot of weak bouncers, but when I connected it felt good.

I didn't know what I'd expected to feel when the terrorists were found. What I felt was a mixture of disgust and relief. I guess any reason for murdering innocent people was going to seem petty or insane. It was over, though. Case closed. Move along, nothing more to see here. Maybe we could all stop talking about it every minute of every day and try to move on now.

CHAPTER 10

I heaved a big, fat sigh and poised my pencil over the first panel. Draw something—anything—to get the ball rolling. On the heels of my epic two-strip output two days ago, I was having trouble keeping the momentum going.

I dropped my pencil onto the Bristol board and went to the window. From my apartment on the second floor of the crumbling drive-in projection/concession building I couldn't tell what season it was. There were no trees, so no leaves, or lack thereof, to clue me in. As far as the eye could see there was only cyclone fencing, weeds, industrial sprawl, and, across Columbia Avenue, a junk yard. Grandma was getting seventy percent of the revenues from Toy Shop, but she was letting me live in the apartment—which had once been occupied by Toy Shop Village's manager—for free. When I first took over the strip, that was a good thing because thirty percent of the revenue from a marginally popular comic strip was not much (certainly not enough to stay in the apartment Lorena and I had shared before she died). I had no idea why I was still here. With Wolfie dolls hitting the stores in a few weeks, I could buy a nice condo in Buckhead and pay cash.

Maybe my new shrink would help me figure it out.

If anyone had told me my first visit to a psychiatrist would not center around living through an attack that killed half a million people, or the drowning of my twin sister, or the horrible death of my wife, but my relationship with my mean old shithound of a grandfather, I would not have believed it.

We'd spent half an hour going over my outbursts, massaging them for significance. The first thing she'd noticed was that they had nothing to do with the anthrax attack, and that surprised her. Evidently the stuff coming up from deep inside me should be rabid, twitching terror.

She noticed that a lot of them referred to Grandpa, and asked if I had unfinished business with him. I admitted that as Toy Shop got more popular, I felt like more of a fraud for continuing it against his wishes. I told her about the argument we'd had the last time I saw him, how I'd gone to his studio clutching my demo strips, full of hope, how we'd gone back and forth, both of us getting angrier until he finally told me I was a hack.

"Just because you have someone in your family who's an artist doesn't make you one," he'd said.

I'd told him he was no artist, that he trotted out the same characters in the same poses year after year, telling the same corny jokes, that the only people still reading were old ladies. That's when he kicked me out.

I turned from the window and pondered the two original strips hanging framed over my drawing table, side-by-side: Grandpa's last, my first.

You can tell a lot about a cartoonist from the final strip (assuming he or she knew it was the final strip). Charles Schulz's last strip was mostly text—a polite, sincere, slightly distant note saying he wasn't able to continue the strip, and that he appreciated his fans' support over the years. I'd been disappointed—I wanted the characters to say goodbye, not Schulz. But it was fitting in a way, because Schulz was a stoic Midwesterner. An emotional goodbye would have been out of character.

Bill Watterson had done a better job saying goodbye to Calvin and Hobbes. Our heroes are in the woods, walking through freshly fallen snow. They climb onto their toboggan, and in the final panel Calvin says, "It's a magical world, Hobbes, 'ol buddy…Let's go exploring!" It says goodbye, but it's also hopeful. And why not? Watterson wasn't dying, only moving on.

In my grandfather's final strip, Tina drops a Christmas ornament while unpacking a box of them. Little Joe, who's in another aisle, calls out, "Holy smokes, Tina, more ornaments??" To which Tina replies, "No, Little Joe, less ornaments." He'd left a Post-it attached to the strip: "A good one. Save for last."

Grandpa's last and my first. The end, the new beginning.

Only it hadn't been a new beginning; not at first. Same old strip, same Little Joe and Tina. I'd even retained Little Joe's two outdated signature exclamations—Holy smokes! and zounds!"

Readers don't like it when you screw with their strips, Steve, my agent, had said. Comic strips are supposed to be comforting—people read them over coffee when they're still waking up and aren't ready for surprises.

I wandered into the kitchen, pulled open the freezer to find something for dinner. I tended to avoid TV dinners and chicken pot pies, not because I didn't like them, but because eating them lent a certain pathetic quality to the act of eating alone. Somehow a frozen burrito or an Amy's rice bowl didn't carry the same stigma; they were lazy meals, but not clichés that made me feel pitiful.

Yet I was holding a chicken pot pie, considering whether to swallow my pride in exchange for something warmer and homier than a Kashi sweet and sour chicken entrée, when my phone rang.

"Yeah, Finn Darby?" the person on the other end said before I had a chance to speak. The voice had a British accent, cockney-thick to the point of parody.

"Yes?" I said tentatively. It didn't sound like a telemarketer.

"Mick Mercury calling."

I laughed while I set the pot pie back in the freezer and closed the door. I tried running down a mental file of people who might really be on the other end of the line, but came up blank. "Mick Mercury. The rock star Mick Mercury?" Steve was my only guess. The accent was impressive.

"Yeah, that's right. I got your number from your agent. Hope that's okay."

I hesitated. I didn't want to fall for a prank; on the other hand the voice sounded an awful lot like Mick Mercury's.

"Of course." I sat at my kitchen table, where I'd already poured a glass of orange juice to go with whatever frozen entrée I ultimately selected.

"Great, great," he said.

I had no idea what to say, or who I was talking to, so I just sat there turning my glass.

"I'm a great fan of your work," Mick Mercury said. "It's art, what you're doing with that little strip."

"Well, thanks," I laughed.

Every time he spoke my suspicion grew that it really was Mercury. He wasn't super-famous any more, so it wasn't totally inconceivable. For a while in the 1980s, though, he'd been bigger than Springsteen, bigger than U2.

I wondered if he was waiting for me to say something. What could I say? I'm a fan? Truth was, I was a fan. I had all five of his CDs. Actually, he'd probably recorded more than five, but I had the important ones he cut back in the early '80s when he was the Bob Marley of punk/new wave.

"That's not really why I'm calling, though," Mercury said.

"Sure," I said, trying to anticipate the real reason. Did he want to do a song that involved Toy Shop? I didn't think he needed my permission for something like that.

"I'm going to tell you something that's for your ears only, yeah?" Mick asked.

"Of course." We celebrities have a code of silence, after all. It really was him. This was beyond surreal.

"Brilliant," Mick said. "So I'll just say it." He took a big breath. "I had a heart attack on the night of the anthrax attack. I was at my flat in Buckhead."

"Oh, wow." I was amazed that he'd managed to keep something like that secret. "Very sorry to hear it," I added.

"I was dead for five, six minutes before a doctor who lives down the hall resuscitated me. Just luck I had a doctor for a neighbor."

"Jeez."

"Yeah, well, I lived too well in my younger years. My middle-aged years as well. Right into my late middle-years, actually."

I chuckled. Mick Mercury's struggles with alcohol and pills were well known to anyone who glanced at the tabloid headlines while waiting in line at the grocery store.

"They're my friends, too." Mick croaked.

I yelped in surprise. There was no mistaking that zombie baritone.

"'Scuse me," Mick said, as if he'd just burped. He cleared his throat. "Maybe you can guess why I'm calling? Can't help saying things I didn't say. If you know what I mean."

My hand was shaking so badly I could barely grip the phone. It wasn't only me. My mind raced with the implications. It had to be a side effect of exposure to anthrax. The hell with the doctor's opinion, and the shrink's. They were wrong.

"How did you know to call me?" I asked, trying not to sound paranoid.

"Funny thing: we've got the same neurologist. He didn't tell me, though—it was one of the birds that works in the office."

I could picture one of the cute young receptionists telling the rock star about me, basking in his gratitude, leaning into the pat on the shoulder he gave her.

"Is yours the same?" Mick asked. "I mean, does your voice sound like mine?"

"Yes," I said. "I nearly dropped the phone when I heard it."

When Mercury finally spoke, he sounded close to tears. "Don't take this the wrong way, but I'm so fucking relieved to hear that."

"No, believe me, I understand." It occurred to me that I should invite him over, to share what we knew. Why not? I opened my mouth feeling like I had when I first asked Lorena on a date. "Maybe we should get together, exchange notes? It might help us figure out what's going on."

"Yeah, brilliant. That's just what I was thinking. You free right now?"

"Sure," I said, flushing with pleasure.

Mick laughed. "Hell, what else would you be doing, yeah? You can't go to a bloody movie without scaring the popcorn out of the rest of the audience. You know anywhere we could get good pancakes and a scotch?"

"I have three good days, then the chemo takes three," I croaked.

CHAPTER 11

My palms were sweating. I wiped them on my napkin, adjusted my mask so the rubber band wasn't rubbing against my ear.

I'd arrived at the Blue Boy Diner fifteen minutes early, got us a window booth with a view of the muddy brown Ogeechee. The Blue Boy was an old aluminum diner that smelled of home fries and cinnamon buns. Usually there was a half-hour wait for a seat; today there were less than a dozen people in the place.

I hadn't been back there since the day Lorena died. I'd expected memories to come flooding in as soon as I drove up, but my mind was preoccupied with the voices—both mine and Mick Mercury's.

Mick Mercury. As I waited I tried to estimate how old he would be. In his heyday he'd probably been in his early 30s. That was twenty-eight years ago, so he'd be in his late fifties.

I wasn't sure what to expect. Mercury had been arrested a few times in the past decade, most famously for heaving a car battery through a bar window, nearly braining a man who had taunted him for the way he was dressed. From what I remembered he wasn't su-perrich any more. Bad investments, divorce, greedy managers, and a lengthy legal dispute with the guy who co-wrote a lot of his songs had all taken bites out of his net worth.

A man appeared at the entrance. My heart began to thump, then I saw he was with a woman, and he was short and bald, and I relaxed. The hostess led them to an open table. It occurred to me that, even when Atlantans began returning to their normal routines, there would be far fewer filling restaurants and subway cars. Close to fifteen percent fewer, at least until others started moving to Atlanta to take advantage of all the job openings and drastically reduced rents. Assuming people wanted to live in a place that had been the target of the worst terrorist attack in history. My guess was that wouldn't stop people. The city would eventually rise again.

"Can I get you something to drink?" The waitress's voice pulled me out of my thoughts. I looked up and was immediately drawn to the tattoos on her forearms: assault rifles morphing into flowers. I laughed, shook my head in disbelief.

The waitress tilted her head, smiled beneath her mask. "What's funny?" She was an attractive woman, with warm, bright eyes and a relaxed self-assurance that was slightly disconcerting. She was in her late twenties, small and thin, black hair pulled into stubby pigtails with orange rubber bands.

"I'm sorry," I said. "You wouldn't remember me, but you'd remember my wife."

She folded her arms, masking the flower on her right forearm, leaving only the rifle. "Why's that?"

"You got into an argument with her once."

The waitress shook her head. "When was this?"

"Two years ago? Springtime. My wife was lactose intolerant," I explained. "She told you to keep all the dairy products off her plate. You forgot to hold the butter—there was a big scoop on the pancakes. She asked you to get her new ones, but you didn't see why she couldn't just scrape the butter off."

The waitress was still shaking her head, no hint of recognition.

"You got huffy. That's when she got in your face, told you she didn't like your tone of voice. She was tall? Latino?"

Her eyes got wide. She pointed at me. "Perfect hair? Expensive hiking boots?"

I pointed back. "That's her."

The waitress let her head loll back until she was looking at the ceiling. "God, that was a terrible morning. My daughter had been throwing up all night, then I couldn't find anyone to watch her and I was late getting to work." She pressed her hand to the side of her face. "By the time I got to the butter thing I had nothing left. I just couldn't conjure up the cheery singsong waitress voice."

"No," I laughed, "you definitely couldn't." I didn't know what it was about this woman. She had an energy that made me wish I could go on talking to her.

She glanced toward the door, widening her eyes theatrically. "She's not meeting you here, is she? Should I hide?"

I felt a pang. "No, no." I shrugged.

"Well, please tell her I'm sorry."

I shrugged. "She died, actually." I had never come up with an easy way to say it. And for some reason it seemed important to add, "Believe it or not, it was the same day as that argument."

The waitress pressed a hand to her chest. "Oh, God, I'm so sorry."

I felt it welling up, but could do nothing to stop it. "I'm telling ya, she's a little tramp," I croaked.

The waitress gasped, her hand flying to her mouth.

"I'm sorry," I said, covering my own masked mouth. "I didn't mean to say that. My doctor says I've got some sort of neurological disorder. He thinks it's temporary. It's not contagious."

"Oh." She reached as if to touch my hand, but didn't quite. "Oh. That's terrible. I'm so sorry. About your wife, and—" she paused, reaching for a word, "your problem." I could see from her face that she was more scared than sorry. She recovered her composure, cleared her throat. "So can I get you something to drink?"

Before I could answer a buzz of excitement rose through the diner. I leaned around the waitress to see the door.

There he was. Unmistakable, speaking into the other waitress's ear, a hand on her shoulder. He still had the spiky blonde hair, and his outfit, though not particularly loud or flashy, announced that he was someone of note: black-rimmed hipster glasses, expensive leather jacket, jeans. He wasn't wearing a mask—the only person in the diner.

I waved. He spotted me, gave me a two-fingered salute, sauntered over wearing a big smile, his hand outstretched. I met him partway and we shook, then he clapped my shoulders as if making sure I was real.

A young woman was hovering behind him, clutching a pen. I motioned to Mick. He turned, exchanged a few pleasantries with the woman as he signed her napkin.

A few other admirers left their booths to meet him. Mercury gave his attention to each of them in turn, listened to their brief testimonials—how they'd seen him at his first Atlanta concert, what this or that song meant to them. He seemed to enjoy himself.

When an elderly woman came forward, her hand outstretched, Mick blurted, "Mom, not in the middle of my show."

The woman let out a startled "Eep"; others gasped in surprise.

"Sorry," Mick said, holding his palm over his mouth. "Been working on a new vocal style. Thinking I might try crossing over into some of that Goth vampire music." He grinned brightly, eliciting a few nervous chuckles. "Finn and me are going to have some breakfast now, so if you don't mind…" He gave everyone a gentle "shove off" gesture.

When everyone was back at their tables, Mick and I settled in.

"So. What the fuck is wrong with us?" Mick murmured.

I took a quick sip of water—my mouth was dry. It was jarring, to realize I was sitting with a rock star. I found it impossible to look across the table at Mick Mercury and see nothing but another guy. It was Mick freaking Mercury.

"Seems to me it's got to be connected to the anthrax," I said.

Mick pointed at me, nodding emphatically. "That's what I said, but the doctor said it ain't possible."

The waitress came over. I stared at the table, still embarrassed by my outburst, and it seemed as if she was standing a lot further from the table than she'd been before. She was wearing gold sneaker-shoes with Cleopatra's face on them.

She gave Mick a level look. "Just so we're clear, I'm not going to ask for your autograph or anything juvenile like that." She shrugged. "But if you happened to sign that place mat for some reason, that would be okay."

Mick grinned. "I've done stranger things."

"Yes you have," the waitress shot back, prompting Mick to cackle madly.

True to his word, Mick ordered a scotch with his bacon and pancakes.

When the waitress had gone, I said, "The doctor told me the same thing. But it's the only thing that connects our cases. That and the fact that we both died for a few minutes."

We compared notes. The things we were blurting were similar in some ways, not in others. I recognized a lot of what I said—it had to do with the strip, people and places I knew, and especially my grandfather. Mick recognized some of what he said—about his music, the lawsuit he'd fought with his collaborator, and so on. Other things weren't at all familiar, like the beauty he'd just uttered.

"Sometimes it's like I got a bleeding anorak in my throat. Pro-grams on the telly, comic books. I go on and on about the most trivial dross."

It definitely didn't fit with my psychiatrist Corinne's theory that my blurting was the result of unresolved issues with my grand-father. If that was it, why would Mick Mercury have the same problem?

"Let me ask you something," Mick said, leaning forward, his el-bows on the table. "You much for getting trolleyed?"

I shook my head, totally lost.

"You know, do you like to get pissed?"

It took me a minute, then I remembered that pissed was British for drunk. "Oh sure, I like a few drinks now and then."

Mick nodded, looked around, as if afraid some of the patrons might be undercover paparazzi. "But when you're done having those few drinks, do you have a few more?"

"When I was in college, maybe, but now it's mostly two or three max." I wasn't sure where he was going with this.

"Harder stuff? Pills and powder?"

"None of that. Why?"

Mick waved it off. "I thought maybe it was from brain damage. You know, brain atrophy and that."

Mick's cell phone rang. He checked it, then held up a finger. "Just a sec."

"My guardian angel! Yeah, I'm with him right now." He nodded at me. "Nah, he ain't angry. He says to say thanks." Pause, then Mick laughed. "I bet, I bet."

The person on the other end—Mick's mole receptionist in our doctor's office, I assumed, said something that lit his face with surprise. "No kidding?"

She went on; Mick fumbled in the pockets of his jacket, then covered the mouthpiece of his phone. "You got a pen?" I handed him the sketching pencil I always carried. He pressed it to the back of his menu. "Can you give me a name?" He rolled his eyes toward the hammered tin ceiling. "I promise, you won't get in trouble. I'll be very discreet." A moment later he jotted a name and number on his napkin. "Thanks. You're an angel from heaven! You've no idea how much this means to me, and Finn Darby too. He just said to give you a big wet kiss for him." Mick winked at me, grinning, as I pressed my hands to my cheeks and shook my head. I'd have to face her again, whoever she was, next time I went to Dr. Purvis's office.

"Jesus flipping Christ," Mick whispered as he closed the phone. "You ready for this?"

"What?"

"Dr. Purvis saw three more cases like ours in the past twenty-four hours."

I wasn't sure if that was good news, but it felt like good news. Mick and I smiled grimly at each other.

"You ever see Planet of the Apes?" Mick asked. "The original, not that shit remake."

"One of my favorites," I said, pleased that Mick and I liked the same film.

"'Where there's one, there's another, and another, and another,'" Mick quoted.

I recognized the line: Three stranded astronauts, crossing a lifeless desert, come upon a single scraggly weed in the rocky soil. I nodded understanding. We weren't alone. We weren't freaks. It was a relief, even if it didn't explain what was wrong with us.

The waitress was back with our food.

"You ever see Planet of the Apes?" Mick asked her. "The original, not the shit remake."

"Take your stinking paws off me, you damned dirty ape," she said.

Mick and I burst out laughing, drawing curious looks from the other tables.

"I bet that line comes in handy for a pretty bird like you, eh?" Mick said.

The waitress just smiled, refilled our coffee cups.

When she'd left, Mick asked, "How long were you, you know, dead?"

"Ten or fifteen minutes, as well as I can figure." Out of the corner of my eye I watched the waitress duck behind the counter, feeling a longing to get to know her, knowing that wasn't going to happen as long as my inner zombie was with me.

"It's something, ain't it? To know you were dead, that you weren't in your body?" Mick said. He seemed to be watching my reaction, peering over his scotch.

"I definitely wasn't in my body," I said.

His eyebrows shot up. "When you were dead, you mean?" He paused, searching for words. "What was it like for you? Do you remember anything?"

"Hell, yes." He was prodding, and I thought I knew why. "It was like I was watching from behind someone else's eyes, seeing what they were seeing."

Mick slapped the table, pointed at me, shouted, "That's exactly what happened to me." He didn't seem to care that people were glancing his way. "Christ, I'm not off my head."

"What did you see?" I asked.

Mick pressed his hands to his face. "I was inside my ex-wife, Blossom." He lowered his voice. "She was, you know, having a romp with her latest beau." He made a sour face. "So there I am, dead, inside my wife while this bloke Peter is also inside her, in a manner of speaking. It was a miserable four or five minutes. Absolute torture."

The pain in Mick's expression made me grin.

"Oh, sure, laugh. You didn't have to go through it."

"I'm sorry," I said. "I wasn't smiling at what happened, just your expression."

"It's all fixed, I'm telling ya. They vote for their friends," I added. The elderly woman who had been talking to Mick during his first outburst dropped her fork onto her plate. Struggling not to stare she scooped the napkin out of her lap and pressed it against her mouth.

Mick ignored it completely. He gestured at me with his chin. "How about you, eh?"

I described what I'd seen in Lyndsay's apartment.

"Do you suppose this is connected to the voices?" Mick asked when I'd finished. He waved to get the waitress's attention, pointed to his empty drink.

"I've thought about that. Maybe we're somehow still connected to the people we were inside. The problem is, some of the things I say are about people I know, but this woman doesn't. I just don't see how she fits in."

"Right, right," Mick said. "That doesn't work." His eyes took on an empty glaze, and he added, "I've got to get it perfect. It's got to be perfect." Ignoring the stares, Mick swirled his drink, gazed thoughtfully into the glass.

His suggestion got me thinking. I had been focusing on mundane explanations for the voice—a physical illness that had screwed me up neurologically, or a psychological problem. But there were those few moments when I was dead, how I learned the attack originated in the subway. Maybe I was looking for answers in the wrong places. What happened when I was dead didn't have a logical explanation, so why should the voices?

Mick looked at his watch. "I'd best get going."

I felt a wash of disappointment.

"Let's keep in touch," he added as he pulled a bill from his wallet, "compare notes on how this thing plays out, yeah?"

I told him I thought that was a good idea.

"I got this," he said, pointing at our plates. "Good choice, by the way. Top-shelf pancakes." Our waitress was behind the counter; Mick went right on back there without hesitation, put a hand on her shoulder as he fished a bill out of his wallet. She laughed at something he said, and that feeling washed over me again, a longing to talk to her. Once I figured out how to stop the vocalizations, I planned to return to the Blue Boy often.

CHAPTER 12

The granite steps outside Corinne's building looked blurry from the tears I'd shed during our session. I wiped my eyes with my sleeve, hoping no one would notice.

Digging up these memories is painful, Corinne had said at the end of the session, but it's like digging up a splinter: you'll feel better once it's out. The thing was, I felt like I'd already dug up and reburied Kayleigh's and Lorena's deaths a thousand times.

I tried not to set Kayleigh's and Lorena's deaths side-by-side and examine the similarities. One at a time was plenty. Sometimes it was hard to resist, though. They were the two most important people in my life, both died on water, and I carried legitimate blame—and terrible guilt—in both cases.

You hear about people who are racked with guilt because they created some benign circumstance that led to the death of a loved one. A woman sends her husband to the store for eggs to finish a batch of brownies, and he's crushed by a semi on the way home. She finds broken eggshells scattered in the car, and thinks, If only I hadn't sent him to the store he'd still be alive. I wish I had to go through such a contorted string of logic to assign myself blame for Kayleigh's and Lorena's deaths.

I don't assign myself all the blame. Sometimes I think I'm more to blame for Kayleigh's death than Lorena's; at other times I give myself a partial pass on Kayleigh's because I was only twelve, and then I think I'm more to blame for Lorena's. Both had to take some of the blame themselves, although they weren't around to do so. It's difficult to apportion blame. It's not an exact science.

Sometimes I wondered what my life would be like if I had backed down from Kayleigh's dare to jump off that pier. If I hadn't jumped, Kayleigh wouldn't have had reason to stay behind on that awful night and try to prove she could do it, too. What would I have done with all of that mental space taken up by guilt?

Lorena's Toyota unlocked with a cheerful bleep-bleep and I hopped in.

I was beginning to wonder how any of this was connected to the voice. I was blurting more than ever; maybe I was digging up all of these painful memories for nothing. Goodness knows I had enough, more recent painful shit to deal with without digging through my past for more.

I turned on the radio to get an update on suffering that put my petty grievances to shame.

The six hundred thousandth victim had been counted. Anyone who hadn't known the population of greater Atlanta before the attack certainly knew it by now. Five million. More than one in nine Atlantans had died. Entire families had been wiped out. Entire blocks, almost. With those six hundred thousand victims had gone all laughter, all joy. The people I passed looked grim, tired. All business. On the plus side the traffic was thinner, the other drivers less ruthless. There was the occasional honk, but it was nothing like the incessant hooting and bleating that had been the background Muzak of the city's downtown both night and day.

"Come here, ya monkey, ya," my unwanted voice opined. Jesus, that was vintage Grandpa. I could picture him saying that as he chased a six-year-old Kayleigh around the yard with hedge clippers, pretending he was going to cut off her toes while she giggled and screeched.

There was no mention of the blurting illness on the news. If my neurologist had seen five cases, there must be thousands, but it would be hard for another story to break through when there was the anthrax story to cover 24/7.

As I pulled onto West Marietta I turned off the news. Enough of this dreariness. I should pick up something cheerful for lunch and eat it while watching last night's episode of The Big Bang Theory on DVR.

Then I remembered that I'd agreed to visit Grandma this afternoon. I let my head slump until my forehead bumped the steering wheel. "Damn it. Damn it." I needed time to acclimate to the idea of a visit to Grandma's, and by forgetting, I'd missed my acclimation period.

Moaning in pointless protest I took a left on Howell Mill and headed for Grandma's house.

It wasn't that I didn't like Grandma, she was just hard to talk to. Sitting on her couch, time crawled in super slow-mo. There were so many things she didn't talk about: politics, religion, relatives' private business, her childhood, sports, feelings, failures, anything bad. The list bordered on infinite. What she liked to discuss was the gruesome but impersonal goings-on depicted on the TV news. She liked to shake her head and tisk. She also liked to talk about how there was nothing on television any more, and about delicious meals from days gone by. I braced myself for two hours of pain.

I'd warned her about the problem I was having with my voice. She suggested I might be coming down with the flu. It hadn't happened while I was on the phone with her, and there was no way anyone could grasp how utterly freaky it was unless they heard it. And Grandma would hear it. The outbursts were getting worse—I was up to thirty since I'd waked that morning. So that was another concern—I didn't want to give her a heart attack.

I was even doing it in my sleep now. I'd wake up four or five times a night, jolted from sleep by that voice. I worried they would keep getting worse until my speech was one long nonsensical rant comprised of things my grandfather might say. I'd be forced to communicate like a deaf mute, writing down what I wanted to say, or using sign language while I blathered on about Toy Shop's superiority over Beetle Bailey.

Corinne suspected that the root of the problem was guilt. More guilt, like I didn't have enough. I had defied the patriarch, and now the child in me was waiting on wobbly knees to be punished. Forgive me Grandfather, for I have sinned. Only I didn't feel guilty. Not about that, anyway. Grandpa dragged Toy Shop into the grave with him out of spite; why should I feel bad for digging it up and breathing life back into it? Who did it harm? In a way he owed it to me after all the verbal abuse he'd piled on me when I was a kid. He owed me something; if not an apology, Toy Shop would do.

Besides all that, this was happening to other people, including Mick. It wasn't about my relationship with Grandpa, it was something in the air I'd inhaled. Or something else.

Grandma greeted me in her singsong Irish warble, entreating me to come in, come in, as she led me into the living room of her spacious but unpretentious home, favoring her bad hip so severely it looked like her right leg was three inches shorter than her left.

She wanted to hear about my accident again, and held her breath through much of my description of drowning as if to share some of my suffering, slapping her cheeks in horror until they were a ruddy pink.

I left out the part about being in a woman's body while I was dead.

"Oh, Finn, that's just terrible!" she said when I'd finished. "This whole business is just awful. All those bodies." She shook her head in dismay as she related some of the more gruesome things she'd witnessed on the news.

To change the subject I asked what she thought of this week's check, her share of Toy Shop's meteoric rise.

"I wish we hadn't waited so long," she half-joked.

The new Toy Shop kept getting more popular. Fan sites were springing up on the web; Steve was working out some new licensing agreements. People loved Wolfie. I guess it was no more surprising than the popularity of the Teenage Mutant Ninja Turtles in their time.

"So you really don't mind the changes to the strip?" I asked, for maybe the tenth time.

Grandma threw her hands up. "What's to mind? The point is to make money."

"Yes it is," I said, though that wasn't at all the point to me. "So, Grandma, what have you been up to?"

"Oh, this and that." She waved at the air as if her activities were nothing but a bad smell that needed to be dispersed. "Staying out of trouble." She laughed her nervous laugh—a tight-lipped, high-pitched giggle.

"You finding anything good to watch on TV?" I asked. "All I can find worth watching are reruns of Lost."

"There's nothing on," she said, sinking her teeth into the topic. "Half the time I watch the Weather Channel—"

"I wasn't there. Do you understand?" I blurted.

Grandma started, the cheery smile melting. She pulled her feet under her as if something had just run by on the carpet.

"I'm sorry. I didn't mean to startle you," I said.

She stared at me, her eyes big and round. Her jaw was trembling.

I wasn't sure what to do. I wanted to comfort her in some way, but I was afraid she'd recoil from me. Everyone was shocked when they first heard it, but no one had reacted like this. She was pale and shaking, like she had a terrible fever.

I felt like a freak, like I'd pulled open my shirt and exposed a secret twin jutting from my chest. I hated this. I wanted it gone.

"It's me first drink today, Frenchie," I blurted.

"Why are you trying to scare me?" Grandma cried out.

"I'm not," I said, holding out my hands in supplication. "I swear to you, I can't help it. It just comes out."

"Things your Grandfather said just come out of you? You expect me to believe that?"

It was a good thing I was seeing a psychiatrist—I was truly messed up.

"What was that first thing you said? Where did you hear that?" Grandma asked.

"Nowhere. Grandma, I know something is wrong with me, but I'm not in control of it. Do you hear how strange my voice is? Do you think I could make it sound like that even if I wanted to?"

Grandma covered her eyes, struggled to stand. "I have a terrible headache. I have to go lie down." She staggered from the couch to the bedroom while I stood, weaving.

I'd warned her about how strange the voice was. I should have warned her about the content. "Goodbye Grandma," I called tentatively. "I'm sorry. I hope you feel better." No answer.

I let myself out, stunned by my last blurt. I'd said "Me first drink today," not "My first drink today." That's how an Irishman would say it. And I'd swear there was a hint of accent in that croak. I was starting to talk like him.

CHAPTER 13

thought that might make a good recurring joke, to have Dave repeatedly sell Wolfie, who has to go through all sorts of effort to get back to the toy shop.

As I put the finishing touches on it I wished there was someone there to share it with. Comic strip fans were mostly a faceless abstraction that couldn't replace having someone to turn to and say, "What do you think?"

I'd never thought of myself as a recluse, or someone who has a hard time making friends, but the paltry list of contacts in my cell phone was hard to ignore.

I decided to call it a day. The vocalizations were driving me nuts; they'd been coming fast and furious for the past half hour. Despite them I'd finished two strips; if I kept up that pace I could work four days a week and take long weekends. It was getting easier to draw the strip again. The characters didn't seem like strangers the way they had a few weeks ago. Part of that may have been my confidence growing because of how people were reacting to Toy Shop. The Cartoon Network was talking about an animated series, for God's sake.

I flipped on the news and fixed myself a turkey sandwich.

The financial markets were nearly back where they'd been before the attacks. As soon as it became clear the attack wasn't connected to a foreign country or some specific terrorist group, the financial world had begun to relax. Life was returning to normal, at least as normal as it could after six hundred thousand people die in the course of three weeks.

"Whiskey! Whiskey!"

I couldn't hear the TV over the rants that were coming out of me, and missed the beginning of the next report. It was about an unexplained malady that was cropping up around the city. Even before they cut to a young woman blurting something in a pitch with which I was horribly familiar, I knew what it was. I put down my sandwich, set the DVR to record. I didn't want to miss a word, and I was having trouble hearing because the damned vocalizations kept coming.

I wiped my forehead with my sleeve; I was sweating like I was in a sauna.

Not sure I could even carry on a conversation between my vocalizations, I looked around for my phone to call Mick.

"Did it occur to you that I might want some hot water too?"

"You're a sight to behold tonight, Helen."

"I'm not paying no forty-three dollars for that."

They just kept coming; I struggled to catch my breath between the outbursts, praying it was going to let up, terrified that this was it, the moment when the voices got so dense they stole my ability to speak.

My hands were trembling like a palsied old man's. I stared at them, mesmerized, as an awful ripple passed under my skin. It was subtle at first, but grew until it felt as if snakes were writhing through my muscles. I wanted to dig into my skin with my fingernails and pull whatever it was out. I spotted my phone, half-sunk between the couch cushions, and decided I should call 911 instead of Mick. But I couldn't get my hand to reach for it; my whole arm was clenched, my whole body.

The writhing gave way to a tingling, as if my whole body was falling asleep the way a foot can. I expected to drop to the ground, but, miraculously, I stayed on my feet while the tingling turned to a thick numbness. I thought I might be having a stroke. I was falling away, losing all sensation.

A sound passed between my lips, a guttural "Uh." My lips moved, but I wasn't moving them. It was like I was wearing a mask. I tried to touch my face to see what was wrong, but my hand didn't come up, it stayed there, trembling.

It was just like the experience I'd had when I was dead, only I was in my own body instead of Lyndsay's.

I felt myself rise from the couch, then look down at my legs. My hand touched one leg, then the other. The hand was quavering so violently it was a blur.

I tried to cry out, to scream in terror, but couldn't.

I heard myself laugh. It was a loose, blubbery laugh, and it was the last sound I wanted to make. I watched myself step away from the couch, put my hands on my hips, and start kicking my legs. They kicked and sprung in a spastic, rubbery parody of dance, the movements utterly unfamiliar to me.

"Diddle de diddle de dee," I sang, my chest hitching, my voice a dead croak.

Just as it began to dawn on me that the dance I was doing was a jig—an Irish jig—I turned my face to the ceiling, spread my arms and croaked, "I got me legs."

Me legs. I wanted to run screaming from the room, to escape this twisted marionette show.

Me legs.

My body stopped dancing. "And now." Even through the thick guttural zombie belch there was no mistaking Grandpa's accent.

I was taken upstairs to my studio, to the drafting table, to the strip I'd just finished.

"You little shit," my mouth said. I watched my grandfather yank a pair of scissors out of a drawer with my hand. "Thieving little shit." He stabbed the strip, hit Wolfie in the face, driving the scissors into the wooden table. "I'll fix you." He pulled the scissors out, brought them down again, and again, stabbing and cursing, until the images were obliterated. When he was finished he retrieved a thumb tack and tried to pin the ruined strip to the wall, but his hands were shaking too badly and he dropped the tack.

The tips of my fingers began to tingle. It was subtle at first, then it ran up my arms. I was feeling something again. It got stronger, until it felt like electric eels in my blood. I balled my hands into spastic fists.

Now that I had my mouth back, I screamed.

CHAPTER 14

The doorbell rang three times before I heard it. It rang a fourth before I could muster the strength to say, "Come in."

Mick found me at the kitchen table, a half-empty bottle of Jack Daniel's and a shot glass in front of me. I'd completely forgotten that he was going to come by.

"All right, Finn?" he said. I was still shaking; I felt colder than the night I was pulled out of the reservoir. Could that have been just over a month ago? That was utterly inconceivable.

"I don't need a psychiatrist," I said. "I need an exorcist." Or was it a delusion? Maybe I was a deeply disturbed individual. That was very possible. In fact, it seemed almost probable when I considered the alternative.

Mick pulled out a chair and sat. "What happened to you?" His voice was soft, calming, the tone you use to comfort someone who's been raped. Which was not far off. I felt violated. I'd been ripped from my own body, pushed to a place where you go in your nightmares, where you try to open your mouth to scream but can't find your own mouth.

"What happened?" he repeated.

I couldn't explain. It would take too many words, too many strange words. Finally, I said simply, "My grandfather visited me."

Mick nodded, not in understanding but to encourage me to continue. Then he frowned. "Hang on, I thought your grandfather was dead."

"He is."

He clapped my shoulder, went to the cabinets, and rooted around, returning a moment later with a mug. He poured himself a drink.

"Can you turn on more lights?" I asked. It had been dark for hours, but I'd been too afraid to move about the house. Grandpa was hiding in every dark corner.

"Yeah," Mick said. His chair scraped the linoleum. "Which?"

"All of them."

Without a word Mick went into the living room and turned on the lights. In the brighter light the kitchen spun slightly, the results of half a bottle of Jack. Mick disappeared upstairs.

"Bloody hell," I heard him mutter.

He returned holding the strip. I looked away—I didn't want to see it. It was evidence that I hadn't imagined it all.

"This was good," Mick said. "Why did you ruin it?"

"I didn't."

"Then who did?"

I shrugged helplessly. "Grandpa." I could still hear him breathing through my nose as he slashed with the scissors. He'd clutched the scissors in his fist the way a child does, just as he'd held a pencil when he was alive.

Mick studied me. "Why don't you take your time, tell me when you're ready?" He poured me another shot of whiskey. I downed it.

Grandpa was in me right now. That's what this had all been about from that first twitch in my throat—it was Grandpa, inside me, struggling to get out.

But that was impossible. It just didn't make sense. I dragged my hands down my face. Who could help me? I was beginning to doubt Corinne could. What if this was real? What if Grandpa had somehow crawled out of the grave and inside me?

I froze, my hand clutching the glass. Suddenly the experience I'd had while I was dead came into tighter focus. I'd been dead, so I'd taken up residence in some unsuspecting person, the way Grandpa was in me. Maybe Lyndsay had felt a twitching in her throat when I tried to speak.

Finally, I opened my mouth. "My grandfather took control of me. All of me. He did that—" I pointed to the ruined strip on the kitchen table.

Mick stared at the strip, his lip curled in disgust, or maybe disbelief. "You mean, he actually took control of your body?"

"Yeah."

He pressed the balls of his hands against his eyes. "I've got to tell you, Finn, this is crazy shit you're talking."

"There are dead people inside us," I said, rolling right over his skepticism. "The voices are the dead people taking control for a moment."

"Christ, don't say that," Mick said. He cupped his hands over his ears, propped his elbows on the table. "You're going to give me another bleeding heart attack."

I reached for the remote and scrolled until I found the news report I'd recorded. "Have you seen this?"

It was only a two-minute piece. They showed people blurting in zombie-speak, their faces in silhouette to protect their identities. A psychiatrist said that cases had been cropping up in the greater Atlanta area for the past few weeks. They hadn't figured out what it was, but believed it was a form of post-traumatic stress disorder brought on by the anthrax attack. He estimated there were several hundred to several thousand cases.

I turned away from the TV.

"You really think we're possessed?" Mick asked. "All of us? Thousands of us?" Mick clutched at my elbow. "Are you sure you didn't imagine the whole thing? Were you on anything?"

"I'm not sure of my own name right now. But I was completely sober." I gestured toward the ruined strip, once again saw my hand reaching for the scissors, stabbing, furious. "And it would have to be one hell of a delusion for me to do that, don't you think?"

Hadn't Grandpa been furious even before he saw the strip? He had, hadn't he? I thought back, tried to reconstruct the events. He'd danced a jig. Much as that was out of character for someone as joyless as my grandfather, it made sense. He'd spent the last fifty years of his life in a wheelchair. Having control of legs that worked, that he could feel, would be wonderful. As soon as he stopped dancing, he said, "And now." Then he went straight for the strip.

He'd already known about it.

"He's watching us right now. Through my eyes." I shut my mouth. It sounded so paranoid.

Mick froze, his eyes wide. "What do you mean?"

I told him how Grandpa had known about the strips even before he set (my) eyes on them.

"Do you see what he's saying about me? Do you see? How can you take his side?" Mick said. He clenched his eyes closed, reached toward the ceiling, fingers clawed. "Christ, I can't take this any more."

I stared through the dark amber of the Jack Daniel's bottle at the pads of my fingertips, debating whether to drink more. I was probably close to vomit territory.

"Wait a minute. Have you noticed that you haven't blurted once since I got here?" Mick asked.

He was right; I'd been so freaked out I'd forgotten about the voice. "I haven't blurted since it happened. That must have been two hours before you got here."

Mick leapt from his chair. "Maybe that's it. Whatever it is," he churned his hands through the options, "a dead person, a nervous tick, whatever, works its way to the surface, takes you over for a spell, and then goes on its way."

There was a certain logic to that. Some viruses waited hidden in cells until they finally showed themselves, then they were driven out of the body.

"God, I hope you're right," I said.

CHAPTER 15

The pitching machine rattled, spit a grey, rubber-coated base-ball. I fouled it off. The impact of ball on metal bat stung my hands, despite the thick gloves I was wearing.

"Shouldn't you be lights out at this, seeing as you've got a batting cage in your back yard?" Mick called from the other side of the chain-link fence. "You've got to listen to The Sonics in the original vinyl," he added.

"I don't use it much," I said. Mick's outbursts were still going strong, but it had been almost twenty-four hours since my last. We were waiting, hoping Grandpa wouldn't return, hoping Mick would have a spell like mine and that would be the end of it.

I hit a bouncer to the left side. "That would've skipped just under the third baseman's outstretched glove for a clean single."

Mick tossed a cigarette butt on the concrete. "Is the third base-man a double-amputee? That's the only way I can picture that."

I laughed just as the next pitch came, causing me to swing and miss badly. The ball hit the padding behind me with a heavy whump.

Mick rolled his eyes toward the sky, grinning at my incompetence.

I leaned the bat against the chain-link fence, let the final pitch go by. "You know, I haven't had a chance to tell you how much I love your music."

"Yeah? Cheers, mate."

I'd been meaning to tell him that, now that it wouldn't sound like insincere flattery, but hadn't had the opportunity, because we had more important things to discuss. By silent assent we were taking a break from talking about our problem, if not thinking about it.

I hadn't slept at all the night before. The thought that Grandpa might be lurking right behind my eyes, watching everything I did, judging me, was intolerable. I hoped Mick was right that he was gone, but what if he wasn't?

"What's your favorite, eh?" Mick asked, interrupting my reverie.

I liked all of his big hits, but didn't want to name one of the obvious songs. "I always loved 'Mystic Messenger.'"

Mick looked pleased. "You've got good taste. That's one of my favorites. Hang on a minute." He jogged off toward his car—a vintage Jensen—popped the trunk, and pulled out a guitar.

"Oh, man!" I shouted, raising my arms in the air. "Are you serious?"

Mick propped a leg on the steel bench outside the batting cage and strummed the opening cords to "Mystic Messenger." Grinning like an idiot, I reveled.

He was still good—his voice had the same power, the same slightly scratchy quality that I remembered. The song was interrupted by the voice three times, but it was pure magic nonetheless. I gave him a standing O.

"I still love the music," he said as he set his guitar against the bench and pulled out a cigarette.

"I wish my wife could've seen this. She loved your music, too." I hadn't thought of Lorena in days, I realized. Too much else occupying my mind.

"How'd you meet her?" Mick asked through the side of his mouth as he lit his cigarette.

"In high school. I had a secret crush on her. Totally debilitating. When I passed her in the hall my heart would hammer. I used to secretly take photos of her with my phone when we passed in the hall." I smiled wistfully, remembering my awkward teenage self. "I thought I had no chance with her. I was a boy, and she was a woman. I sat in the back of the class and only talked to my friends, making boy jokes and talking about The Fantastic Four. Lorena had conversations with our teachers after class about Dostoevsky." I shut my mouth, suddenly realizing I was babbling. Mick hadn't asked for a history of my adolescence.

"How did she die, if you don't mind me asking?" Mick said.

"Lightning," I said, feeling no desire to elaborate.

His eyes got big. "She was struck?"

I nodded, though Lorena hadn't been "struck." Few people are truly struck. Reluctantly I told him about the canoe trip; Mick listened attentively until I got to the point where Lorena screamed that there could be snakes in the tall grass.

"Snakes?"

I nodded. "She had a terrible fear of snakes. I jumped into the water and pulled the canoe to the bank, but she wouldn't get out. I made a show of looking all around to show her there were no snakes. I told her I'd carry her up the bank." I blinked away tears. "I think she was about to let me carry her when lightning hit the far bank." I could hear the rain pelting down, feel my soaked shirt pasted to my skin.

Mick nodded understanding. I couldn't describe the moment Lorena died. I'd never described it to anyone.

"Were you hurt?"

"I was ten feet up the bank." Up the bank, where it was safe. I didn't remember taking those steps; somehow it was the only aspect of the event that wasn't emblazoned in my memory.

"It's hard to believe she was thinking about snakes in the middle of all that lightning."

I thought of my car skidding off the road and sinking in the icy lake in the midst of an anthrax epidemic. "I think sometimes what we're afraid of and what can actually kill us are very different things."

"That's nice," Mick said. "If I still wrote, I'd use that."

"So you don't have a secret cache of songs you've been working on? I thought all musicians did," I said.

Mick scratched his temple at the hairline. "Most of them don't, actually. It's a lucky few who can keep writing good songs." He retrieved his guitar, plucked a single string, watched it vibrate. "For most of us it goes, and it doesn't come back. Maybe it's the drugs and booze, I don't know."

He set the guitar back down. I wasn't sure what to say; I couldn't imagine what I would feel if my ability to draw abandoned me.

Mick glanced at his watch, signaled it was time to go. He had an appointment with Dr. Purvis, and I had one with Corinne, so we were driving downtown together.

"Truth be told, I wrote very little of my last successful album, Little Tripe," Mick said as we climbed into his car. "It had all dried up by then."

"Who wrote it, then?"

"My lyricist. Bloke named Gilly Hansen. I never wrote the words, was never very good with words. I was a music fellow. Gilly always did the words, then slowly took over doing the music."

I'd heard of Gilly Hansen. He'd had a nervous breakdown or something, became a recluse and never wrote again.

"What's it been, a day and a half since your last ghoulie voice?" Mick held up crossed fingers.

CHAPTER 16

I pulled to the curb along Piedmont Park. Parking near Piedmont on a weekday used to be impossible. Now the streets were filthy with spaces.

"I take it you fancy a walk? We can get a lot closer to the doc's office than this," Mick said.

I reached back and retrieved a plastic grocery bag from the back seat. "I've got some business I want to take care of, then, yeah, I thought it might be nice to walk. Do you mind?"

Mick smiled. "Sounds good to me."

There were more police and National Guard than civilians in the park. The mood was muted, devoid of the usual festive cocktail of musicians, Hacky Sackers, and joggers. The smattering of civilians walked with their heads bowed, stepping carefully among the shoes.

The sidewalk running along the lake was covered with shoes, set in pairs. Mick and I walked in the grass alongside, silent save for Mick's blurts. The shoes demanded silence.

The swimming pool, drained for the winter, was covered with

shoes, even the sides. The tennis courts were carpeted as well.

There was a running track around the ball fields. I found a spot where the track was relatively bald of shoes, squatted, and withdrew Annie's running shoes and a tube of crazy glue from the plastic bag. Mick stood by, head bowed, while I set them in place, two nondescript white shoes, the tread worn most deeply along the outside edges. Annie had an odd, ducklike jogging gait.

No one knew who started this memorial to the dead, but I thought it was a good one. In a few years the powers that be would come up with some concrete obelisk to honor the dead, but it would never have the power, the honesty, of this one. Standing, I turned in a complete circle. How many of the dead were represented here? Probably not even half.

"Let's go," I said.

As we turned, Mick clapped me on the back, left his arm across my shoulders as we walked. I started to tear up, swallowed, shook it off. How foolish that the lump in my throat was as much about having made a new friend as losing my old one. I hadn't realized just how alone I'd felt.

We were just within earshot for me to hear a woman whisper, "That's Mick Mercury" to her companion, reminding me of how unlikely my new friendship was.

"I haven't heard anyone else with the voice," Mick said.

"When it first started in me, I hid in my apartment. I was afraid of people hearing," I said.

Mick dropped his arm, fished a pack of cigarettes from his jacket. "Hang on. I stayed in my apartment most of the time, but I did go out once." He looked at me.

"To a doctor," I said.

Mick nodded. "Should give us an idea of how widespread it really is." He picked up the pace.

The electric doors whooshed as we entered the medical building that housed Dr. Purvis's office. Mick paused just inside, held up a hand.

"What is it?" I asked.

"Listen."

It reminded me of frogs in a pond on a rainy night. A muffled croak, followed by another, then two on top of each other. We moved down the hall, pausing in front of each door until we reached a pediatrician's office. The voices were coming from different directions, but the bulk were coming from in there.

I felt sheepish wandering into a doctor's office to check out the patients, but Mick evidently didn't have the same qualms. He marched right in with me scurrying to keep up. Mick seemed to push through life ignoring all of the social proscriptions that kept the rest of us in line. I admired his balls, but it also made me cringe.

The waiting room was packed with stone-faced parents and wailing kids. A few heads turned as we stood hovering near the doorway, but if anyone recognized Mick they didn't show it. All of the kids were crying—even the older ones.

"Take it off; I want to see you strip." We turned in unison toward the voice. She couldn't have been more than three; it seemed impossible that her little throat could produce such a low, gravelly tone. The little girl screamed, buried her face in her mother's shoulder.

"It's okay, sweetie," the mother cooed, stroking the girl's hair, the expression on her face contradicting her soothing tone.

"If I can just make it to Christmas," a freckled, red-haired boy croaked, then resumed crying.

"I need to talk to him in person," Mick chimed in.

"Come on, I can't stand this," I whispered, pulling open the door. "Several hundred to several thousand cases? Bullshit," I said.

CHAPTER 17

Corinne didn't buy that I was possessed.

"But I had no control over my body. I was trapped inside myself, moved around like a puppet." I said. "How could that be psychological?"

Corinne looked at me for a moment, as if considering. It flustered me that she didn't look at all like a psychiatrist. She was in her early sixties, bleached-blonde hair and too much eye makeup. Abruptly she pulled a fat book off the shelf and flipped through the pages before setting the open book in my lap.

The heading was Dissociative Identity Disorder.

"What's Dissociative Identity Disorder?"

"Read it," Corinne said, walking to the window and peering into the naked grey branches.

I read until I got to the part where it said Dissociative Identity Disorder used to be called Multiple Personality Disorder.

I looked up. "You're kidding me."

Corinne turned from the window. "Why? The symptoms are consistent."

I rubbed my eyeballs. "You're saying I created a personality that represents my grandfather and set it loose inside myself, and it took on a life of its own?" Actually, it did fit the symptoms. It didn't feel like that's what was happening, but if I stepped outside myself, it made sense. "But what about the thousands of other Atlantans? We're all doing the same thing at pretty much the same time?"

The escalating number of cases was hard to ignore. Every news station had a different estimate, and different talking heads speculating about the cause of the new epidemic.

Corinne gave me her kind smile. "Isn't that more likely than your explanation—that you've all become possessed at pretty much the same time? The trauma must have triggered the epidemic."

Corinne's voice faded to a murmur. My hands were trembling, the snakes were crawling under my skin. It was happening again. My grandfather hadn't left me. Crushing disappointment and curdling terror was mixed with just a tinge of satisfaction at the timing. Corinne could tell Grandpa he was a construct of my psyche.

Corinne noticed my quavering hands and stopped. "Finn, are you all right?"

"Finn's on a little trip," Grandpa said. He slapped his thighs and stood. "And I'm going home." He looked around, grabbed my coat from the arm of a couch. "Hundred forty dollars an hour for this. You've got a lot of nerve, missy."

Corinne tried to intercept Grandpa at the door. "Please, Mr. Darby. Stay for a few minutes. I'll waive the fee if you're concerned about it." She seemed concerned that I was leaving, but maintained a professional calm.

Grandpa waved at her in disgust. "I don't want what you're selling even if you're giving it away." He brushed past her, slammed the door behind him.

Not again. My arms swung with a wide, unfamiliar arc as Grandpa crossed the parking lot. "Maybe we should pay your grandma a visit. Don't you think, Finnegan?" He glanced at my watch. It was one thirty. Grandma's place was maybe ten minutes away; it was possible he could make it, but if this spell was no longer than the last he wouldn't have much time once he got there. Mick was waiting for me in the park; hopefully he'd guess what happened.

Grandpa drove like a demon escaping hell. He took the first turn too sharply, his quavering hands jerky on the wheel, and we bounced over the curb, just missing a stop sign. I felt like I was watching the scenery pass by on a screen, slightly removed from all of the sensations. I could hear, see, smell, but it was as if all of it was being piped in.

"You stole from me, the both of you. Well I'm gonna straighten you out, buddy boy." The light ahead turned yellow, then red; Grandpa pressed the gas, flew through the light. I pondered what he'd just said. Grandpa had never been a violent man; he relied on his mouth to inflict the wounds. I hoped that hadn't changed now that he'd spent time in a grave.

We pulled into Grandma's driveway, stopped just short of the garage door with a hard jerk.

Grandma eyed us warily from behind the screen door.

"Hello, Frenchie." That's what he'd always called her—a not-so-affectionate nickname he chose because her grandfather had been French. Not waiting for an invitation Grandpa opened the door and pushed past Grandma into the living room.

Grandma hovered by the door, looking confused and scared. "Why would you call me that, Finn? I'm your grandma."

"You're a traitor is what you are." Grandpa pointed a shaky finger at her. "I told you, no one gets Toy Shop. Not Finnegan, not anyone. How long was I in the grave before you cashed me in?" He grunted. "Not long."

"This isn't at all funny, Finn." Her eyes darted around the room nervously, looking anywhere but at us. "I don't appreciate this. Not one bit."

"Don't be stupid. I'm not Finn. It's Tommy. Don't you even know your own husband?"

Grandma was still clutching the door knob, as if hoping we

couldn't stay long.

Grandpa leaned in close to her. "Would you like to have your old Tommy back?"

Grandma looked up at us, all business despite the bald terror in her eyes. "That's enough, Finn."

"I ain't Finn," Grandpa hissed. "I'm your God damned husband." He gripped Grandma's shoulders, pulled her forward and kissed her tightly on the mouth. Grandma writhed with alarm, trying to pull away, and so did I.

As I tried for the first time to get away from the outside world rather than struggling toward it, Grandpa receded. I felt the tingle of waking, surged back into my body, felt my lips on my grand-mother's, my hands clutching her loose shoulders.

I leapt back, shouting in dismay as Grandma hid her face in her hands.

"I'm sorry, I'm sorry," I babbled. "It really is Grandpa. He's inside me and I can't get him out."

Grandma hobbled away from me, toward the kitchen, where she always went to get away from Grandpa when he was alive.

I wanted to hide under the couch. Instead I sat on it, resisting the urge to pull myself into a ball. The sound of clanking pots emerged from the kitchen.

I opened my mouth to say something. It took all of my willpower to get words out. "Grandma, it really is him. I swear to you."

Sounds of rattling silverware, clinking glasses. Was she having a dinner party I didn't know about?

"Grandma, I'm scared to death."

"Tommy died. I watched them put him in the ground."

I threw my hands in the air in frustration. "All I know is he's inside me. He takes over, and when he does I'm trapped inside." It sounded preposterous when I said it out loud, like one of those people who went on Oprah claiming they'd been abducted by aliens.

The faucet went on. Sounds of a pot filling.

"It's him. It really is," I said impotently.

She was out of sight, her words half-drowned by the running water, but I was sure she said, "I know it is." The cacophony went on. I wondered what she could possibly be cooking. Surely it wasn't for me. I only wanted to get out of there, and wondered as the moments stretched if I should slip out.

The sounds stopped abruptly. "Can he hear me now?" Grandma asked.

"Yes."

She appeared in the doorway, her eyes squinted with rage that I instinctively knew was not directed at me. "You haven't kissed me in fifty years. What makes you think I'd want you to now?" As she disappeared back into her kitchen, I slipped out, stunned and embarrassed that Grandma, of all people, would reveal something so intimate in front of me.

Grandma's greatest fear had always been making a scene—standing out in a way that might make the neighbors frown and tisk. For sixty years she'd been married to a man whose specialty was making a scene. When I think about it, my grandparents had been remarkably incompatible. Grandpa lived to stand out, whether through his accomplishments or through blunt pronouncements delivered at high volume. Grandma spent her life doing everything she could to stifle him. He was making quite a scene now, and I didn't think Grandma was going to be able to keep him at bay.

Just before I closed the door, she added, "Leave me alone, or I'll tell them a few things. Don't think I won't."

I almost went back in to ask what she meant by that, but I desperately needed to get out of there. My lips tasted of menthol Chap Stick.

I slammed the car door and, trembling, hugged my shoulders and rocked. He wasn't going away. Some part of me had known it, had sensed him peering through my eyes, waiting.

I called Mick. He'd guessed why I stranded him and was in a cab on his way home.

"So that's not the end of it." Mick sounded profoundly disappointed. "Guess my turn's coming."

Is that how it would go? If so, everyone else who had the voice would follow. It was hard to imagine hundreds of thousands of people being dragged around Atlanta by the dead.

As I drove I fumbled through the compartment between the seats, desperately looking for gum or mints, but there was nothing. I wiped at my lips with my shirt sleeve.

The anger, the disdain that burned right through Grandma's fear at being face to face with her dead husband, shocked me, even if it didn't surprise me. I hadn't been there when Grandpa died, but Mom had recounted the scene at Grandpa's death bed. Grandpa kept repeating, "This is miserable," as one by one his family sat beside him to say goodbye and pay respects. When it was Grandma's turn, Grandpa glanced at her, rolled his eyes in disgust, and turned away. It was clear in that pivotal moment that Grandpa despised Grandma, that he had stayed married to her only because people of his generation did not divorce.

People from my grandparents' generation ridiculed my generation for our reliance on therapists, our namby-pamby navel-gazing, but it was astonishing to me that a couple could be as dysfunctional as my grandparents and never seek help.

When Grandpa had first taken control, he'd spoken directly to me, knowing I could hear. Now I felt the urge to reciprocate. I inhaled to speak, feeling vaguely moronic, but pushed on.

"What will it take, Grandpa? What do I have to do to get you out of me?" I paused, as if expecting him to answer, but this wasn't that sort of conversation. It was more like the conversations NASA used to have with astronauts when they were on the moon—one side talked for a while, then waited half a day for a reply.

"I was wrong, okay? Is that what you want to hear? I shouldn't have resurrected Toy Shop." Again I paused, waiting. Maybe that's all he wanted; maybe he'd leave me alone if I apologized. "Okay?"

Who was I kidding? Grandpa wasn't going to give up his foothold on a second life without a fight to the death. Shouldn't I at least try to negotiate, though? Weren't you always obligated to attempt diplomacy when the alternative was war? I had an uneasy sense that this was already war, and that the worst was yet to come.

CHAPTER 18

I jolted upright in bed, my heart pounding.

Lorena.

If Grandpa was back, and thousands of others as well, couldn't Lorena be back?

If I could have just five minutes to talk to her. How many times had I thought that? One of those pointless, impossible wishes that fill the dark hours after you lose your life partner. That it might actually be possible made me want to run through the city knocking on every door. I wanted to search for her, now, this instant. Whatever it took, I'd do it to have those five minutes. There must be some way to find her if she was out there.

I got out of bed, went into the living room and paced, thinking.

If she was back, she could be anywhere in the city, and she was nothing but a disembodied voice repeating random pieces of her past. Of course assuming everyone with the voice would follow the same path as me, Lorena would eventually be able to contact me. I didn't want to wait, though. If she was out there I wanted to find her now and be there when she came out.

I wandered into my studio, sat at my drafting table. My heart was racing, keeping me from thinking clearly. Drawing calmed me.

I drew Wolfie clutching a magnifying glass, searching for Lorena. Then I drew Lorena's face in the upper margin, then Little Joe, peering upward, a bladed hand shading his eyes. Where was she? She was outside the boxes of their little world, just as she had been outside my world until the anthrax attack. But if she was here, she was a needle in a haystack. A speck of dust in a smokestack. I'd have to talk to everyone in the city.

I stopped sketching.

I stared at the page, not seeing it, letting an idea take shape.

If Lorena was out there, she could be inside anyone in Atlanta. How many Atlantans read Toy Shop, or had friends or family who read Toy Shop? What if this person read in my strip some of the words that were bursting unbidden from her or his mouth? If Lorena was out there, there were certain words she must be repeating.

Finn, I jotted in the margin beside my sketch of Lorena, underlining it twice. Snakes. Lightning. Annie. Chile. Toy Shop.

I could have gone on, but I wasn't sure how I could work even those words into a strip without making it awful. Toy Shop was the only easy one—that would be on the masthead. I pulled out a clean sheet of Bristol board.

#

I winced as I read over the finished strip, reminding myself that I was doing this for Lorena, that if she was out there this was my best chance of finding her. But I hated making a joke out of her death. Before the strip was published I'd have to contact Lorena's family in Chile and explain why I'd done it, just in case they saw the strip. They'd be mortified, but I thought they'd understand, assuming I could convince them the dead were returning, and she might be one of them...

I put my pencil down. They'd think I was insane. Everyone who read it would be horrified, and if I tried to explain why I'd done it they'd have me committed.

As long as Lorena understood why I'd done it, let the rest of the world think I was crazy.

CHAPTER 19

A thirty-foot-tall Jeff Bridges held a sobbing twenty-eight-foot-tall Rosie Perez, right in my back yard.

When we were deciding what movie to order three days earlier, Mick had lobbied for Planet of the Apes, but in the end I'd won out with Fearless, about a guy who walks away from a fiery plane crash without a scratch, and is profoundly changed.

A year ago it seemed like the most amazing thing to screen movies on the drive-in screen—both awesome and somehow terribly frivolous. Tonight it was a minor diversion, a way to take the edge off the cutting reality of what was happening to us.

In the papers and on TV the feds were maintaining that the voices were part of a new mental illness dubbed Post-Traumatic Stress Vocalization, but stories were running on CNN and FOX about people who swore the vocalizations were the voices of dead friends and relatives.

A story of a missing nine-year-old girl whose body was recovered after twenty-five years was getting a lot of attention. Her mother claimed the daughter's fourth grade teacher (who died in the anthrax attack) was speaking through her, and told her right where to find the body.

Mick, sweating profusely and blurting incessantly, looked like a man waiting to be led to the electric chair. He had already put a substantial dent in the bottle of Glenlivet he'd brought.

"You okay, Mick?" I asked.

"Mm hm." He stared at the movie, but I knew he wasn't seeing it.

I pulled out my laptop and checked my email. Most of the messages were from people I didn't know—fans of the new Toy Shop. I got more of them every day, lately more than I could possibly answer.

Some of the subject lines were amusing:

Wolfie is my new BFF!

Please kill Little Joe!

Looking for an assistant? I'm your guy.

I came to a message from my Aunt Therese. The subject line was How could you??? I really, really didn't want to open it, but I knew it would just eat at me until I did.

> Is that lousy comic strip all that matters to you? How could you use Lorena's death as a punchline? What's happened to you? I hope you enjoy your fame and success, mister big-shot.

I really couldn't blame her. From the outside it looked like I'd used the circumstances of my wife's tragic death for comic strip fodder. That would be reprehensible, no question about it.

I considered replying, explaining why I'd run the strip, but it would make me sound insane. If I found Lorena she could call Therese and set the record straight. Of course if Lorena was able to use a phone she could call me. Maybe I would be the only one who would progress that far.

Another message halfway down my email list caught my eye. The subject line was Are you looking for me???

I opened it.

> Mr. Darby,
> Is it just coincidence that all sorts of things from yester-
> day's strip keep coming out of my mouth? I hope not, be-
> cause if it is, I will have to question my sanity even more
> than I am now. Please call.
> Summer Turnbull
> 404-878-0320

I leapt to my feet, stared at the message as if it might disappear if I took my eyes off it. "Oh my God."

Mick turned. "What?"

"Lorena. My wife. I think she's—"

I punched the number, pressed the phone to my ear and jammed my finger in the other. The ring sounded so far away. Two rings. Three, and then to voice mail. A woman's voice—a low, throaty timbre.

I left a frantic message for Summer to call me back as soon as possible. With Mick standing beside me I Googled Summer Turnbull, hoping to find her address. My heart was drumming. Every moment it took to find this woman was going to be excruciating. Was it possible? Was Lorena back, or at least her voice?

My phone rang.

In my eagerness I lost my grip on it, sent it clattering across the floor. By the time I retrieved it, it was on the fourth ring.

"Hello?"

Mick sidled up to me and pressed his ear near the phone.

"Hi. You just called me?"

"Hi," I said. "This is Finn Darby." I didn't know what to say. "I—. You—."

All that for a kiss? Summer croaked.

All of the strength drained from my legs and I slid to the floor. It was her. I remembered the exact moment she uttered those words.

"Lorena?" I whispered into the phone. "Can you hear me?" I knew she could. Just as Grandpa could hear all of this, because now I knew with perfect certainty that this was no delusion, that my grandfather was really and truly possessing me.

Mick stood over me, his face questioning.

"It's Finn," I whispered to Lorena. I almost expected her to answer, to storm her way out and blurt my name.

"Who are you talking to? Who's Lorena?" Summer demanded, her voice shaking.

"She was my wife. She died two years ago, on the Chattahoochee River."

Summer's breath hitched. "I don't understand. What are you saying? Are you trying to say I'm possessed? Please tell me you're not trying to say that."

Mick handed me a glass filled to the brim with scotch. I nodded my thanks and took a lavish gulp. Nothing would ever be the same. I felt like I'd been pulled inside-out. "I'm sorry. That's what I'm saying. The same thing is happening to me, and to all those people on the news. I'm pretty sure we're all possessed."

She tried to speak, but couldn't. I waited patiently while she got hold of herself. "Well, can you please tell your wife to get the hell out of me?" Her nose was badly plugged. She sounded so lost, so desperate.

It was hard to think of Lorena terrifying someone, even when she sounded like she was speaking from the bottom of a swamp. But I knew what it was like to have the voice. It had scared the hell out of me, too.

"I'm sorry. I know what you're going through." I felt guilty, because I wasn't sorry—I was elated. I'd found Lorena. Maybe I'd be able to speak to her eventually. There were so many things I wanted to say. "Look, can we meet? I know how hard this is for you, but..." I left it hanging there.

"I've still got it in me. I'm sure of that much," Mick blurted.

"What was that?" Summer asked.

"A fellow sufferer. Friend of mine," I said.

"Oh."

I waited, hoping Lorena would say something else. Summer was probably a week or two behind us, like most of the afflicted, so Lorena probably didn't speak often. Yet.

"Look, can we meet?" I repeated.

She seemed hesitant. "Will you help me? Will you try to get her to leave me alone?"

"I'll try. But she's just echoing things she said when she was alive. I can't have a conversation with her." Not yet, at least.

"But if I meet with you, you'll try? That's all I'm asking."

I said I would. What else could I say? I'd been focused on the possibility of talking to Lorena; I hadn't considered how the person she was haunting would feel.

Mick wanted to come along, but I told him I needed to do this myself.

"How do you know it's her? What was that she said? 'All that for a kiss?'"

"I'll explain when I get back," I said as I swept up my keys.

I was in my car, MapQuest directions to Summer's apartment in hand, when I saw that Summer's apartment was up near the Chattahoochee River where Lorena had died. It might be coincidence, but maybe the dead ended up inside people who were near the spot where they died. If it was all about location, though, how did I end up with my grandfather haunting me? There was more to it, but maybe proximity was one piece.

It was dark, and raining, and I drove too fast. I pounded the steering wheel at red lights, which stayed red for eternities. I thought about what I wanted to say to Lorena. I'm sorry? I've never stopped loving you? I took your advice on Toy Shop, and now I'm a big-time cartoonist? All of that, but mostly I just wanted to be near her. If and when she could speak, would she have things to tell me, about the other side? The thought terrified me. Maybe there was no other side. Maybe her last memory was the lightning.

I jerked along Paces Ferry, watching for the turn into Summer's apartment complex. When I spotted the faded, pockmarked sign for Park Place Apartments I flew into the parking lot, bouncing through potholes. It was an immense complex, all concrete and blacktop. The unit two doors down from Summer's was boarded up, the steps to the front door missing. I parked next to a dumpster that had a warped mattress and box springs leaning up against it.

Summer opened the door before I knocked.

We stared at each other for a long, frozen moment, each of us trying to make sense of what couldn't possibly be a coincidence.

It was the waitress from the Blue Boy. My pounding heart found a higher gear.

"You," she whispered. "You're the cartoonist?" The circles under her eyes were so dark it looked like she had smeared her mascara. Fear and exhaustion looked as if they had taken up permanent residence on her face since we'd last met. "What the hell is going on? You—" she closed her eyes, squeezed the bridge of her nose with her thumb and forefinger, trying to pull herself together. "The last time I saw you, you told me it wasn't contagious, but now I have it. Whatever it is."

I waved my hands. "Hold on. I didn't give it to you."

Summer laughed, a little hysterically. "But it's your wife who's inside me. Isn't that what you said?"

"I know. I can't explain that, but this isn't like a virus where you can sneeze and pass it on."

Summer studied me for a minute, then turned, drawing the door open to let me in. There were tattoos behind her ears—Chinese characters.

The living room was scattered with kids' toys—a stuffed dog, big Tinkertoys, a plastic train big enough for a toddler to ride. In the corner two sagging particleboard book shelves were crammed with books of every shape and size. It was mostly New Age stuff— The Tibetan Book of the Dead; Living Zen; The Gnostic Gospels. The apartment was small and cramped, the carpet dingy and worn.

Summer had done everything she could to make it cheery, hanging colorful rugs on the walls and lining the kitchenette's counter with McDonald's happy meal toys, but still, if I had to live there I'd stick my head in its 1970s-era oven and turn on the gas.

I gestured at the room. "You have children?"

Summer nodded. "A daughter." She lifted a scruffy brown teddy bear from the couch, set it aside, and sat down. She seemed to be all knees and elbows. "When the voices started I sent her off to stay with her father in Savannah. She's only four; I don't want to scare her."

"I understand."

Summer stared at the teddy, contemplating it as if it held some terrible secret.

"So when did it start?" I asked.

She looked up at me. "A week ago." She was so thin the ribs in her upper chest were visible above the hem of a wide-necked Janis Joplin t-shirt, looking like rows of extra collar bones. "I was waiting a table. It was horrible." She swept her hair back. "Do you know who's inside you?"

"Yeah, I know who mine is," I said. "My grandfather."

She considered for a moment. "So, assuming this thing really isn't contagious, there must be another explanation. I met your wife before. Your own grandfather's inside you. It can't be coincidence."

She was right, of course. The hauntings couldn't possibly be random.

"Maybe she's still mad at me about the butter." Summer blew a loose strand of hair out of her face. "I'm being possessed by a woman who was mad at me about her pancakes." The look of disbelief on her face was priceless.

It hadn't been about the pancakes, it just upset Lorena that nobody seemed able to pay attention to details any more. Lorena's dad was in the Chilean military—a high-ranking officer—and Lorena had adopted his love of efficiency.

"I had an argument with my Grandfather the day he died. Maybe it has something to do with anger."

Summer smiled, sort of. It was more of an ironic squiggle. "I meant it as a joke. Surely this isn't about me serving her unwanted dairy products."

I shrugged. "It was on Lorena's mind right before she died. She was worried that you might get fired." I was eager to ask about Lorena, but I felt awkward, a bit like a ghoul.

"Have you by any chance written down the things you've been saying?" I ventured.

Summer cast about, yanked a sheet of paper from under a pair of books on a cluttered end table and handed it across to me.

I scanned the list, nodding. "Fatima is Lorena's sister. Lorena was an attorney who worked in youth civil defense, so some of these are references to cases." I paused, chuckled. "Notting Hill was her favorite movie."

Summer didn't smile. "When I first saw that strip, I lost it. I thought the words were appearing there just for me, that everyone else who read it was seeing different words."

"Sometimes I wish I was delusional," I said. "At least then I'd know what to do."

Summer inhaled, about to say something, but instead she croaked, "If one more person assumes I'm Mexican..."

I'd forgotten that Lorena was here with us, right now. I leaned forward. "I'm here, Lore." I desperately wanted to talk to her, to reach in and pull her out and take her with me, but she was merged with this other person, this stranger. I felt an irrational surge of propriety, that Summer had no right to be carrying her around, keeping her in a strange place.

"It's disconcerting when you do that," Summer said.

"Do what?"

"Talk to me like that, like I'm her."

"Sorry."

Summer waved it off. She was fidgety sitting, looking like she wanted to pace. "She wasn't Mexican, I'm assuming?"

I nodded. "Chilean. It bugged her that people assumed if she was Latino, she must be Mexican."

"Mm."

Why this woman, I wondered. Why was Lorena inside this stranger? Could it really be the argument they'd had?

"She was a wonderful person. She had a good heart," I said.

Summer ran her hand through her bangs, which fell across her forehead like a veil. "I'm sure she was very nice." She didn't look at all sure. "To be honest, though, that's sort of beside the point, you know?" She gave me an imploring look, broke into a half smile. "You know?"

I smiled wanly, nodded. "I know."

"I mean," she laughed, "I guess it's better to be possessed by a nice dead person than a mean dead person, but still…"

"Yeah. I'm sorry."

"Do you really think she can hear you? That she can hear what we're saying, right now?" Summer looked mortified by the notion.

I leaned back on the couch, crossed my leg, then uncrossed it. It would upset Summer to hear what had been happening to me, but there was no getting around it. She looked exhausted, like she was hanging by a thread. I leaned forward, folded my hands.

Summer's eyes went vacant, the thousand-yard stare that was becoming so familiar, and added, "Can I say something that's kind of sneaky?"

I felt a stab of recognition. I could see from Summer's face that I hadn't masked my reaction very well.

"Lorena said that just before she died," I explained.

Summer swallowed thickly, touched her throat. "I just can't get a grip on what's going on. Do you know what's going on?" There was a pleading look in her eyes.

"I'll tell you what I know," I said. "I'm pretty sure I was one of the first who got the voice. I think that's because of an accident I had on the first night of the anthrax outbreak. I was clinically dead for ten minutes, and while I was dead I was inside someone else, in the same way my wife is inside you."

Summer opened her mouth to speak, but nothing came out, so I went on.

"The voice got worse and worse—"

"Hold on," Summer interrupted. "I haven't heard your voice once. If you're ahead of me—"

"I know. Mine stopped—"

She leapt out of the chair, her face bright with hope. "It stopped?"

I shook off her enthusiasm. "It's not a good thing, believe me." I motioned toward the couch. "You might want to sit."

Summer sat.

"The ghost doesn't go away. It starts taking over your entire body, a few minutes at a time."

She froze, and stayed perfectly still, like I'd just told her there was a huge spider on her head. "What do you mean?"

I told her about Grandpa. When I finished, Summer closed her eyes, steepled her hands under her chin for a moment. Then she stood. "I'm going to drink now. Do you want one?"

"Whatever you've got. Thanks."

On her way back she made a detour to her bookshelf, came back with two glasses half-filled with caramel-colored liquid in her hands and a book tucked under her arm. "Rum and Coke?" I guessed.

"Rum and rum. Dark rum."

"Ah." I took a swig, as Summer flipped through the book, felt the rum burn a trail down my throat and hit my belly in a warm rush. Grandpa was probably doing a jig inside. I took a second swig, set the glass back on the coffee table. "What's that?"

She held up the book so I could see. The title was Seth Speaks, by Jane Roberts. "Seth was very big in New Age circles forty years ago. Jane Roberts claimed that Seth spoke through her—it's called Channeling."

I motioned toward her bookshelf. "I noticed you were interested in the occult."

Summer waggled her head. "Well, Eastern mysticism. I'm less

interested in Western stuff."

I had no idea what the difference was, but nodded anyway.

Summer pulled up clips on YouTube of Jane Roberts channeling Seth. There were similarities between Seth and what was happening to me—he took Jane over completely, spoke in a somewhat different voice from her—but Seth didn't sound like something half-human and half-frog.

We speculated about what might cause thousands of people to suddenly start channeling the dead, but neither of us had any good answers. Then we chatted for a while about other things, mostly catching each other up on who we were, what our lives were like—a tacit acknowledgment that we would be seeing more of each other. The rum relaxed us past the awkwardness, until I felt like I was catching up with a friend.

My phone interrupted us. It was Mick.

"It's Mick," I whispered to Summer. I felt a stupid rush of pride saying it.

Summer nodded, pointed, indicating that she'd go into the bedroom to give me some privacy.

"You're not going to believe who I just got off the phone with," Mick said as soon as I answered.

"God?" I joked.

"Almost as good. A bloke working for FEMA. He filled me in on what they've learned."

"How did you pull that off?"

Mick chuckled. "You haven't been famous long enough, mate. Doors open magically when people recognize your bloody name."

"What did you find out?"

"Not over the phone."

I almost laughed; it sounded so cloak and dagger. But maybe he had a point. I was torn—I wanted to stay and talk to Summer, and be with Lorena, but I needed to hear what Mick had learned. I arranged to meet Mick at his place in an hour.

I called to Summer as I pulled on my coat. "Mick has new information that might help us understand what's happening. I'm going to meet him."

She nodded. "Well I'm sure I'll see you—" she paused, raised her finger to her lips and considered. "Would you mind if I came along? It's okay if it's not, it's just—"

"No," I interrupted, "that would be great." I wanted to stay close to Lorena and, now that Summer understood what the voice was, I imagined the thought of being with others like her was comforting.

Suddenly I had to pee. Maybe the rum was getting to me, or maybe it was this latest jolt. "Can I use your bathroom before we go?"

Summer motioned toward the open door, then croaked, "Annie called. She met a guy at Cosmic Charlie's."

The bathroom was as old and decrepit as the rest of the apartment, the linoleum stained and peeling up around the toilet. All around the mirror were index cards, each with an ornate, handwritten epithet.

Walk with the noble. Avoid fools and assholes.

Never give up. Never ever ever give up.

There is no hurry. Nowhere else to go. Nothing else to do.

The cramped space around the sink was jammed with soap, cosmetics, toothpaste, an Elmo toothbrush holder with two toothbrushes in it: a grown-up one with badly frayed bristles and a kid's toothbrush with a cartoon fairy handle. I felt like I was intruding on a very private place, but I had to go, and this was the only bathroom.

"Ready?" I asked as I hurried toward the door. Summer was already wearing her coat, her purse dangling against her elbow.

CHAPTER 20

"It must be hard to be away from your daughter," I said as we pulled out, an attempt to make conversation.

"It's very hard. Will this be ready by the thirtieth? It's for my husband's birthday. Rebecca likes going to her dad's house, though. He's the fun one—he swoops in every other weekend, a month in summer, and takes her places I can't afford." She'd kept on going after the blurt, not missing a beat.

"That doesn't sound fair. Doesn't he pay child support?" I asked, struggling to carry on the conversation. I resisted the urge to tell Lorena that I knew which birthday she was talking about. I was wearing the engraved watch she'd bought me.

Summer laughed sardonically. "He was just a poor college student when I had Rebecca. I had to drop out of high school to raise her while he went on to a comfortable if boring and empty life as an insurance salesman."

"Ah."

"Are you sure you'd even be happy drawing Toy Shop?"

Summer pressed her hand over her throat. "This is worse than it's

116

ever been. Tell her she's scaring the hell out of me. I can't sleep. My hair is falling out."

"I will," I said. I braked to avoid a cardboard box lying semi-flattened in the wet road. The rain had mostly stopped. "You just told her yourself, though. Remember, she can hear us."

Summer threw her head back. "I'm sorry about the butter! Please, please, leave me alone."

"Do you…" I wasn't sure how to put it. "Would you mind if I talked to her?"

"Yes. I mean no. Go ahead."

I cleared my throat, feeling nervous, like I was on stage. How many imaginary conversations had I had with Lorena since she died? Thousands. I wasn't sure what to say.

"Hello, Lore," I began. "I know you can hear me. I miss you. Your sister and mom and dad are doing well. I keep in touch with them a little. They miss you, too."

Enough platitudes. What did I want to say? I found myself dropping to a whisper, as if I could speak to Lorena without Summer hearing. "I'm sorry I wasn't there for you. I should have been watching out for you. I'm so sorry."

Summer glanced at me, then out the window, then down at the floor mat. It was strange: I was talking to Summer, or at Summer, but she was only in the way. She didn't know what to do to get out of the way.

"I don't know what's happening, how you've gotten inside this woman. Summer. But we'll sort it out. I'll stay close so we can figure it out."

Summer's head was bowed, like she was in prayer. "I'm done for now," I said to her.

She nodded, lifted her head. We drove in silence for a few minutes, swishing through puddles.

"I don't think I would want to talk to the loved ones I've lost," Summer said, her voice soft.

"Why not?" I asked.

She pulled her knees up, wrapped her arms around them. "It's hard to put into words." She bit her fingernail, thought for a moment. "There's an order to things. We love people while they're alive. When they die, we mourn them and move on. They're part of the past, and we're not." She shook her head. "I know that sounds like something out of Chicken Soup for the Soul."

I wasn't sure how to respond. If I disagreed she might think I was arguing that it was okay for Lorena to be inside her. I didn't agree with her, though. She didn't understand because she hadn't lost someone like Lorena.

"What does it feel like when they take over? Does it hurt?" Summer asked.

You'll never be the same, I might have said. You'll never recover from it. "It doesn't hurt, exactly." I said instead. "But it feels bad, almost like there are snakes under your skin."

Summer gaped at me.

"Just for a second," I added quickly. "Then you don't feel anything; you're numb."

"Numb is good. Better than snakes under my skin." She rubbed her thighs, as if warding off the prospect of snakes. "Your wife keeps talking about snakes."

"She was afraid of snakes. Terrified." I considered telling Summer how Lorena's fear of snakes had been instrumental in her death, but decided it was too personal.

I studied Summer out of the corner of my eye. She was wearing red Keds high-tops, one foot propped on the dash. Lorena was in there. Some essence of her was right beside me, inside this woman. Incredible. Maybe part of the reason Lorena had been drawn to Summer was that, despite their differences, they seemed to have some similarities. Both were high-energy, self-assured. Maybe it went even deeper than that, though. There was something about Summer—an appealing something that she radiated.

"I'm not sure how much I want to know about her," Summer said. "If she becomes a person to me I might feel sorry for her."

"Maybe you'll also feel less scared of her," I suggested. "You might sleep better."

"I don't want to sleep better, I want her out of me."

I didn't know how to respond to that. I didn't want Lorena out of her, not if it meant losing Lorena again. It was spectacularly unfair of me to feel that way—I knew that, and I knew how badly I wanted Grandpa out of me.

"I was sure I was developing schizophrenia," Summer said. It took me a moment to realize she was changing the subject. "I have an aunt who's schizophrenic. She hears voices that aren't there. This seemed close." She drew her purse into her lap, fished out a pack of gum. "Then I saw the reports on TV, about how it's a type of multiple personality disorder." She held out the pack, offering me a piece.

I pulled a stick out the pack, nodding thanks. "Did you see a doctor?"

Summer shook her head. "No health insurance. If I'm calling a doctor, I'm standing in a puddle of my own blood."

I laughed out loud. "Here we are." I pulled into the private parking lot under Mick's building on Peachtree Street. The attendant motioned me to roll down my window.

"Afternoon, Mister Darby," he said, leaning in the window. "Ma'am." He nodded to Summer before turning back to me. "You still owe me a Wolfie." He mimicked sketching.

"I'll have it for you when I come down. What's your daughter's name again?"

"Alison. Allie." He thanked me, patted my shoulder. I rolled up the window, feeling the warmth of celebrity roll through me.

"Congratulations, by the way," Summer said. "Toy Shop seems to be everywhere. Wolfie's like the new Snoopy."

I chuckled, wondering if Grandpa was getting this.

Mick's apartment was one giant room, a converted warehouse with exposed steel beams and huge windows. It was a mess. Large swaths of the hardwood floor were barely visible under layers of designer clothes, paper, pizza boxes, musical instruments, and dust bunnies.

Mick looked as if he'd been getting about as much sleep as I had. To my surprise he immediately recognized Summer. He reached out, hugged her with one hand (he had an open beer in the other). "Another kindred spirit. Or maybe that's kindred with a spirit, eh?"

Summer pressed her head to Mick's shoulder. "It's nice to see you again."

We talked about what it might mean that Summer and Lorena had met the day Lorena died, then Mick turned to me, eyebrows raised.

"So tell me now: 'All for a kiss.' What's that about? You knew it was her just from that?"

I felt embarrassed to tell the story, but I could see that Mick wanted to know.

"When I was in tenth grade, the drama teacher came to my Social Studies class begging the boys to try out for the lead in the drama club's production of Bye Bye Birdie. I had absolutely no interest in acting. In fact the idea of standing in front of an audience—of being looked at by rows and rows of people—was about the most horrible thing I could imagine. But then the drama teacher mentioned that Lorena Soto was playing the female lead."

Summer turned, wandered toward the windows. I lowered my voice, suspecting that she'd moved because she didn't want to hear the story.

"After class I went to the library and read the script, until I found what I was looking for: there was a kiss in the play. Without giving myself time to think about it I went to Ms. Camasso and told her I wanted to try out.

"I was no actor, but I acted my heart out. I wasn't a singer, but I warbled out the songs with my heart hammering, all for the chance to kiss Lorena. I got the part, and I got to kiss Lorena. Three times, actually: during the dress rehearsal, and during the two performances."

Grinning, Mick lifted his hand to my face and patted my cheek.

"You're a true romantic. The genuine article."

Blushing, I steered the conversation toward what Mick had found out.

"They're baffled," Mick began as Summer sidled back into the conversation. "My friend at FEMA said they recruited a few hundred volunteers who've got the voices, and one experiencing the full Monty like you—"

"Then it's not just me?" I interrupted. Why hadn't Mick flung open the door and shouted this the moment we arrived?

Mick nodded morosely. "That's right. It looks like we're all headed that way. Anyway, they're trying everything to drive out the bloody ghosts: drugs, radiation, noises, electroshock, and—get this—exorcists."

"Catholic exorcists? Guys in black robes carrying valises of holy water?" Summer asked.

"That's what the gent said." Mick took a long swig from his beer.

I gaped in disbelief. "You've got to be kidding. Are they all completely nuts?"

"How about a few witch doctors and Wiccan priestesses?" Summer said. "If they're going to get religious, a little diversity wouldn't kill them."

It was good to hear they were doing something, but exorcists? It sounded like they were as lost about what was going on as we were.

"So they know this is more than mental illness?" I asked.

"Some do. Most still buy the multiple personality/post-traumatic stress angle, but they're working all the angles."

Summer and I digested this news.

Mick had a framed poster hung on the pitted concrete wall that I hadn't noticed before—The Beatles' Let It Be. I wandered over to admire it. "An original?"

"Absolutely," Mick said.

"One of my favorite movies," I said, admiring the portraits of the Fab Four in their later, long hair phase. "Right up there with Planet of the Apes."

"The last scene in the film, the rooftop concert, was the last time they ever played together," Summer said. She was at my elbow, looking at the poster.

"I didn't know that," I said.

"Adds a darker edge, don't it?" Mick said.

I turned away from the poster. Summer followed.

"So, did your friend tell you anything else?" I asked Mick.

Mick nodded. "Seems it's one ghost to a customer. He said the voice is always one distinct person."

That made sense. "If there's one ghost to a customer, and a bunch of ghosts went to possess the living all at once, it would be like a game of musical chairs, wouldn't it?" I said. I tapped the notes Mick was holding. "Even if the ghosts are drawn to people they had some business with, or connection to, the most likely suspects might be taken, and they'd have to find someone else."

"Mick, do you even know who yours is?" Summer asked.

Mick blew air through pursed lips, making a fart sound. "Maybe. Maybe not. I don't know."

No one pointed out that he might find out soon enough.

I was still thinking about how our ghosts were brought to us. I pictured it almost as a scent the ghosts we were linked to could smell on us. I wondered if the intensity of the conflict increased the likelihood that a particular ghost would find you, or if being close to the spot where they died was a bigger factor. Lorena's tiff with Summer had been superficial, but Lorena had died in a place where she knew very few people. That may have made distance more of a factor.

"How many of these bloody things are we talking about?" Mick pointed at me. "You were able to find your wife. One single solitary person out of the countless masses who've died. Does that mean everyone is back? Everyone who ever died around here?"

We considered.

"That doesn't seem possible," I finally said. "Six hundred thousand people died in the anthrax attack. Add all the people who've lived and died in Atlanta, even just in the past twenty years, and you're talking about millions. There aren't that many cases. Unless there are a lot more to come."

"No," Mick said. "My insider says no one has developed a brand new case in a couple of weeks. The existing ones are just getting progressively worse, so they're getting noticed."

"So why would some people come back, but not others?" Summer asked.

We looked at each other. What did Lorena, Grandpa, and untold thousands of other dead people have in common? None of us had any idea.

"There's one other thing I keep wondering," I said, breaking the silence. "If we can't stop this, what's going to happen to us?"

Nobody spoke, but I think we were all thinking the same thing. The pattern was clear: the dead were stealing a little more of us each day.

⸸

As soon as the car door slammed and Summer turned toward her apartment, I let Grandpa have it.

"So what do you think of that, old man?" I said as I pulled out of the parking lot. "My 'spic wife' is back, too. Maybe the four of us can go to dinner sometime."

I hated the thought of being away from Lorena for a moment, let alone the rest of the day and evening, but I couldn't expect Summer to sleep at my place, or invite me to spend the night at hers. I'd see her tomorrow; that would have to be good enough.

"You know what?" I continued. "My treat. I'll take us all to the best restaurant in Atlanta. With all the money that's pouring in from Wolfie's popularity, I can certainly afford it."

It had been almost forty-eight hours since Grandpa last took over. A faint hope was beginning to flicker inside me that I was shouting into an empty car. God, I hoped so. If not, the old man would visit soon, and I'd be banished to that numb twilight place.

I flicked on the stereo, shoved in an Abney Park CD because I knew Grandpa would despise it, and cranked up the volume until my ears crackled.

CHAPTER 21

Thanks to Mick and Grandpa, I was spending a lot more time in bars than usual. Mick's taste was substantially more upscale than Grandpa's: The Regis had an authentic art deco-period bar, original oil paintings, plush chairs, and a grand piano. Mick and I sat at the bar watching the news, transfixed. The momentum on the news had clearly shifted; so many people were turning up with the blurt-like-a-zombie disease that it was supplanting the anthrax attack as the top story. The disorder was still being described as a post-traumatic stress response. That it was extreme and unprecedented only reflected the extreme and unprecedented nature of the anthrax attack itself, according to psychiatrists and people at the Center for Disease Control.

"If they think this is extreme, wait till they get a look at act two," I muttered to Mick just as Summer appeared in the doorway. She scanned the bar, looking for us.

When she spotted me she hurried over, holding up a beat-up brown book missing its dust jacket. "Wait till you see what I found." I gave her my barstool and stood behind her as she thumbed through pages. "When we were talking last night, I had this niggling feeling that all of this was somehow familiar. When I got home I remembered. This mystic, J. Krishnapuma, comes awfully close to describing our situation." She flattened the book on the bar, ran her finger under a line of heavily underlined text. "He said that consciousness persists after death, and that consciousness had what he called 'osmotic properties'—under the right conditions the dead could get sucked in and out between the world of the dead and the world of the living."

I read along where Summer was pointing. His language was gaudy, but it did sound eerily familiar.

"According to him everything has consciousness," Summer went on, "animals, plants, planets, stars—but the various forms of consciousness aren't interchangeable. The consciousness of a star can't inhabit a human body, and vice-versa.

"So if they came through, the dead would have nowhere to go but into people," I said.

"Charming," Mick said.

Two months ago I'd have rolled my eyes at this sort of supernatural stuff. I was still skeptical that some mystic's fifty-year-old book held the answers we were looking for, but it didn't seem all that far-fetched, either.

"Why would I pay to eat food in a restaurant that I can cook myself?" Mick blurted. Heads turned to stare, but we ignored them. Mick was probably used to people staring at him.

"How did he figure all this out?" I asked. "Does he say?"

Summer tilted her head back to look at me, breaking into a wide smile. "Oh yeah, he says." She flipped through more pages, stopped on a page with multiple exclamation points in the margins. She tapped the page. "He claims he visited the other side. 'The world of the dead' he called it. Actually saw it."

I guffawed. Couldn't help it. Even with my grandfather taking up residence in my body, this sounded way over the top.

"How did he do that?" Mick asked, eyeing the pages as if they might explode at any moment.

Summer flipped to the next page, which was marked by a pow-der-blue Post-it. "He spent years fine-tuning his consciousness un-til he could enter a deep trance state, aided by mescaline."

Mick leaned back, chuckling. "I figured heavy drugs had to be involved somehow." He tapped the page with his fingernail. "I think I've been to the very same place a few times, only it was heroin that got me there. I preferred the opiates in my high-flying days."

Summer smiled at the joke, flipped a few more pages.

I skimmed the browned pages of Krishnapuma's book, catching random snippets as they flew by:

…gathered up in the darkening wind…drawn by the dwindling dead…my bodiless presence…

He had a melodramatic delivery, that much was certain. Whether any of it was true…at this point I didn't know what to think.

"Maybe this guy visited this land of the dead and maybe he didn't, but how does it help us?" I asked. "How does it get my grandfather to go away?"

Once again Summer craned her neck to grin up at me. "Easy. You're going to go there."

"Go where?"

"The world of the dead."

I laughed, because I thought she was joking. "How the hell would I do that? I don't have years to fine-tune my awareness. Or any mescaline."

Summer held up the book, her finger holding her place. "Krish-napuma didn't have this to guide him. And Krishnapuma wasn't halfway there to begin with."

"I'm halfway to Deadland?"

"The world of the dead," Summer corrected. She flipped open the book and read a passage: "'Those who have touched death, however briefly, tread with one foot in the world of the living and the other in the world of the dead.' That's why you and Mick are ahead of the others who have this thing. You were in the world of the dead when it happened."

"Lucky us," Mick said, exhaling smoke from his cigarette. He had been blurting so often he seemed reluctant to speak for long, like a person with hiccups who is tormented by anticipation of the next one.

Summer flipped through her notes. "There's so much more. Krishnapuma predicted that it might be possible for a rift to open between the two worlds, allowing the dead to pour into the world of the living." She held up a finger. "And listen to this: 'When a conscious being leaves its physical form, it dissolves back into the all, the place from which all consciousness arises. This process takes time; how much depends on the being's willingness to let go of the illusion of his own individuation.'"

"That's lovely. I have no idea what it means, but it's lovely." Mick heaved a big sigh. "Is it possible we're all just going mad? Doesn't that make more sense than thinking we've each got someone dead inside us?" As if to underscore this, he blurted, "Is it mint? If there are scratches I'm not interested." A red-faced guy in a white windbreaker glanced at Mick from the adjoining stool, swept his drink off the bar and moved away. It was becoming clearer it was a man's voice; the tenor was coming through stronger than ever.

"The thought has crossed my mind," I said, "but that wouldn't explain how Summer could know so much about Lorena."

"I know, I know." Mick drained his glass. It made a solid thunk as he set it back on the table. "Wishful thinking."

"But how did it happen?" I asked. I lowered my voice. "I mean, if we're all possessed, why are we all possessed?"

Mick shrugged. "Has to be the anthrax attack. No way the timing's a coincidence." Another blurt followed—something about wanting pizza before bed—then another almost on top of the first.

"What if it's not so much the anthrax, but so many people dying at once?" Summer suggested. "Have so many people ever died at once before?"

I opened my mouth to suggest Hiroshima, or the fire-bombing of

Dresden, but neither had killed six hundred thousand people. Millions may have died from the bubonic plague in the middle ages, but that was over a couple of years. Plus the deaths were spread over a much larger area. Same with the flu pandemic of 1918.

"I don't think so," I said. "Over half a million people in four or five days?" Something was niggling me about all this. I rotated my glass, thinking, trying to get a grasp on it. Then I had it. "But hold on—Grandpa didn't die in the anthrax attack. Why would he come back?"

I had to raise my voice to talk over Mick's blurts. His forehead was damp with sweat. "Mick? You all right?" I asked, putting a hand on Mick's back. Around us the buzz of bar patrons was rising.

Mick raised his arm like he was going to gesture at something, let it drop. His hands began to shake. "Oh, bloody," Mick blubbered. His face was so slack he looked like he'd had a stroke. He inhaled deeply, jerkily. His hands were jerking like fish just hauled into the boat.

People left their seats. A dozen headed for the door in quick order.

I knew just what Mick was going through, and I felt for him. Maybe it was easier for him because he knew what to expect.

The bar stool squeaked against the wood floor as Mick stumbled off it. He looked at us, wide-eyed.

Summer put a calming hand on his arm. "Can you tell me your name?"

"I thought I was dreaming." His voice was the same deep, crude thing mine had been when Grandpa spoke, but he spoke fast, spitting and blubbering so you could barely understand. He looked at the mirror behind the bar, pressed his hands to his face. "I'm Mick. This is unbelievable." He looked at me. "He can hear me, right? Isn't that how it works? That's how it was in the dream." He stuck his hands under his arms like he was cold.

"That seems to be how it works," I agreed.

"Mick!" He called, looking at himself in the mirror. "Gilly here." He held up his hands as if warding off a blow. "Now don't get mad.

I'm sorry about all that legal stuff. That's all behind us now, okay?"

"I'm sorry," Summer said. "Gilly?" She held out her hand. "I'm Summer." Gilly studied Summer's palm, then held out Mick's quavering hand, dangling loosely at the end of his wrist. "Hey."

"Can you tell me your last name?"

"I've been watching you." He pointed at the mirror.

Summer nodded. "Can you tell me your last name?"

He touched Mick's lips. "What's happening to me?" He had a thick New York accent that came through despite the wet, croaking timbre of his speech. There was no trace of Mick's cockney British.

"Hansen," I said. "His last name is Hansen." Summer looked at me, her head tilted, questioning. "He co-wrote most of Mick's big hits."

"I was also in the band for a while." He looked around the bar, as if he'd just noticed where he was. "Did I die or not?"

"What's the last thing you remember, before you started seeing through Mick's eyes?" Summer asked.

"The wind," he said. "Music going through my head, on and on and on and on and on. That's why I'm back. I need to find my notes and get back to work." He looked at the mirror, raised his voice. "I been working on something new for you, Mick. It's good, really good. I promise. Not just a retread—"

"Wait a minute, back up," Summer said. "Why are you back?"

Gilly held his outstretched palms over his head. "Because the gods, or the cosmos or whatever, wanted Mick and me back together. How could that be any clearer? We're in the same fricking body." He turned back to the mirror. "Mick, no hard feelings, right? I worked on it on the other side, in my head. It's weird but it's not, you know what I mean?"

"Hang on," Summer said, grasping one of Gilly's hands and tugging, trying to get his attention. "The other side? Can you tell us about it?"

My hands were shaking. That awful crawling sensation started up.

"Me and you, man, together again." Gilly shook his head.

"Summer," I interrupted, before the tingling swept over me, numbing me like a full-body shot of Novocain.

Summer looked at my hands, gave me a look that said "Don't leave me with two dead people."

Grandpa turned to the bald bartender, shouted, "Whiskey, neat." He nudged my drink toward the gutter of the bar. "Scotch is for sissies and Englishmen, which is the same thing." He pulled his stool closer to the bar as if it offended him.

"Mr. Darby, my name is Summer Locker." She motioned to Mick. "And this is Gilly Hansen." Gilly offered Mick's wobbly hand.

Grandpa looked at it. "I was listening. I know who the hell he is."

Alarmed, urgent voices carried from the far end of the bar. Someone was sobbing, "I don't understand what's happening" over and over. Grandpa glanced at them. Most of the patrons remaining in The Regis were standing, packed toward the entrance as if watching an avant-garde play. Most looked scared shitless, though a woman with dyed red hair was snapping pictures with her phone.

"Do you remember the other side?" Summer asked Grandpa.

Grandpa shrugged. "I got nothing to say to you, missy. Why don't you jump in front of a bus and go there yourself." He jerked a thumb at the door.

"Wait. You were dead too?" Gilly asked.

The bartender ventured within a few paces of us. "I think you should leave."

"I think you should go to hell," Grandpa shot back. "Pour my drink, and be quick about it." The bartender retreated down the bar.

"Really, what was it like?" Summer persisted, staring Grandpa down, daring him to engage her.

The bartender slid Grandpa's drink down the bar from ten feet away. It slid past Grandpa's spastic grip. Summer caught it, set it in front of Grandpa without dropping her gaze.

Without bothering to thank her, Grandpa took a swig, exhaled loudly as the whiskey burned the back of my throat. "It's like nothing. At least after a while it is. At first it's like a drunken dream."

His voice was still a croaking mess, but not as bad as last time. He was learning how to use my mouth, forming sounds more clearly with practice. The slackness was leaving his face as well. I barely recognized my face in the mirror behind the bar. The muscles around my eyes were pinched, my lips pulled into a frown. My grandfather's features seemed to be bleeding through—his cheeks like angry boils, his beady eyes.

"So what are you doing back? Usually when you die, that's it. You know?" Summer asked.

Grandpa took another pull, swallowed the thick whiskey. "How the hell do I know? They don't hand out instruction manuals over there." He motioned to the bartender, pointed at his empty glass. "But if I had to guess, I figure there's going to be a little less Finnegan Darby and a little more Thomas Darby every day." He smiled with satisfaction, checked my watch.

The significance of what he said roared in my head. He couldn't know for sure, but it made sense. It started as just a voice, and each day it got worse. What would happen to me if he took over for good? Would I stay in here, helpless, for the rest of my body's life?

Summer turned to Gilly, who was watching the proceedings with dumbfounded fascination.

"How about you, Gilly? What was it like for you?"

"What is this?" Grandpa interjected. "Who are you, Larry King?"

"What was what like?" Gilly asked.

"Being dead."

Gilly shook his head. "I heard what you were thinking of doing. You don't want to go there. Not if you don't have to."

A camera flashed. A guy with a high-speed camera was halfway to our table, snapping photos.

"Hey, stop that," Summer said. The guy ignored her.

Mick's face began to shake, the loose skin under his chin jiggling. Gilly moaned, shut his eyes.

The slackness in Mick's face vanished into a grimace. "Bloody hell!" Mick cried. "Christ." He pounded the bar with his fist as the camera flashed again.

Summer pushed his scotch in front of him. "Welcome back."

Mick downed the scotch. "We have to sort this out. I don't want to go back in there." He wiped his mouth with the back of his hand, signaled for another drink.

"I'm with you," Summer said. She turned. "Where are my manners?" she added, dripping sarcasm. She flicked her hand in Grandpa's direction. "Mick, this is Finn's grandfather, Thomas Darby."

Mick pulled a pack of cigarettes from a vest pocket in his jacket, shook one out, and lit it with a badly trembling hand. "Fuck off."

Grandpa lifted his glass. "Well pardon me if I don't shed a tear. Lousy drug addict."

That blessed vague tingling, like a low-level electric current, spread down my arms and legs. The glass dropped from Grandpa's hand, splashed whiskey on my jeans before shattering to the tile floor.

I took a deep, ragged breath. "No, it's me. I'm back, too." I buried my face in my hands, stifled a sob of relief. "So now we know who Mick's ghost is."

"I knew who it was," Mick said, lighting his cigarette with still-shaking hands. "I just didn't want to admit it to myself. The sodding bastard was trying to block me from performing my own songs when he keeled over. I was glad to see him go. I threw a bloody party."

"Did he die in the anthrax attack?" I asked.

"Him?" Mick rolled his eyes. "He ate himself to death. Diabetes or some such. You heard him mention he used to be in the band? That was in the early days, before we made it big. The wanker kept putting on weight until we had a four-hundred-pound bass player. Then he went strange on us. Stopped playing in the middle of songs, wandered the stage, went all bug-eyed and hid behind amps. A complete embarrassment, he was. Then ten years ago he slaps me with the lawsuit."

"Um, Mick?" Summer shook her head tightly, as if attempting to signal Mick without Gilly seeing. "Sounds like he's willing to let bygones be bygones. This might go easier if he's on our side?"

Mick grumbled under his breath, tipped his head back and drained his glass.

Flashing red lights appeared outside the bar. A police cruiser had pulled up. Summer tugged my jacket. "Time to go." With Mick on my heels, we stumbled out.

CHAPTER 22

A skinny, exhausted-looking kid handed me a white bag through the Wendy's drive-through window.

"I still get the fever on a Saturday night," Gilly sang from the passenger seat, his eyes closed, head lolling. He sounded terrible, trying to sing with that voice.

I unpacked my spicy chicken sandwich while I pulled out of the lot, burned the roof of my mouth on the first bite. I was eating too fast because I didn't want to waste time eating. It had been almost sixteen hours; who knew how much longer I had before I'd be driven back inside?

"Sorry. Don't mean to be rude," Gilly said. "I'm working hard when I'm inside, but I can't write anything down, and I forget stuff. It's frustrating." He plucked a few fries from their cardboard basket.

"Did you find the notes you mentioned?"

"Not yet. I need to make some calls. It's hard when you only have half an hour, you know?" He licked his fingers like a dog cleaning his front paws. "I worked on this for eight years before I died. I was going to surprise Mick, give it to him as a peace offering, you know?"

I nodded. I wondered if he was delusional, or if he was actually composing decent music. Mick said Gilly had lived with his mother for the last twenty-odd years of his life, in the same room he'd occupied as a child.

Gilly waggled his head, brayed sort of like a horse. "Man, wish I could clear my head. I'm not used to the pills and the booze." He twisted the rear-view mirror so he could look into it. "Not that I'm criticizing, Mick. It's your body; I'm just along for the ride, as long as it lasts." He held two fingers up in a peace sign. "Back to the top, man. Me and you."

My phone rang. It was Mom, but I wasn't going to get to talk to her. The snakes were running free. Damn it. I was pulled back into cottony numbness.

Grandpa closed the phone, signaled, parked along the curb.

"Why are we stopping?" Gilly asked, peering out his window.

Grandpa got out without a word.

"Hey Finn?" Gilly had one foot on the pavement, his hand on the hood.

Grandpa crossed the street with its neon signs and honking cars. I had no doubt he was heading for a bar.

He turned into Cypress Street Pint and Plate on the corner of Fifth Street, stormed up to the bar and ordered a whiskey, his tone all business.

"Finn?" Gilly pulled up the stool next to Grandpa.

"I ain't Finn," Grandpa hissed, turning a shoulder to Gilly.

I tried to ignore their interchange; it was time to get to work, looking for Deadland. I couldn't stomach Krishnapuma's melodramatic and cumbersome "world of the dead," so I had shortened it.

Summer had laid out a plan based on Krishnapuma's book, and had practiced with me for two hours. I smiled inside, remembering how she would reach up and feign choking me when my natural skepticism came out. I didn't expect to get anywhere. I wasn't a mystic, and I wasn't dead.

Despite my reservations, I took a few imaginary deep breaths, tried to bring my mind to a single-pointed focus on the back of my head. I felt ridiculous, like I was on the ultimate snipe hunt, sent by a mystic who'd been dead fifty years.

Turn around and peer out your third eye. And tremble. That's what Krishnapuma had written.

My third eye. Right. How do you turn around when you don't control your body? I tried to visualize the third eye in the back of my head, while Grandpa chewed out Gilly, who didn't understand why Grandpa had to be like that.

Again, I imagined the breath I couldn't actually take, willed myself to drift, to grow lighter. Those were Summer's directions. When Mick heard the directions he waved a dismissive hand and went for a cigarette, and later refused to even consider trying it. I couldn't tell if he truly thought it was dumb, or if it was a front because he was scared. In any case it seemed unfair that it was left to me.

It felt sort of good to drift, actually. Rather than feeling pinned beneath Grandpa I felt like I was floating free, even rising a little, toward the top of my head...

I returned to myself with a jolt. For a moment everything had gone dark. My eyes had stayed open, because Grandpa was the one controlling my eyelids, but the me floating around inside had closed off the connection. I had drifted away from the windows of the eyes. That's what it felt like, anyway.

I relaxed, found that I could close my eyes again. I let myself drift. It was unsettling, as if I was in deep space, floating away from the mother ship. It felt as if I was rotating, moving slowly clockwise. Without knowing why, I felt certain I was now facing my right ear.

Breathe. Relax.

The darkness began to lift, like the first hint of dawn. Trying to stay calm, I continued rotating toward the back of my head.

A sliver of silver light broke through.

I jolted with surprise, and I was instantly pulled back behind Grandpa's eyes.

There was something back there.

I didn't want to see what it was. I desperately didn't want to see what it was. Had I just glimpsed the place you go when you die? I'd never felt so utterly petrified. I had no choice, though. I had to look again. If we didn't know where the ghosts had come from, how could we find out how to send them back?

Reluctantly I tried again, drifting, turning, until the darkness turned grey, then light broke through.

The bar drifted into view.

I panicked. I was seeing the same room, but not through my eyes, through the back of my head.

This bar was empty, or nearly so. There was a man sitting on the end stool, facing the bar. Something was very wrong with his head. It was flattened at the top, as if it had been worn down to just an inch above his eyes. His handless arms ended in smooth stumps; his feet and ankles were gone, too.

There should have been a great deal of blood, but there was none, and somehow that made it worse. I wanted to squeeze my eyes closed, but I had no sense of my eyes, no sense of my body. I looked at the man on the stool, trying to understand what I was seeing. It looked like he'd been sanded away at the extremities.

I wanted to get the hell out of there. Every fiber of my being screamed run, or spin, or whatever it would take to get away. Instead I noticed tiny flecks lifting off of the man at the bar, like dust brushed off a mirror, or ashes lifting out of a bonfire.

"Bunch of cheaters," he muttered. Only his mouth moved—his cheeks remained perfectly still, his eyes stared dead at the mirrored bar, his pupils dilated to big black donuts.

He chuckled as if he'd just thought of something funny, but managed this chuckle without the hint of a smile.

"Forgot my pills," he said. I could believe that. I had a hunch he had keeled over right there on that stool, dead of a heart attack. I was sure that was it; I was looking at the corpse, the soul, of a man who had died in that spot. That was the only explanation that made sense. He looked fused to that stool, as if he hadn't moved in years.

The bar was otherwise empty as far as I could see. I couldn't see or hear the people I'd just left; instead I heard a softly howling wind, as if I was on an open plain. And, I realized, I could see the wind, or at least see the distortion it caused—horizontal static, like the imperfections you see in old unrestored film. The color of the room was off—everything was muted sepia tones—and everything seemed flat, lacking depth. The bottles behind the bar stacked up back-to-front like cardboard cutouts, the planks of the wood floor tapering too quickly to thin lines at the far end of the bar. I had the sense that if the strange man at the bar ever reached for the bowl of Chex Mix sitting there, they would taste like rubbery nothing, and he wouldn't be able to swallow them.

My vantage point lifted higher, then began to recede, toward the door. Grandpa was leaving. That was fine with me. I didn't want to talk to the man at the bar who was slowly wearing away to nothing, who spoke like a ventriloquist's dummy and seemed to be nothing but an empty shell.

Outside, a woman lay spread-eagled on the pavement, her face a concave blank from the nose up, her arms and legs trailing away to nothing above the joints.

"Those cookies smell delicious," she said just as Grandpa turned the corner onto Cypress Street.

The dead were scattered along the wind-blown street. An old man with a beard leaned up against the wall outside a parking garage. A baby wailed flatly from inside a dumpster. A man and woman, both young, lay entwined in the middle of the street, repeating snippets of non sequiturs to each other like Dada poets.

If these were all of the dead, there weren't many for a city this size. Most, I assumed, were inside. I couldn't imagine what it must be like inside a hospital; the dead must be piled twenty deep in each room.

No—there was more to it than that. If I visited Grandpa's studio I was sure I wouldn't find him hunched over the drawing table, wearing away. His spirit, or ghost, or whatever these things lying in the street were—was inside me, not in his studio where it should be.

None of the dead I passed were dressed in out-of-date clothes, no men sporting 1940s fedoras, no flapper women.

We passed an undifferentiated pile of something, bigger than a dog turd, smaller than a terrier. It was slowly, inexorably blowing away.

All at once I realized what that pile was: a person. I thought of the man in the bar, the woman lying on the sidewalk, how they were wearing down. They would keep wearing down until they became piles, then, one day, the last of them would disappear on the wind. That's why there were no men in fedoras.

I tried to get a sense of myself in this place, of my eyes moving, where my mouth was, but I was nothing in this place, an invisible observer peering from behind a window.

The street stretched, swirled as if I was viewing it through a black and white kaleidoscope. I felt a tug that was almost physical, followed by the familiar tingling in my hands and feet that told me I was coming back

Now my heart was hammering. Images of the place I'd just escaped danced behind my eyes; I doubted they would ever leave.

Gilly was nowhere to be seen, probably driven off by Grandpa. Spinning from the four or five glasses of whiskey Grandpa had downed, I searched until I located the spot where Grandpa had parked, and headed home, haunted by images of the dead blowing away in that silent, empty world.

That was where Grandpa had come from. Or maybe more apt, had escaped from. One day I would go there. It might be a week, a year, or fifty years, but I would end up there in the end. The bald truth of it was like barbed wire pulled up my spine. It wasn't an abstract, philosophical question any more—I knew beyond a shadow of a doubt what happened when we died. It scared the shit out of me.

I tried calling Mick's phone, but he didn't answer. That was okay, because I wanted to talk to Summer first, in person. I wanted her to help me make sense of what I'd seen.

How had dead people gotten out of that place? I couldn't imagine. And the voices—they were in there doing just what they did at first on the living side, blurting out bits of unconnected conversation, almost like they were emptying it all out for the last time. It reminded me of how people often say their lives flash before their eyes in the moment just before they thought they were going to die.

I pulled into the parking lot of Summer's apartment, called to her as I got out of the car. I kept calling as I stumbled up the steps. The apartment door burst open and Summer came out, eyes wide.

"I was there. Everything he wrote is true," I said. "Oh, shit. It's all true."

Summer shook with excitement, or maybe fear. "You saw it?"

Huffing, out of breath, I nodded. "I saw it. It was awful. So strange. I can't tell you—" I took a deep breath and let it out, trying to collect myself.

Summer put her arm across my back, helped me sit on the steps. There were tears in her eyes. "You're back now. You're safe." She wiped under one eye. "My God, it's like you just walked on the moon. Bigger. I can't believe it."

"I can't either."

"I'm so scared."

"Yeah. Me too."

She turned to look at me closely. "Are you okay?"

There was a slight delay between when Summer's lips moved and when her voice reached me. Everything seemed very far away. "No. Not even close."

She put the back of her hand on my forehead. A heartbeat later I felt her cool skin there. It felt nice—soft, and real. "I think you're in shock." She touched my shoulder. "Come on, let's go inside and you can lie down."

That sounded good. I knew she wanted to hear everything, but right now I wanted to stop thinking about it.

CHAPTER 23

"What do you think happens to those people over there?" Mick asked. He was still stunned, and sounded like a lost kid. When I told him what I'd seen he'd gone grey and begun to sweat. I thought he might be having another heart attack. Now he was working his way through a bottle of Drumquish single malt at his dining table.

"I think they blow away," I said.

Summer was frantically flipping through Krishnapuma's book. Now that we knew it was all true, his cryptic paragraphs were our map of the landscape. We'd gone round and round, piecing together what I'd seen, poring over Krishnapuma's writings.

"So what do we do now?" Mick asked.

"I think we need to talk to some of the dead who are back. Try to figure out what happened to bring them here," I said. "I doubt Grandpa is going to help, so that leaves Gilly."

Summer lifted her head from the book. "We could also contact some of the others posting online." Summer had come across a website that was sort of a support group for people with the voice, and a few had posted accounts of full-body possession in the past few days. She glanced at her watch. "Hell. I have to get to work."

"Oh, hell no," Mick said, rising from his chair. "Here." He pulled his wallet from the back pocket of his jeans, extracted all the money in it. "I'll pay you this to stay and help save our arses from eternal sanding."

"I can't," Summer said. "I called in sick two days in a row, and that screws everyone else, because they have to cover for me." She looked at me. "Can you give me a ride?"

I nodded. "Sure. But Mick's right—we need you. Can you quit on short notice and let us pay you to help us? Our Eastern mysticism specialist." I didn't add that I also wanted to stay close to Lorena. Before too long she would be out.

"I don't know. Can we talk about it later? I really need to get going." It looked like the topic was making her uncomfortable, and I guess I could see why. From her perspective it might seem like two guys with money offering a handout to their poor newfound friend. It wasn't like that at all, at least not for me. To me it was a life or death situation, and she seemed to have a better handle on what was going on than anyone.

#

We crossed the underground parking lot, my shoes clacking on the concrete, Summer's worn sneakers silent.

"Your grandfather seems like a complete jerk, if you don't mind me saying," Summer said. "Was he that bad when he was alive?"

"Careful," I laughed. "He can hear you. You don't want to get on his bad side."

"Yeah. Seriously, that wasn't his bad side?"

I considered. How to sum up Grandpa? "He never hit us or anything, not even when my mom was at work, but he was mean. Cutting. Whenever he was around there was tension in the air. You'd be doing something innocuous—washing the dishes, turning the channels on the TV—and suddenly he was letting you have it, calling you lazy or stupid."

Or a sissy. How many times had he said that to me? You're nothing but a sissy.

"He did it to both of you? You and Kayleigh?"

I shook my head. "Kayleigh always got a pass. She was the only one who could get a kind word to slip past that clenched jaw. He could be nice to my mom as well, but they argued a lot as well."

"What did he look like?" Summer asked. "Was he a big guy? I picture him as a big guy."

"I wish I had a picture with me—"

"You don't carry a picture of him in your wallet? I'm surprised."

I threw back my head and laughed. It felt good, especially because we were laughing about Grandpa. It made him seem less terrifying.

"He wasn't particularly tall, but he was built like a laborer—Popeye arms, a thick middle, a ruddy red face. He'd been a laborer before the accident."

Summer frowned, turned in her seat to face me. "The accident?"

"I haven't told you about the accident?" I asked. We paused as we climbed into the car. "Yeah, he was in a wheelchair. It happened sixty years ago, but we were reminded of it constantly. No one in the family could skin a knee without being told how sometimes what seems bad at the time was actually a blessing in disguise, as if we should raise our hands and thank God for every bout of diarrhea."

Summer laughed.

"Of course only physical bad fortune counted. No one in the family would dare suggest that Grandpa's bankruptcy after Toy Shop Village failed might be a blessing in disguise. Only accidents counted, because if Grandpa hadn't been burned and crippled he wouldn't have needed to find a way to make a living sitting down. And, as the twisted logic goes, if it wasn't for Grandpa's release from a life of manual labor, the rest of us would now probably be working as laborers, fast food workers, or whores—"

As soon as it was out, I tried to gulp it back, realizing how snooty that sounded to someone who waitressed for a living. "Not that—"

Summer waved me off. "I know what you mean. Go ahead."

Embarrassed, I tried to pick up the thread. "So we all lived in the shadow of Grandpa's semi-fame. That was another insufferable thing about him—he was always, always telling people who he was. In the time it took for the movie attendant to tear his ticket and point him toward the correct theater, Grandpa would find a way to let the ticket-tearer know that he was the creator of Toy Shop. He managed to do this without being friendly for a second—no smile, no 'So glad you're a fan,' just a simple declaration that he was someone important."

"Did you at least get to hang out with other cartoonists? Did he know Charles Schulz?"

I laughed again. "Oh, now you're really going to get on his bad side. He despised Schulz. He also hated Mort Walker, Hank Ketcham, Chic Young, Dik Browne, all of them. He hated the newcomers even more. As far as he was concerned Gary Larson was lazy; that's why Far Side was only one panel, and why Larson quit after 'only' fifteen years. Same with Bill Watterson and Berke Breathed. Neither of them had the fortitude to stick it out for fifty years the way Grandpa had. Of course both earned a lot more than Grandpa, so they could afford to retire early."

"It's ironic that the changes you made to the strip moved it into their league." She put her red Keds sneaker on the dash, retied a loose lace. "It's amazing that he's angry at that. You're doing just what he supposedly valued. Initiative. Business prowess."

I threw my head back. "Oh, now he hates your guts."

"What?" Summer laughed.

"You're giving me credit for something." Inside, I was glowing from Summer's praise. "Hasn't Grandpa told you? I'm a no good slacker who lets women take care of him. First Kayleigh—when we were little she used to talk for me half the time. Then Lorena, who supported me while I tried to make it as an artist."

Summer leaned back in her seat. "It sounds like he resents your success more than he resents you resurrecting the strip, or the changes you made."

I shook my head. "I don't know. Maybe. It's hard to know what goes on in his mind. I barely know what goes on in mine. Sometimes I think I made all those changes to the strip as a way to get back at him."

CHAPTER 24

"**C**an you at least tell me why you're leaving?" croaked a woman buying lottery tickets at the register. I gave her an understanding smile.

The voices of the dead seemed to be everywhere.

A trickle of cases had become a steady flow, and now a torrent. Some tipping point had been reached. On the streets people reacted to the vocal epidemic with hollow-eyed shock. You could smell the panic on people as they passed, acrid and foul. Thousands of people were fleeing the city, rushing for the exits as the horror show got really scary.

I set my coffee on the counter, feeling like the veteran soldier welcoming raw recruits to the front line. You think the voices are hard? I wanted to tell them, Wait till you see what comes next.

Back in my car I checked the news. NPR's Lakshmi Singh was discussing the epidemic with someone from the Center for Disease Control.

"This is not a disease caused by a contagious pathogen. We're sure of that."

"How can you be sure?" Lakshmi asked.

"Contagion of disease follows a pattern; it spreads from a point. No one who was not in Atlanta at the time of the anthrax attack has developed this new malady, so it cannot be contagious."

I could hear Lakshmi inhale as she formed her next question. "The CDC, the Federal Emergency Management Agency, the White House are all saying this is psychological. Is there any evidence to support this?"

"The evidence is by process of elimination. It's not a physical illness. It's not some second secret supervirus the terrorists planted. That rumor is completely without merit. Given the symptoms, it's clearly psychological."

I stopped at a light. A girl whizzed by on a red Huffy bike. She reminded me of Kayleigh. Kayleigh had insisted on a red bike; she hadn't wanted a girly color.

"There are rumors that there is an advanced form of the disorder…"

I turned the volume way up, leaned forward.

"…victims report not only losing control of their voices, but of their bodies. Do you have any information on this? Can you confirm these cases?"

"We have encountered a few of these cases. It appears to be an advanced form of the same disorder."

"Bullshit," I growled. The feds were probably afraid people would panic if they knew what it really was. They had to know by now.

On second thought, the feds were probably right to keep it quiet. Let people get used to the voices first.

Summer was waiting on her front steps. She hopped up when she saw my car.

"Have you seen WSB News?"

"No, what?"

"They've got footage of a full-on possession, and proof it's not this post-traumatic stress thing. The woman's hands are trembling like mad, she's got the zombie voice, and she answers detailed questions only the dead person would know—How tall was your first wife? What was your grandmother's first name? They checked the answers and all of them were right." Summer shook her head. "The whole thing is about to blow. They can't pass this off by saying we're all crazy or traumatized any longer."

Summer stared out the passenger window, watching pedestrians hurry by, hunched in the cold.

"My guess is they'll insist it's a mental illness to the bitter end," I said. "I just can't picture the president on national TV, saying 'The dead have taken over half a million souls in Atlanta. We're doing everything we can to save them.'"

"I see your point," Summer said. She opened her window a crack, sending a burst of cool air through the car. I turned the heat down, in case she was too warm. "I was awake most of the night wondering what happens if they can't save us. And we can't save ourselves."

I only nodded; I wondered that myself, and I didn't have any answers. Grandpa's gleeful prediction played between my ears.

A little more Thomas, a little less Finn every day.

Until, what? No more Finn?

"I've always been comfortable with not knowing what happens when we die," Summer said. "Maybe there was something, maybe nothing. I was a true agnostic—I liked believing that anything was possible and I wouldn't know the answer until I died." Her head drooped. "Now I know the answer, and I can barely breathe I'm so scared. You actually saw what happens when we die. I can't get past it."

I sighed deeply. "I try not to think about it. When I do it's like the ground has given way and I'm falling into a bottomless pit."

"What do you think is happening over there? Have you thought any more about it?"

I grunted a laugh. "All I do is think about it. I don't know, maybe it's hell, and the people who rescue dogs from the pound and recycle go to a different place."

Summer burst out laughing. "Shit, I need to adopt a pet in a hurry."

We stopped at a light; an old man, his spine curled so deeply he had to crane his neck to see, hobbled past the Avalon's bumper. His hands were trembling. It was not the tremor of the aged, but the blurry vibration of the possessed.

I gestured through the windshield. "That's what it looks like."

"What?"

"That old man. Look at his hands. He's got a hitcher." That's what people were calling them; it seemed to have started on the support group website.

She watched, transfixed. "I keep trying to imagine what it would feel like, but I can't."

The old man stepped onto the curb; the light turned green.

"No, you really can't." Again, I struggled to wrap my mind around the contradiction: Summer's tormentor was Lorena.

I spotted another, about two blocks further on, a blocky young guy in a charcoal suit. He looked all wrong in a suit. This was a flip-flop and shorts guy, a beer in a Styrofoam holder guy. I didn't bother pointing him out to Summer, though she may have noticed him on her own.

"Can I ask you something?" Summer said.

"Sure." As I spoke a spasm laced down my back, like a rope being pulled under my skin. "Oh, no."

"What?"

I pulled the car toward the curb as the rippling spread, followed by tingling. I tried to warn Summer, but couldn't get it out.

Grandpa finished pulling the car over. "This is where you get out, Missy."

"What?" Summer asked, confused.

"You heard me."

She looked at my hands, quavering, clinging to the steering wheel. "Here? I don't even know where I am."

Grandpa looked up at the street sign. "You're on Forsythe Street. Now get out."

Summer got out. Grandpa lifted a hand in farewell as he drove off.

He glanced at my watch, though the Avalon had a clock two feet from his nose and the watch bounced as if it was on the end of a spring. "Let's see if we get more than forty-seven minutes this time."

He turned right at the light. "We're gonna have a little talk, you and me. But not just yet." He drove around the block, headed back up Forsythe. Even before we pulled up in front of the Cypress Street Pint and Plate I'd guessed where we were going.

When I was a kid Grandpa would often volunteer to drive me somewhere—to buy school supplies or whatever—then take a detour through the Pint and Plate. I didn't mind because he always bought me a Coke, and he was unusually nice to me on those detours. "Don't tell Grandma, now," he'd say as he boosted a drink to his mouth, chasing each swig with a long, satisfied "Aaaaah." He always knew the bartender, was warmer, more animated than he ever was at home. In the course of twenty minutes he'd down three whiskeys, then we'd be off. If someone asked what took us so long Grandpa would say I'd had trouble deciding, or the store had been out of what we were looking for and we had to go somewhere else. If no one was watching he'd wink at me when he said this, and after a while I'd watch for the wink. The wink was like a vitamin I was deficient in, and I drank it in.

If Grandpa knew the bald, unshaven man who was tending bar that day he didn't let on. All he said was, "Whiskey, neat." The bartender started at the sound of his voice, but set a cocktail napkin down, then the drink on top. He quickly retreated down the bar.

Inside I cringed as he let out that first long raspy "Aaaaaah" and set the shivering glass back on the napkin. The plan was for me to return to Deadland, to explore further and see what I could learn, but I was curious about the "little talk" Grandpa had promised. Besides, I didn't relish going back to Deadland. It was scary.

The bartender was staring at Grandpa's hands. Grandpa folded his arms, pinning the hands under his elbows. "Let me ask you something. Which is right: The yolk of an egg is white, or the yolk of an egg are white?"

The bartender peered at the ceiling. "Is white."

Now I knew Grandpa didn't know this bartender. Every bartender who'd ever tipped a bottle for Grandpa knew this one.

"You're not so bright," Grandpa said humorlessly. "The yolk of an egg is yellow."

The bartender smiled nervously, nodded. "Got me."

Grandpa set his empty glass down. "Hit me again. See if you can't get a little more in the glass this time. You're charging me for a whole drink, aren't you?"

The bartender's face grew stony. If he'd been dealing with a normal customer he looked like the sort who wouldn't take any crap. Instead he poured noticeably more into the glass, then turned and walked to the farthest corner of the bar.

Grandpa drained the glass in three gulps, pulled out my wallet and hooked a twenty. "Keep it." The twenty fluttered to the bar.

"You're a big tipper," Grandpa chuckled as he pushed open the door.

"So," he said as he walked, "dinner's on you, is it? Because of all the money you're making." A young couple heading toward us paused. They looked alarmed, whispered to each other, then hurried across the street. The bartender may not have heard yet, but word was spreading about what shaking hands meant. "There's only one problem, buddy-boy. It's not your money. It's mine."

He turned into a clothing store called Enki Mikaye. A skinny guy with a square jaw met him right at the door and asked if he could be of service.

"Yes, I want a suit. A solid three-piece, double-breasted. Classic. None of this new styles crap." Grandpa made it sound like changing fashion in men's suits was entirely this salesman's fault, but I didn't think that was why the salesman took a step back. Besides the hands, Grandpa's voice still held an unmistakable croak.

Appearing visibly nervous, the salesman helped him choose a suit, plus an ensemble to go with it. It was an outfit I would never be caught dead in, and it cost me $1800.

When he presented the salesman with my credit card, the guy slid it through, glanced at it, then at Grandpa.

"Finn Darby. Toy Shop."

"Yes, that's right." Grandpa lifted his chin, as if daring the salesman to question it.

The salesman slid the card across the counter. "It's a wonderful strip. Wolfie is a hoot."

Grandpa was breathing out of his nose so heavily it was almost deafening. "Go fuck yourself." He turned and headed for the door.

"You're an ungrateful little mutt," he said as he slammed the car door. "I took you in when your no good father walked out on you. I fed you, I tried to show you how to get along in this world, and what thanks did I get?" He threw the Avalon into gear. "I want your comic strip," he said in a whiny baby tone. The tires squealed. "And when you get hold of it, what do you do? You use cheap tricks— bells and whistles—because you're not clever enough to do it the right way. You're not a man, Finnegan. You're still a boy, hanging on to everyone's shirt tails. Mine, your mother's, your spic wife's. You expect everything to be handed to you."

Grandpa fell silent. He had quite a take on things. He took us in and fed us? He charged his own daughter rent. Mom had to buy all of our groceries separately; there was a separate part of the fridge for Grandma and Grandpa's food, and we were not to touch it. Bells and whistles? The strip was a hundred times more popular than it had ever been under his hand, and that was right into the teeth of a huge decline in newspaper circulation.

And the truth of it was, I had to change the strip. I'd felt boxed in by a strip frozen in time, with only two major characters and a finite stable of timeless toys (jump ropes, bicycles, teddy bears) to work with. I'd dreaded each return to that musty little toy shop, to those two earnest little twits, to my dead grandfather's tight, Victorian humor. I'd been falling farther and farther behind my deadlines when I finally decided to defy my agent and the syndicate and update the strip, creating new characters and having a big chain buy out the little toy shop.

I stewed, and waited for my body to return to me. How long had it been? An hour and a half, at least.

Grandpa pulled out my phone, punched 911. The 911 operator asked what his emergency was.

"My emergency? I don't have a damned emergency. I'm calling information."

The operator told him information was 411, not 911.

"Oh, that's right." He hung up without apologizing, dialed 411, and asked for the number for CNN.

As he dialed, repeating the number in a whisper as he did so, my mind raced. What would Grandpa want with CNN?

Grandpa said he wanted to talk to someone about Toy Shop, specifically how Finn Darby had stolen it from him without his permission. He was transferred, told the story again, then was transferred again. This final listener, a young woman with a Long Island accent, asked how he could be the creator of Toy Shop when the creator was dead.

"I know I'm dead. You don't have to tell me I'm dead," Grandpa said. "I've come back. Now, will you run the story or not?"

"How have you managed to come back?" she asked, sounding amused.

"A lot of us have come back. The dead are everywhere, missy, or haven't you noticed?"

Sounding less amused, she said she'd have to look into it, and took his number. I could only hope they'd check with my agent, and he would deflect them.

Our next stop was a jewelry store, where Grandpa bought two Rolexes at full retail and a set of gold cufflinks before ducking into another bar. Then we were off again.

"It's really something, to be young again," he said as he drove. "I tell you it's no good getting old. When you hit seventy, that's it," he made a chopping gesture, "blow your brains out and be done with it. Ah, here we are." Grandpa pulled into Maserati of Atlanta.

"I've always wanted an expensive car," he said as he swaggered toward the showroom, flipping my keys in his palm. "I might as well spend it, right? I'm the one who earned it."

The son of a bitch. When he was alive he was so cheap he rinsed out and re-used plastic baggies. Now that he had my bank card he was going to live it up. Or maybe he was intentionally trying to bankrupt me, to get revenge for Toy Shop.

A miniature poodle met us at the door, yipping and spinning in circles. Otherwise, the dealership was deserted. Evidently not many people were buying Maseratis, at least in Atlanta.

"Can I get some help here?" Grandpa shouted.

A young woman in a grey suit appeared. "Sorry, I was in the rest room. Can I help you?"

"Yes. I'm Finn Darby, I have a lot of money, and I want to buy a Maserati."

The woman frowned. She was staring at Grandpa's hands. "I don't think I can help you. Please come back some other time." The croak in his voice and tremors in his hands were definitely less severe; in another week or two he might pass for one of the living. But not yet.

Grandpa froze. "What do you mean? I want to buy a car. You sell cars, don't you? Isn't that what you do here?"

She took a step back. "Please go." She was clutching her phone. My guess is she was debating whether to dial 911.

Grandpa threw his hands in the air. "For God's sake, I won't bite. I just want to buy a car. Here—" He pulled my bank card from my wallet, held it out. "I can pay cash. Ten minutes and I'll be out of your hair."

"I'm sorry. Just, please leave me alone." She looked terrified.

Grandpa lunged at her, clutched her jacket sleeve where it was hanging under the wrist. In a low voice he said, "I want a God damned Maserati. Now get your little ass in gear and sell me a car, and we'll get along just fine."

It took Grandpa five minutes to pick out a wheat-colored four-door Quattroporte from their inventory. He didn't want to look at the interior, only under the hood. When the saleswoman popped the hood and quickly stepped back, Grandpa peered at it, scowling with concentration before nodding once and saying, "That's a beaut."

I groaned inwardly. My grandfather knew nothing about engines. He used to take a rag and a spray bottle of Formula 409 and clean the parts of his engine he could reach from his wheelchair, because he liked the idea of working under the hood of a car. Cleaning it was all he knew how to do.

After strong-arming the terrified saleswoman into forgoing all of the usual paperwork, he headed to Grandma's house, the Maserati growling in a low, unfamiliar rumble.

Grandpa rapped on the locked front door, then peered in the window to be sure Grandma wasn't hiding inside; he pushed behind the overgrown bushes in front of the house and retrieved a key hidden in one of those fake rocks.

He headed straight to his studio, where his drafting table still sat, empty of pens, ink, paper. Cursing, he went to the empty shelves lining the far wall, where there had been tens of thousands of original strips, stacked floor-to-ceiling.

"You sold them all, didn't you?" He traced the grain of the wood with his fingers. "You rotten stinkers. All you care about is money. You're a pair of God damned profiteers, I'm telling you."

Yes, I had sold them. Except for the really important ones, and the ones I'd kept as models for drawing new strips. I'd given the proceeds—over sixty grand—to Grandma. I felt a little guilty about it now, but when you dispose of dead people's possessions it's with the assumption that they're going to stay dead, so there is no one to hurt, no one who'll miss those things. Sure, you keep sentimental things, but not ten thousand original comic strips. Besides, he'd only kept them out of spite. He had no use for them, and certainly could have used the cash I could have raised selling them, but when I'd told him they'd bring maybe forty dollars each for the dailies, seventy-five for the Sundays, he'd scowled and asked what I got for a Peanuts original. Peanuts originals sell for twenty thousand and up. He knew that. He'd curled his lip in disgust, said if I couldn't sell his strips for what they were worth, he'd keep them.

He sat at his drafting table and opened the bottom drawer. It was empty, except for a tattered brown photo album.

"Did you throw everything out?" Grandpa asked. "How long did you wait? A week?" He set the album on the table and flipped it open.

"Hm." He pinched his nose. "Hello, Mother dear." His mother was a bland woman who looked like she was sucking on a sour-ball. He sighed heavily, flipped to the next page, muttering softly to himself. There was a photo of two ruddy boys standing in the mud, each holding a pail. Milking time. One of them must have been Grandpa, the other probably his brother, who died in World War II. He turned the page and grunted. There he was, singing in a pub. My mom once told me Grandpa wanted to become a singer, but once he married Grandma she put an end to that foolishness.

This was a side of him I never got to see, because he'd been angry at me since the day I was born. It was strange that he'd hated me so much, yet loved my twin sister. How many times had I walked past his studio as a child and seen Kayleigh sitting in his lap while he drew? Come here, ya little monkey, ya, he'd say, intercepting Kayleigh as she passed, to comb her hair with a black fifty-cent comb he bought at the barber. That Grandpa was kind to her was one of the few things I'd hated about Kayleigh.

Grandpa rose from the desk, stretched to open the door on a cabinet built above his book shelf. He cursed when he saw it was empty, grabbed the key to the Maserati from the desk and headed for the door.

He'd had a bottle stashed in that cabinet; I remembered coming across it while helping Grandma clean out the room. He was losing his buzz. The life of a closet alcoholic must be tedious—all those trips to procure booze, afraid if you buy a case at a time it will be too obvious.

Grandpa hadn't checked my watch in a while, but he'd been in control for a long time—it seemed much longer than the last. I was getting anxious. Maybe I wasn't going to return this time.

My phone rang before he reached the Maserati. He fished it from his pocket and held it up to see who was calling. "It's your new girlfriend. She's probably still standing on the street corner where I unloaded her."

He opened the phone, pressed it to his ear. "What can I do for you, girlie?"

"Finn?" The voice was a swamp creature with no tongue.

"Who's this?" Grandpa snapped.

"I waited for you. On the bank. But you didn't come."

Inside, I wailed. I thrashed and cried.

"Jesus," Grandpa muttered. "I know that lousy accent, even fresh from the grave."

"Finn?"

"Welcome to the party, senorita burrito," Grandpa said. "You're late, as usual."

She was here, right here on the phone, and I couldn't speak to her.

"Grandfather-in-law," Lorena croaked. Rough and unformed as the words were, the contempt was unmistakable.

"Ahh, I don't have time for you." He snapped the phone closed as inside I screamed "no." She was back. My Lorena.

Instead of returning my phone to his pocket, he examined it in his quavering hands. Poking buttons, he found my phone book and scrolled down the names until he reached Mom.

Again, I was screaming "no," but I couldn't reach him as he dialed Mom and brought the phone to his ear.

"Hey," Mom answered, expecting me.

"Hello, Jenny, me gal."

Mom laughed tentatively. "That's not funny."

"It's not Finn, Jenny. It's your father."

There was a long pause. "Finn, you told me you were better.

You're not, are you?"

Grandpa exhaled into the phone. "Finn doesn't have no disease, Jenny. He's got me. I don't know how it happened, but it did and there's nothing any of us can do about it."

This was intolerable. I was torn apart by the dual horrors of what he was putting Mom through while simultaneously being kept from Lorena.

I heard computer keys ticking through the phone. "I'm coming up there right now. I'm going to take care of you, sweetie." She was probably looking up flights. What was he doing? I'd worked so hard to save my mother the agony of witnessing this, now here he was, ruining everything.

"I'll say it again. This is not Finn. This is your father, who used to sing you 'Wild Irish Rose' and 'Take Me Back to Dear Old Blighty' when you went to bed, who took you to the top of the Empire State Building and put a quarter in the viewer and held you up so you could see."

"I'm coming, Finn." She was crying now. "I know you can't help it."

"Jenny, don't you even know your own father? Listen, remember when I used to sing you 'Take Me Back to Dear Old Blighty'?"

"No."

"Oh yes you do," Grandpa said. "I know you do. Listen."

He sang it, carrying a tune like I never could, his resonant Irish brogue coming through despite the graveyard croak, spewing convoluted lyrics I'd never heard from an obscure song that only a man who was Irish and alive seventy-five years ago could possibly know. Mom kept telling him to stop, but he pushed on until she screamed it, prompting Grandpa to pull the phone away from his ear.

"Now Jenny," Grandpa said in a soothing voice. "Everything's all right—"

"This isn't happening. Where is Finn? I want to talk to Finn."

"He's safe."

The connection went dead.

Grandpa cursed, snapped the phone shut. He dragged his hand across his mouth, sighed. "Jenny, Jenny. What are we going to do?"

Finally, finally, I felt tingling in the tips of my fingers, a rush of warmth. I inhaled gratefully. I dialed Lorena while I raced for the car.

She answered on the fourth ring, crying into the phone, unable to speak.

"Lorena?"

"No," Summer managed.

"Are you all right?"

"No." She was nearly whispering.

No, she wouldn't be all right. "I'm on my way. Where are you?"

"At the High Museum. The French Impressionist exhibit."

I couldn't stifle a laugh. "You got dumped on a corner by my grandfather and hopped a bus to the High?"

"This is where I go when I feel like I'm drowning."

I pictured her sitting on one of those incredibly solid wood benches, surrounded by Monets and Gauguins. "I'm going to remember that," I said. "When everything seems darkest, go to the French Impressionist room at the High."

"Don't make fun of me, Finn. I'm hanging by a thread right now."

"Sorry. I'm on my way."

As soon as I hung up I called my mother. There were honks and rumbles of traffic in the background

"I'm on my way to the airport."

"Mom, for God's sake, don't come here. This place is a nightmare. They're all coming out, the voices are coming out. The whole city is going to be filled with dead people."

I managed to scare the shit out of myself, imagining the city brimming with hitchers, their hands shaking, those horrible voices fouling the air.

"I'm not losing you," Mom said. "He'll listen to me. I'll make him listen."

She had a point. As far as I knew she was the only person alive

Grandpa didn't hate. If anyone could talk him out of me, it was Mom.

"Where is Grandma?" I asked.

"She's staying with Aunt Julia." That didn't surprise me. She probably started packing the moment Grandpa and I left her house.

"It's probably best if you stay with her, too."

"Why is that?" Mom asked.

"Because I'm not home much. I'm spending all of my time trying to figure this out with help from some friends."

I told her to call when she arrived, tried to assure her that I was okay.

I found Summer sitting cross-legged on a bench, her coat draped across her shoulders, gazing at Monet's water lilies but clearly not seeing them. She was rocking slightly.

"Hey," I said softly, putting my hand on her back.

Her eyes lost some of their thousand-yard stare and fixed on me. She made a vague sound that was mostly vowel.

I sat next to her, looked up at the Monet. It was the one with the green rainbow-shaped bridge. "My twin sister Kayleigh had a print of this in her room. She kept bugging Mom to take us to France so she could see the real bridge."

"I'd like to see France," Summer said listlessly. "I've never been anywhere. Except Disney World." After a moment she added, "And Nashville. I saw Graceland." Abruptly she turned and looked at me. "Can I ask you something personal? I won't be offended if you don't want to answer."

"Sure, anything." Anything to get her mind off what she'd just been through.

"What happened to Kayleigh? I asked Mick, but he said you haven't told him, except to say she drowned."

My eyes filled with tears. It surprised me that the question could stir up such emotions with everything else going on, but thinking about her now filled me with such a profound sense of loss and shame. "I try not to think about it. But I'll tell you if you want me to."

Summer turned to face me more directly, waited. I realized that, painful as it was, I wanted to tell her my story. I wanted her to know. I started in a low voice, though there was no one else in the room at the moment.

"The summer Kayleigh died had been the best of our lives. Grandma and Grandpa had invested in this rooming house on Tybee Beach, sort of a downscale B and B, with the idea that Grandma would run it (making the beds, cleaning, running clean towels up and down four flights of stairs with her bad hip) while Grandpa drew his strip. Tybee was a blue-collar place back then—t-shirt shops, beer joints, lots of chipped paint—but Kayleigh and I fell in love with it. Bare feet all day, dark tans, hunting for shells in the dunes, begging quarters from Mom to play the games on the boardwalk. We won this big stuffed tiger we were dying to have, always playing the number twelve, because we were twelve.

"The shift from magical summer to the blackest despair I'd ever known was so quick it nearly snapped me in half. One minute I was with my folks, wolfing down fried clams dipped in tartar sauce from a paper plate, on top of the world. The next, my sister was dead.

"Grandma was the one who called. I can still hear seagulls screeching in the background, fighting over French fries when Mom answered her cell, the way she stopped chewing, the way her face suddenly shifted to an expression I'd never seen before, one that made my heart start hammering. It's an expression I became very familiar with, because Mom wore it every day for the next three or four years, and still wears it sometimes, nineteen years later.

"I can still see Mom's phone clatter to the boardwalk. She was saying "No" over and over. "No. No. No. No." Dad picked up the phone, and after talking for a minute he started crying. That's when I knew something awful had happened, something that meant summer was over, that my life would never be the same.

"It just kept getting worse. First, I learned Kayleigh was at the hospital, then I learned she was dead. Then I realized it was my fault."

A couple of elderly women entered the room and I stopped. We sat in silence as they circled the room and eventually slipped out into the next.

"Why was it your fault?" Summer prompted.

"Kayleigh jumped off the pier because I did," I said. "It was Kayleigh's idea to begin with. She dared me to jump, and said she would if I would. But she didn't think I'd really do it; it was a thirty-foot drop, and you had to jump out away from the pier to clear the wooden pilings." I shook my head. "She was just talking. Sitting on the pier pretending we were going to jump was just something to do.

"So we squatted with our toes curled around the edge of the wood planks, and the longer we stayed, the more I thought maybe I could actually do it. I thought about how impressed everyone would be, maybe even Grandpa. I was as surprised as Kayleigh when I launched myself off that pier. The fall seemed to go on and on, and when I hit the water I hit hard. The soles of my feet stung and my balls ached. But I was ecstatic. I felt strong, and brave, and I didn't often feel that as a kid. I was a shy, anxious kid. When we were younger I used to whisper things to Kayleigh when we were around other people, and she would say them for me.

"Kayleigh admitted she couldn't do it. I didn't taunt her. I didn't tuck my fists under my arms and flap them and go buck-buck-buck. We didn't do that stuff to each other. But I did strut. I told everyone how I had jumped off that pier."

I was getting to the hard part. I put my hand over my mouth, tried to calm my pounding heart.

"It must have eaten at her, that she agreed to jump and then backed down, and after dinner when Mom and Dad decided to go to the Shoppies—that's what we called the outlet mall out by the interstate—Kayleigh stayed behind with Grandma and Grandpa.

"I jumped off the pier on a calm sunny day, the waves just bumps with occasional slivers of white at the crest. Kayleigh jumped just after sundown, into big, black, crashing waves."

I stared down between my feet, at the swirling grain in the polished wood.

"Mom and Dad's marriage lasted a year to the day from Kayleigh's fatal jump, and we moved in with Grandpa. Dad disappeared for a while after that, only to reappear long enough to convince Grandpa to invest in his insane Toy Shop Village idea. When it was clear the village was failing, he disappeared again for good.

"It was all my fault, and everyone blamed me. At least, that's how it felt to me. That's when I started drawing. I'd come home from school and go straight to my room and draw my comics until dinner. And when I wasn't drawing I was reading comics; I had hundreds of compilations—Peanuts, Ziggy, Nancy, Dilbert. You name it. While most guys my age were playing baseball and sneaking peeks at Playboy, I was obsessing over Pogo."

I looked at the Monet. How hard it must have been for Mom to take that print down from Kayleigh's wall, to pack all of her stickers and clothes and stuffed animals in boxes.

"I'm sorry," Summer said. "For what it's worth, I don't think you're to blame. You didn't put her up to it. You jumped for your own reasons. You didn't push her to follow you. It doesn't sound like you really cared whether she jumped or not."

"Honestly? I didn't want her to. I wanted it to be my thing." I studied the bridge, the calm, shallow, comforting water beneath. "Next time Grandpa called me a sissy, I could remind him of how I jumped off that pier."

Was that really what I'd thought? I wasn't sure. Maybe I was adding it after the fact because Grandpa was so much on my mind.

"I appreciate you telling me. Thanks," Summer said.

"Sure."

We sat side by side, each seeking solace in Bridge Over a Pond of Water Lilies.

As Summer wrestled with her demons, I fantasized about making my grandfather dead again.

Or, barring that, hurting him.

By the time I left the High I thought I knew how to do it.

CHAPTER 25

My pencil seemed to draw Little Joe by itself, leading my shaking hand. For a change it was shaking in anger, not because Grandpa was coming.

"You want to play? Let's play," I said. Fuming, my breath rushing through nostrils that suddenly felt too small, I drew Little Joe, the tired old standard, the center of Grandpa's universe.

I drew him for the last time.

"How do you like that? Little Joe is dead." I dipped my shading brush, watched plumes of black ink leach into the clear water. "Dead, dead, dead. Croaked. Deceased. Pushing up daisies." I could run with this plot line for weeks. I didn't understand why no one was calling the government on such a transparent lie. No one who was actually in the city still believed this was a mental illness. There were dead people running around; there was no debating it. Yet the national press still led with the mental illness take.

I packed the strips and arranged for a UPS pickup that day. They needed to be out before Grandpa returned, so he couldn't cut them up.

The thought of Grandpa's return sent a wave of dread through my belly. I went to the living room and turned on MSNBC.

Tamron Hall was interviewing a hitcher, standing in the sea of shoes in Chastain Park.

"Do you remember where your mother bought them?" Tamron asked. The shot switched to a close-up on a pair of tiny, white, girl's dress shoes, the size a six-year-old might wear.

"Yes. Stride Rite in the Lenox mall." The woman who answered was fiftyish, with long black hair streaked with grey and a little girl zombie voice.

Tamron looked off-camera. "Mom, would you?" She reached to draw another woman into the shot, a heavyset woman in her thirties. I turned it off, then hurled the remote across the room for good measure. This was so messed up.

"Why was it so hard to act like a decent human being?" I shouted at Grandpa. I went back into my studio, stared up at those two framed strips hung side-by-side. "A normal grandfather would have taken me under his wing. He would have been proud to have me follow in his footsteps. You were never there for any of us." I grunted a humorless laugh. "You weren't there for Kayleigh, that's for sure." I'd never had the guts to say that to him when he was alive. It felt good. Sure, I was the one most responsible for her death, I could admit that, but there was plenty of excess blame to go around. "How could you let her go out to a pier alone, at night? You knew she'd been trying to get up the nerve to jump off that pier. How could you let her go out there alone? Where were you?" He'd probably snuck out to a bar.

Maybe I'd get my answers when Grandpa took over again, maybe not. Either way it felt good to ask questions I'd been swallowing for years.

It occurred to me that I could look for Kayleigh. After sixteen years she was probably gone, but I could drive down to Tybee Beach and check. She would have hung on to the world with both hands, the way Lorena had.

If there was anything left of her, though, it couldn't be much. And she'd still be eleven. I didn't think I could bear to see that.

The doorbell rang. I wasn't expecting anyone. Mick would just let himself in, and Summer wouldn't be along for another hour or so. That left my mother. Maybe she'd changed her mind about going to Aunt Julia's house. It was awfully quick for a flight from Phoenix, though, not to mention the ride from the airport.

I opened the door to a woman with a microphone. Behind her a man was pointing a TV camera at me. "Mr. Darby? I'm Kimberly Perkins of CNN."

I stared at her dumbfounded, giving her my best shocked, blinking, deer-in-the-headlights look. "I don't give interviews at my home. Talk to my agent."

"Mr. Darby, CNN—"

I closed the door and flipped the lock, but Kimberly Perkins only raised her voice and went on talking. "CNN received a call originating from your phone, from someone claiming to be your late grandfather, Thomas Darby. I'd like to speak to you about it."

I pressed my forehead against the door, not even daring to breathe heavily.

"Mr. Darby? Was it your grandfather?"

I waited until Kimberly stopped calling through the door, then watched through the curtains as she headed back to a white van.

Propping a foot on the bumper, she turned to talk to her cameraman. He pulled out a cigarette, cupped his hands around a lighter, nodding at something Kimberly said. They weren't leaving.

This I didn't need. I was sort of famous, had developed a reputation for being reclusive because I wasn't making any appearances in the wake of Toy Shop's growing success. If they could confirm that Grandpa was possessing me (or that I was suffering from post-traumatic identity disorder and thought he was possessing me), they would be all over it. I needed to call Steve, see if there was anything he could do.

I was just about to turn when Summer pulled up behind the van.

"Don't talk to them, just come straight in," I said aloud as Summer stepped out of her car and Kimberly and the cameraman rushed over.

The car keys dropped out of her trembling hand. Her face was flat, expressionless—a flesh mask.

I bolted out the door. "Lorena!"

She pushed past Kimberly Perkins, stumbled. "Finn?"

I wrapped my arm around her, led her toward the door. Tears streamed down her cheeks. "I waited for you. I was sure you'd come." I wanted to tell her not to speak until we got inside, away from the reporter, but I couldn't bring myself to silence her. "The wind kept blowing but I tried to hold on." Her voice was a watery horror. Despite how badly I had wanted to talk to her, despite everything, I was afraid. My dead wife was here, returned from two years in that place.

"I couldn't get to where you were," I said as I closed the door and led her to the couch, my heart breaking at the thought of Lorena waiting by that river. "I would have if I could."

She took my hands in hers and squeezed. "I know that now." Her head dropped; she shook it slowly. Summer's pigtails swayed with each turn. "I kept forgetting I was dead." She raised her head, reached to me and gathered me toward her. "Please hold me. I want to feel that I'm really here."

It made my skin prickle with involuntary dread, but I hugged her, felt her shoulders bounce as she cried into my neck, felt Summer's small breasts pressed against my chest. It was strange to be holding my Lorena but feeling Summer's thin arms, seeing skin so pale the blue of veins shone through where Lorena's warm brown should be.

"I'm sorry I left you in the boat. I'm so sorry. I should have been there."

She laughed spasmodically. "I'm such an idiot. Why didn't I listen to you? I died of stupidity. It's not your fault I'm stupid."

"You're not stupid. You have a phobia." Or was it had a phobia? How do you refer to someone who's both alive and not? I squeezed her tighter, wanting to cherish every second, wishing she smelled like Lorena. I closed my eyes, pictured my Lorena the first time I held her, on our first date. I'd taken her to Ele, the best restaurant in the city where I could get a reservation, and spent a fortune trying to impress her.

Lorena pushed away from me, hard.

"Get your hands off me!"

"I'm sorry. I'm sorry." I held up my hands. Summer was shaking hers as if she'd just touched some horrible bug. "I was holding my wife. I thought I'd lost her forever, and I had a chance to hold her. How could I not?"

"This is not your wife's body. Don't you ever—" She made a fist, raised it to punch my shoulder, then lowered it to her lap, gasping for breath.

I thought of Grandpa kissing Grandma, how violated it made me feel. "You're right. I really am sorry. I wasn't thinking. Can you see how you could forget, if someone you loved suddenly came to life right in front of you?"

Summer rubbed her face with both hands. "It feels like being buried alive."

"That's a good way to put it."

"God, I don't want this to happen any more. I can't."

I was stinging from the disappointment of Lorena leaving so quickly. I wanted to see her again. At the same time, I knew what it felt like, and I didn't want Summer to have to suffer it again. Somehow I was able to separate those two desires and wish for both.

"She's come back because of you," Summer said.

"What?"

"'I waited for you. The wind kept blowing but I tried to hold on.'" Summer was staring off toward the staircase, her tone listless, almost plaintive. "The ones coming back are the ones who don't want to be dead. The ones who find it most intolerable. Ghosts haunt because they're not at peace. They desperately don't want to be dead. Or they have unfinished business, like Gilly."

I thought of Lorena. If there was a way to get back to the world of the living Lorena would be the first in line. Grandpa had been drawing the day he died, clinging to this world. Not even death would snuff that much ambition. And Gilly—as soon as Gilly came out, he started working on The Album, the one that was going to relaunch Mick's career and make them friends again.

"Yeah. That sounds right." And it seemed important. "What was it Krishnapuma said? Under the right conditions, the dead might get pulled back into the world of the living. Maybe if enough dead in one place wanted back in, they could storm the gate, so to speak."

Summer didn't look like she was in the mood to muse on the motives of the dead. She nodded absently, hugging herself and rubbing her upper arms as if she was freezing.

It made me uneasy that we'd be running with a conclusion based on so little evidence, though. If we wanted to drive the hitchers back to where they came from, it seemed important to be sure we knew why they were here. We should hunt down other people who knew who was haunting them, see if they were all restless souls, not ready for that wind to take them up. If Annie were back, for instance, we were on the wrong track. She'd wanted to die.

"Hang on," I said.

Before I could voice my idea, I was gone again.

CHAPTER 26

Grandpa drove right back to Grandma's house. On the way he tried to consult with his attorney about getting an injunction to block the publication of Toy Shop. His attorney had died in the anthrax attack. When Grandpa tried to explain to another member of his attorney's firm that he had been dead for two years, the attorney hung up on him.

"Ah, ya stinking rotten—" Grandpa pounded the dashboard with my phone. "You think it bothers me, what you did, don't you? Well, it doesn't. Little Joe doesn't go away just because you put it in a strip. How many times did Tina run him over with a bicycle and leave him all bent up? He doesn't spend a month in a cartoon hospital after that, now does he? He's back the next day. It's not a story. It's not a book. It's a God damned cartoon, for God's sake."

I glowered inside, feeling cheated. It had been less than eleven hours since I'd regained control, and I was already back in my prison, forced to listen to his rants. If I'd had another hour I could have set up my plan.

"And another thing—I want you off my property," Grandpa said as he hung a left onto his block. "You've got a lot of nerve, living there." There was a car I didn't recognize in Grandma's driveway. "Now who is this?"

The front door swung open; Mom stepped out. She folded her arms, waiting. Grandpa's hands tensed on the wheel; for a moment I thought he would cut and run. He turned off the ignition.

"Hello, Jenny gal," Grandpa said as he stepped out of the Maserati.

Mom looked him up and down, her arms still folded. She looked exhausted. "Who are you supposed to be?"

"I'm your father, Jenny. I've come back to you." He opened his arms as if waiting for her to run into his embrace. "I don't know how it's happened."

"You've come back." Mom yanked her hair out of her face, shook her head violently. "No. You don't come back. That's not how it works." I couldn't have said it better. "What the hell is going on? Tell me what's going on."

Grandpa closed the distance between them, put his hands on her shoulders. "Jenny, I don't know. It's a miracle."

"It's not a miracle. It's an abomination." She shrugged his hands off of her. "Where is Finn? Where's my son?"

Grandpa pinched his lips together, studied Mom. Or maybe he was buying time while he thought of how to phrase it.

"He's here. We got stuck together somehow; I don't understand it any better than you. It's a miracle, is what it is."

I wished I had eyes to roll. Suddenly he was a victim in all this; an innocent rube, a confused old man. What was it about my mother that led him to rein in all of his venom?

"I want to talk to him," Mom said.

Grandpa shook his head sadly. "It isn't up to me who gets to talk when."

She pierced Grandpa with a look that made me flinch. It was a very familiar look from when I was a boy and I was misbehaving. "I want you to leave Finn alone. You had your life. You can't have Finn's. I won't let you."

Grandpa held his open palms in the air. "I told you, I had nothing to do with it. I just found meself here, like I was dropped from the sky."

Mom put her hands on top of her head. "I can't believe I'm having this conversation. You died. I was there; I saw you die."

"Come inside and sit down." Grandpa tried to steer her through the door, but Mom didn't budge.

"This isn't your house. You don't live here and you have no right to invite me in."

Grandpa held up the key. "I paid for this house. Every penny, with my sweat and blood. Don't you tell me it isn't mine."

Mom didn't respond; she just glared.

Grandpa huffed. "Well, I'm going in. If you want to come in and have a cup of tea, you're welcome." As he unlocked the door with the spare key Grandma had given me to replace the one I'd lost at the bottom of the reservoir, he turned, held the screen door open. Mom stood with arms folded, staring toward the street. I heard her sniff back tears as the screen door swung closed.

CHAPTER 27

Within hours, Lorena and I were on CNN.

"You can clearly hear Finn Darby call 'Lorena,' although the woman he's addressing is Summer Locker, a waitress who lives in northwest Atlanta. Lorena is the name of Darby's late wife, who died two years ago in a boating accident…"

They played a tape of Grandpa's phone call and covered that angle as well. There were probably a half-dozen news vans parked outside my apartment; fortunately I went straight to Mick's apartment when I regained control of myself. Summer was there, watching the news while Mick talked to his mole at FEMA.

They were quarantining the city. They had secured Route 285—the perimeter—but if we could trust what the feds were saying it was to protect the victims of this new "disease" from throngs of superstitious miscreants whose threats against us were growing louder each day. (For good measure MSNBC aired a few clips of sundry extremists airing their opinions of what to do with the afflicted.) People with good reason to move in or out of the city would be allowed, according to the news. Still, the images of National Guard troops lining the perimeter was disconcerting.

MSNBC also reported two separate multiple homicides, where the only thing that connected the victims was all of them were known to have hitchers. There was some debate about whether these could be classified as hate crimes.

"Shit, shit, shit," Mick growled as he closed his phone. He flopped onto the couch. "They've documented at least two cases of people who've left and not come back. The bleeding hitchers appear to have taken them over permanently."

We digested this in silence.

"So now we know," I said.

"Now we know," Mick echoed. He turned his face toward the ceiling, expelled a plume of cigarette smoke.

The news didn't chill me the way I might have expected, probably because deep down I already knew how this was going to end if we couldn't figure out a way to stop it. I didn't have much faith in FEMA or the CDC; this was too bizarre for a federal agency to get a grip on it.

"Summer has a theory about what's happening, and I think I've figured out a way to test it," I said, trying to strike a positive note.

We drifted into the space that served as Mick's living room and I explained. It hinged on my late friends, Annie and Dave. As I talked I pulled out my notebook, wrote their names on opposite sides of the page.

"One of the last things Annie said to me was not to feel bad for her, because she wasn't all that sorry about dying." I underlined Dave's name a half-dozen times. "Dave had a wife he loved like crazy. Just a flat-out happy guy." If Dave was still on the other side, we were probably on the wrong track.

"So you want to check to see if these people are in Deadland, eh?" Mick said.

"That's the idea," I said.

Mick nodded. "Annie should be there, Dave shouldn't, because Dave should be back here."

"How are you going to get Grandpa to go to the places where Annie and Dave died?" Summer asked.

"How am I going to?" I laughed. "I'm not. My job is to float around on the doorstep of the dead and look for these people; you and Mick have to get me there."

Mick flexed his bicep, looked at Summer. "We're the muscle."

Summer shook her head. "It's simpler if I go this time; Lorena would probably go willingly if you asked."

She had a point. The thing was, I wanted to do this. I wanted to see the evidence (or lack thereof) firsthand. "I see what you're saying, but I'm hoping I can communicate with Annie if she's there. She'll help us if she can. You don't know her."

"I had a brother who drank himself to death about a year ago," Summer countered. "We could use him instead. If he returned to the world of the living, we're definitely wrong, because he hated it here."

"Where did he die?" I asked.

"Piedmont Hospital."

I shook my head. "There'll be thousands of dead in a hospital. Locating him would be dodgy." Then I remembered something Summer had said. "Plus, I have one foot in Deadland already, remember? There's no guarantee you can get there."

Summer kicked at the spine of a paperback lying on the floor. She sighed. "You're right. But I'm still going to try to find Deadland next time I'm inside. Anything's better than being trapped in there."

I handed Summer the spare key to the Maserati. Now there was nothing to do but wait for Grandpa.

"So have you found out anything that could help Finn when he gets over there?" Mick asked, gesturing at the stack of books Summer had brought along.

Summer fidgeted with a corkscrew somebody had left on the coffee table. "I don't know how it could help, but it's all here. Krishnapuma spent entire days watching Deadland, and by the time he died he saw it for what it was."

"Which is?" Mick asked.

Summer shrugged. "A waiting room. We go on from there."

"We go on in little bits, blown away," Mick said. "That's not very reassuring, is it?"

Summer pulled one leg onto the couch, steepled her hands under her chin. "We don't just blow away, it's much more than that. We return to where we came from, back into the..." she swept her arms in a grand gesture—"into the all. Our individual selves are just an illusion, just a game we play, and we remember this, one fleck at a time. It's beautiful. Very Vedic."

"The way you interpret it, it is," Mick said. "Why couldn't it be purgatory? When the last of you blows away, you go to hell."

"You know," I said, "right now I couldn't care less where we go. I just don't want to go there any time soon." I wasn't in the mood for a theological debate. "Does he say anything that can help us—"

I was going to say "help us boot these damned hitchers," then I remembered one of those damned hitchers was Lorena, and she could hear me. It was like a riddle I would never solve—I wanted Grandpa out, I wanted Summer to be free, but I didn't want to send Lorena back to that place. Yet here I was, plotting to boot her back to that place.

"Nothing about reclaiming your body from hitchers, no. In a few places he suggests it might be possible for the dead to possess the living, but I don't think he ever saw it firsthand." Summer spun the corkscrew; it rotated, slowed, stopped with the sharp end pointing at me. "He did write this weird entry about what he called soul eaters."

"Soul eaters?" I didn't like the sound of that at all.

"I don't know if he meant it literally or figuratively. So often his writing blurs the lines between the two. What he said was that some people just can't let go; they'd rather stay in the land of the dead, whole, than reunite with God—"

"Blow away, you mean," Mick said.

"So as they blow away they replenish themselves by absorbing others..." Summer trailed off.

This was getting weirder and weirder. If I had come across Krishnapuma's book in a used book store before any of this happened I might have bought it for a laugh. I could picture myself in a bar with Dave, flipping through the pages, saying, "Wait, wait, listen to this one..."

CHAPTER 28

The phone jerked me awake. Or maybe I had been in a half-sleep, churning through my fears as I drifted. I hurried across the bedroom toward the phone's solitary glow, stumbled on a shoe.

"Hello?" I answered, my stomach clenching in anticipation. When your phone rings in the middle of the night it's almost always bad news.

"Finn?" It was a corpse-voice, sputtering my name like he'd just had a shot of Novocain at the dentist.

"Who's this?"

"Dave. It's Dave."

I turned on the light. "Where are you?" It was so good to hear his voice, awful as it was.

"I'm homeless. What happened? I'm old."

The pain and confusion in his voice was unbearable. "Where are you? I'll come and get you." I slid one of my shoes on my bare foot.

"Where's Karen? I tried calling…"

If my mind had been clearer, if I wasn't so exhausted, I probably would have deflected the question. Instead I said, "She's gone. I'm sorry, Dave. She's gone."

"She's dead?" I thought he was coughing—there was a deep, phlegmy rolling—then I realized he was crying.

"She may have come back, though. Like you. Don't give up hope." I pulled my coat off the hook, shrugged it on. "Tell me where you are. I'm coming."

He was downtown in Pitman Park, in a phone booth, using change he'd begged. He was cold, and all alone. As I drove I tried to explain what was happening to him, to us, to Atlanta.

Before I even got to Route 85 I was on the phone with the homeless man, who shouted at me, sounding just as confused. Somehow he was convinced this was all my fault.

He promised to wait by the phone, but by the time I got there the receiver was dangling from its cord, swaying in the wind, and the man was nowhere in sight.

Dave would be back, though. Next time he'd have a little longer, maybe enough that I could reach him. It was no surprise; Dave would not have gone gently into Deadland. We were on the right track. I felt even more certain now. If I found Annie in her apartment in Deadland I'd be absolutely certain. I'm not sure where we went from there, but it was a start.

On the way home I made a call I'd been putting off, one I promised Lorena I'd make.

"Hola," Lorena's sister answered.

"Fatima, it's Finn."

"Finn, hello!" she said, switching easily to English. "It's good to hear your voice. Are you all right? Are you out of Atlanta?"

"No, I'm still here." Fatima and I hadn't spoken since the funeral, though we'd exchanged a few emails.

"Why? You have to run while you can. The dead…" She trailed off breathlessly, the dread pungent in her tone.

"It wouldn't help me to run. Unfortunately one of the dead is in me. My grandfather."

She gasped, horrified. "Oh no. Oh, Finn."

"But that's not why I called, Fatima." How could I say this? I struggled to find words. "It's about Lorena."

Fatima went silent.

"Are you still there? Fatima?"

It was a long moment before she answered. "Yes." There was so much dread in that one word; she must have suspected what I was going to say.

"She's back, Fatima. Lorena has come back."

Without seeing her face I had no idea how she made the sound she made. It was an ululating wail that tore my eardrum. "No. Don't say that. I don't hear you."

"She wants to speak to you—"

"Oh, God. Help me, God." She hung up.

I closed my phone, dropped it on the passenger seat. I hadn't been sure how Fatima would react, but I'd guessed it might go like that. The world was terrified. The dead were rising. It was Revelations, The Exorcist, the nightmares of our collective unconscious reaching out of the dark and grabbing our collective ankle. Fatima didn't want to talk to her dead sister, because to her the emphasis went on dead, not sister.

CHAPTER 29

It would have made more sense for us to go over to Annie's ahead of time and wait for Grandpa to show up so I could look for Annie, but Annie's power was surely disconnected, and we decided we'd rather drag Grandpa over than wait in Annie's cold apartment with no TV for who knew how long.

When Grandpa did finally show, he went straight for Mick's liquor cabinet.

"Hello, Grandpa." Mick was leaning against the counter, holding the bottle of Jack Daniel's Grandpa was looking for.

Grandpa turned, eyed the bottle, his hand still clutching the cabinet door. "I'm not going anywhere with you. You can forget it."

That was the problem with the dead witnessing everything that went on. You couldn't surprise them.

"Oh, come on, Grandpa," Mick said. He sauntered over, offered him the bottle. "What's the worst that could happen? We send your sorry arse back to hell. We're all heading there sooner or later, eh?"

Grandpa accepted the bottle, unscrewed the cap, lifted it in a mock toast. "Mickey boy, you can go there any time you want.

Me, I'm staying put. Get Toy Shop straightened out, keep it going for another fifty years. By then no one will even remember who Snoopy was, and we'll all be watching 'A Toy Shop Christmas' on TV." He took a long swig, made a satisfied "Ahhhh," then set the bottle down and turned toward the stove, patting my pockets. "In fact…" He pulled out the pad with the notes I'd been taking, turned on a burner and held it over the flame.

Mick took a step toward the stove, saw it was already too late and stopped. "Lousy pyro," Mick muttered as flames licked the edges of my note pad. Grandpa dropped it into the sink. He retrieved the whiskey bottle and took another pull.

Mick turned to Summer. She'd been watching Being John Malkovich as a break from long sessions online and poring through books, making cracks about how polite and not-dead the intruders inside Malkovich were. "He's not cooperating. A little help?"

Summer got off the couch, pulled a length of thin rope out of her back pocket. "Why am I not surprised?" Mick's arms came around from behind, pinning Grandpa's arms to his sides. Grandpa shouted, tried to jerk free. They toppled, with Mick landing on top of Grandpa.

Summer grappled to get hold of Grandpa's wrists. "Hold him," she said, fumbling with the rope. She straddled Grandpa's legs as Grandpa twisted and bucked, cursing them as he tried to break free. I'm not a particularly large or strong person; I never would have guessed my body could put up such a fight. Still, there were two of them, and Summer was surprisingly scrappy for someone her size.

They dragged Grandpa out to the Maserati. I decided to put off turning toward Deadland until we were actually in Annie's apartment. I wanted to spend as little time there as possible. It astonished me that Krishnapuma had gone to Deadland dozens of times. Hundreds. He and I clearly had little in common.

Summer told me that Krishnapuma had been tagged at age twelve to be the spiritual leader of some esoteric spiritual society in the early 1900s. An orphan, he was adopted by the founders and groomed to assume the role. When he turned twenty-one and was of age to lead, they held a huge convention. Two thousand members gathered to hear the words of their spiritual prodigy.

He told them to disband.

He said he had nothing to offer them, that they should go home and sit in silence in order to experience the numinous. They were wasting time with conferences and doctrine and hierarchy. He turned his back on fame, on the regard and approval of his followers.

I, on the other hand, couldn't get enough regard and approval. I was basking in the success of Toy Shop; I spent every free moment Googling my name to see how my latest strip was being received. It was mesmerizing, to be noticed, especially after spending so much time drifting, unable to catch a break. I'd tried so hard for so long to become a successful cartoonist, and now I was one. There was a bitter edge to it, though, because I was standing on Grandpa's reluctant shoulders.

My phone rang. Summer retrieved it from Grandpa's pocket. It was Dave. Summer gave him Mick's address, told him to meet us there in a few hours. She asked for the name of the guy Dave was inhabiting, just in case, but there was no ID in his pockets. All Dave knew was that people on the streets called him Salamander. Dave asked Summer something before disconnecting.

"Dave, I'm sorry. We haven't heard from her yet," was Summer's answer. Then, "Yes, Finn checked with her family. I'm so sorry I don't have better news. Don't give up hope."

If Karen hadn't surfaced by now, I doubted she would, unless she was in a situation similar to Dave's and had no access to a phone. It didn't make sense that she hadn't come back. How was she different from Dave that she would be content to stay in Deadland?

Maybe I was thinking too absolutely. In the world of the living so much relied on chance—a missed train, a coin flip, a freak storm. Maybe it was the same in Deadland. Maybe a million souls pushed to get through the rift that opened between the worlds, and some of them simply hadn't made it through before it sealed up. Maybe Karen had still been alive when the rift opened, and died the next day. Hell, maybe people with certain blood types couldn't come back. There were a million maybes. I started to doubt the point of this whole operation; did it prove anything if Annie was or wasn't there? Still, what could we do but try to understand what was happening? There was nothing to be learned sitting on the couch.

They whisked Grandpa into the lobby, then dragged him up two flights of stairs, with Mick panting and cursing his tobacco-clogged lungs with each step.

If the population of Atlanta hadn't been devastated by the anthrax attacks, Annie's apartment probably would have been rented, and this operation would be much more complicated. As it was, Annie's door was sitting open, and we were in business.

The furniture, and many of Annie's possessions, were still in place, including the huge abstract paintings she'd done herself, and her Pez collection.

I couldn't put it off any longer. I took a mental breath, sought that relaxed, dreamy, disembodied state, and willed myself to rotate.

It was easier this time. So easy it unnerved me. Was it easier because each time Grandpa took over I was one step closer to taking up permanent residence in Deadland?

I'd expected her to be there, but it was still a shock. She was lying curled on the couch, her lips pressed to her knee, her brown eyes distant, pupils huge. Wisps of her frizzy hair waved in the perpetual breeze.

I choked up at the sight of her, alone in this place. I also felt sure now. The knife that had cut a passage from this world into ours was the longings, the desires, the dreams and ambitions of the dead.

"Annie." It was the first time I'd tried speaking in Deadland. It came out a raspy whisper, like dead leaves stirring in a fall breeze.

Annie lifted her head. She didn't seem surprised to hear my voice. "I was wondering." Her features were softer, maybe because the wind had sanded them down.

"Wondering what?"

She closed her eyes. "If you died."

"No," I said. "Just visiting."

This didn't confuse her the way I thought it would, or maybe it just didn't register. There were so many things I wanted to ask, but I only had a few minutes. We had another stop to make, and couldn't be sure how long Grandpa would be in the driver's seat.

"A lot of the dead have come back," I said. "Did you decide not to? Did you have a choice?"

"Hm?" Annie asked. She sounded as if she'd dozed off and my voice had waked her. This was going to be difficult. She wasn't as far gone as the man I'd seen sitting at the bar, but she was on her way.

"Did you decide not to come back to the world of the living?"

"I'm dead. It's not so bad."

I decided to try another tack. "How do you feel?"

I didn't think she was going to answer, then her eyes seemed to focus for the first time. "The hum is gone."

"The hum?"

"Gone."

Grandpa started to move, or, more likely, to be carried toward the door. Time was already up. "What's the hum?"

"It's gone."

"But what is it?" It seemed important to understand what it was, if only because Annie was focused on it. She opened her mouth to answer and I stretched toward her. I didn't want to miss what she said. I leaned, leaned...

My head popped. All of the air went out of me. I felt myself fall like a dropped penny, hit the floor, circling and circling until I settled and was still.

I'd never been so still. There was no sound except the whistle of the wind. And suddenly I could see my feet, my hands, the tip of my nose, as if I had a physical presence in this world.

I'd fallen out of my body. There was no other explanation.

"Gone," Annie whispered.

Now I remembered what the hum was. Annie once told me that she never felt completely at ease. There was always a hum, a sense that all was not well, a guilt driven by her own sense of inadequacy.

My own hum was not gone. I felt very heavy, like a block of iron, but a very unhappy block of iron.

"Annie, I fell out. I need to go back to the world of the living. How do I get back?"

Slowly, Annie lifted her head. "I can see you. Hi."

"How do I get back? What do I do?"

"You blow away."

"I don't want to blow away." I tried to stand, but I felt way too heavy, and I couldn't get a sense of my legs. I tried turning. It was like trying to turn while encased in concrete.

I tried wobbling from side to side, and found that I could rotate ever so slowly, as if the air was mud. Eventually I managed to face the door.

It was closed. They were gone. They had no idea they'd left me behind.

"Annie?"

"Mm?"

"Please. How do I get back into my body?"

"You're dead. No bodies. It's fine."

I was dead. I would blow away now. I would never see Summer, or Mick, or Mom again. I'd never speak to Lorena again. Grandpa had won.

A Hello Kitty Pez dispenser stared down at me from Annie's book shelf, its plastic smile taunting, the color bleached away by the curtain that separated the living and the dead. Or maybe my eyes had been scrubbed of the ability to see colors. What need do the dead have of bright colors when their purpose is to let go of the physical world and blow away?

I was about three feet from the door. If I could reach it, maybe I could open it and get into the hall and down the stairs.

I wobbled again, and as I rotated I leaned. After a few minutes of this I could see that I was inching across the carpet toward the door.

As strenuous as moving was, I didn't feel fatigued, but it was hard to stay focused. I kept forgetting what I was trying to do, kept drifting off. To combat it, I pictured my friends. Mick. Summer. I tried to picture Lorena, but it didn't work as well. Deadland was a part of her.

After what seemed like hours I reached the door and tried the knob. My fingers stopped at the polished metal, but I couldn't feel it, let alone turn it. Staring at that knob I thought of something Summer had told me. Krishnapuma had written that he sensed the things in the world of the dead were not really things, only reflections of things, or echoes of things that only existed because of the collective memory of the dead. He speculated that places where no people had died—remote stretches of ocean or desert—didn't exist in this world. I could believe that.

The door swung open.

Startled, I cried out, raising my hands in supplication to whomever was passing through in the world of the living. I saw no one, but knew it had to be my friends.

I felt a pull, like the head of a vacuum cleaner passing close by. I leaned into it, reaching, felt the suction. I was lifted off the carpet, but I couldn't gain enough traction and I dropped back down with a plop. Frantic, I splayed my fingers and stretched until it felt like I was a foot taller.

My last chance; I knew they wouldn't come back again.

I caught a cone of suction, felt myself twist and spin as I was drawn up. And then…

pop.

The heaviness was gone, the sense of floating returned. I was back in my body. Struggling to stay calm I rotated back toward the front of my head until color and life flooded back into my field of vision.

"No, no, lassies first." Grandpa was saying as he extended a hand, waving Summer toward the bathroom. "But try not to steal anything while you're in there."

"Shut up, you prick," Mick interjected.

Summer glared at Grandpa. "If you were in your own body I'd break your neck." From the first syllable I knew it was Lorena.

"My own body is rotting in a grave," Grandpa said. "So is yours." He cupped his hands to his chest, forming imaginary breasts. "You won't have these to help you this time around." He spit on the carpet at her feet. "I knew it was your idea to steal my strip. You can't trust a spic."

Mick swung an arm around Grandpa's neck and put him in a headlock. He pulled us down the hallway. "Take your piss before I gag you." Grandpa struggled to break free, but Mick twisted his neck. My view spun crazily. "If you weren't wearing Finn's pants I'd leave you to piss in them." He shoved Grandpa into the bathroom and slammed the door.

Grandpa struggled to unzip my jeans with his quavering hands, then relieved himself with a grunt and an urgent stream.

They'd come back because Grandpa had to pee. I was alive because of Jack Daniel's.

Grandpa glanced at my watch. "It's only a matter of time, laddie. More me and less you every day. Only a matter of time." The croak in his voice was getting even less pronounced, and he now fell at the midpoint between a beast from hell and someone with a bad cold. He broke into a mutter of Irish music, a snappy "Dum de diddle dum dum" as he zipped my fly. "Need to put on some real pants," he muttered as he opened the door.

Mick was waiting at the door with the rope.

Grandpa eyed it. "You think you can get that on me when I'm ready for you, eh?"

Mick lunged for Grandpa's wrist. As if in slow motion I watched Grandpa lift my clenched fist and punch Mick in the eye. Mick slammed into the wall, dropped to his hands and knees.

Lorena leapt at Grandpa, wrapped her arm around his neck from behind and squeezed. Grandpa reared back, threw his shoulders; Lorena's head hit the wall. Her grip relaxed and Grandpa headed for the door. Behind us, Lorena shouted for him to wait.

Grandpa strode out to the parking lot and hopped into the Maserati. "It's good to have legs that work," he said as he fumbled the key into the ignition. "Everything is harder from a wheelchair." His head lurched forward, then backward as he sped out of the parking space. "You just can't get away from people when you want some peace and quiet."

I couldn't believe how cavalier he was about pounding someone's head into a wall. He was talking as if nothing had happened.

"I could never get any peace and quiet when I was alive. Between Frenchie trying to control my every move right down to when I bent my pinkie, and the rest of you blaring the TV and yammering back and forth like chimps, I never got a moment's peace." He wheezed mocking laughter. "I'm the selfish one?" He barely slowed taking the turn. "So why did you keep hanging around after you grew up? I didn't ask you to come by, but there you were every couple of days, coming to butter me up, ready to pick my bones as soon as I hit the ground."

Why did I keep coming around? I guess I thought that's what families did. They ate meals together once in a while, exchanged gifts at Christmas. Silly me.

"You think I was going to hand over my life's work to a sissy like you? Still hanging by your mother's apron strings when you were shaving? Letting that Mexican pay your bills while you brought in nothing, drawing your crap cartoons. For God's sake, make your way like a man! Don't whine and complain and wait for women to wipe your nose for you."

Grandpa peeled through Toy Shop Village and up to my apartment in a cloud of road dust. Three news vans were waiting.

"Ah, shit. I don't need them hanging around." He jerked the Maserati into park while it was still moving, went around to the trunk, pulled up the carpet and retrieved the crow bar.

He turned to the closest news team. "Get out," he said, brandishing the tire iron. "This is private property. Get off it before I spill your brains."

A cameraman held out his hands. "Relax—"

"Now, God damn it!"

Grandpa watched as they pulled out, breathing like a bull after his charge. "That's how you handle them."

Satisfied they were gone, he headed inside. "I told you I wanted you off my property. But did you listen? You're nothing but a leech, just like your God damned father." He turned on a burner, grabbed a grocery list off the refrigerator and held the tip of it to the burner until the tip burst into flame.

"You want to play, Finnegan? Let's play."

The flame crept toward his hand as he carried the burning paper to my studio, to the stacks of papers piled on my desk—the contracts and financial statements that had been rolling in as a result of Toy Shop's success.

He wouldn't, I thought. He wouldn't light my desk on fire inside his own building. He held the burning paper to the edge of a document leaning off the desk. The flames crept across the page and lit others.

There was a poof. My desk was a bonfire. Grandpa backed out of the room.

He found lighter fluid under the sink. I'd barbecued in the drive-in lot exactly once, so it was almost full. He sprayed a trail from the kitchen right into my study, then dropped the canister and headed outside.

Everything I owned was in that apartment. All of my photos, everything I'd ever drawn. He'd just torched my life.

Summer and Mick were waiting outside by Mick's car, surrounded by newspeople and cameras. There was a black welt under Mick's eye that looked like it wasn't nearly finished swelling. They pushed their way over to Grandpa. "Is it you, Finn, or still the old man?" Gilly was back. He looked at Grandpa's hands, frowning in concentration.

Grandpa peered up at the apartment. "Me and Finnegan are

playing a little game. Aren't we, Finnegan?"

Inside, I screamed and raged and swore I'd get him for this.

A roar erupted inside the apartment. A window shattered. Flames leapt out the broken window and climbed the stucco wall.

Summer pulled my phone out of her pocket, opened it. It was hard to believe no one in the news crews had bothered to call, but she was right to make sure. Who knew what they would do?

Grandpa swatted the phone from her hand. "Let it burn. It's mine, I can burn it if I want." He turned his face toward the flames. "You want to play, Finnegan? I told you to get the hell off my property. Now you're off. How do you like that?"

CHAPTER 30

Grandpa was driving back to his house from Murphy's Pub when I finally regained control, six hours after he'd burned my apartment. He'd downed five drinks at Murphy's, and as I headed back toward Mick's place in the Maserati I felt like I was driving on a ship at sea rather than a level road.

The traffic going the other way—out of town on Route 85—was crawling. Every day more people were fleeing. I couldn't blame them—every day more hitchers walked the streets of Atlanta, seeking out friends and loved ones who didn't recognize them, returning to their old haunts (pun intended), and generally scaring the shit out of everyone who was not afflicted. No doubt about it, Atlanta was getting weird, and if I wasn't afflicted I would pack up my stuff (if I wasn't afflicted I would still have stuff to pack) and join the bumper-to-bumper traffic fleeing this giant morgue.

"You're a real piece of work, you know that?" I said aloud. "Lousy drunk. Mick is the drug addict? You want to see a drug addict, take a look in the mirror." I tried to point at the rear-view mirror and poked it instead, then had to readjust it. "I think I finally figured

196

out why you hated me so much. It's because you saw yourself in me. Oh sure, you were the man, except you had to sneak to the bar so your wife wouldn't find out. You handed over your paychecks to her and got an allowance. That's it, isn't it? You harp on my weaknesses because it's easier than owning up to your own." I took a deep breath, tried to calm down. I had a feeling I'd hit a nerve with that last observation, and it felt good. I'd shut up now, and let the bastard stew.

The lampposts just off the exit were papered with flyers of people seeking dead loved ones. I'm sure they realized that if a dead loved one had returned, he or she could simply pick up a phone. It was hard to give up hope, I guess, and I imagined most of the unafflicted who were staying in Atlanta were doing so because they hoped to find a dead loved one.

National Guard troops stood on a corner, watching over protesters who wanted all of the hitchers rounded up and put in a camp, or shot on sight.

When I got to Mick's, Mick was back and Lorena was with him. Lorena leapt from the couch with a jubilant shout, flew into my arms. After a moment of cheerful reunion she gestured toward the TV. "Have you seen this?"

They were watching my apartment burn on CNN. I was suddenly big news—the celebrity face of a horrible new plague. Well, me and Mick. They'd already run a couple of stories on Mick, but he was used to it and didn't seem to care. The police wanted to speak to me about the fire. There was a debate on the Rachel Maddow show about whether a person was culpable for a crime (arson, for example) if he was either suffering from post-traumatic identity disorder or possessed by the dead. Rachel and her guests didn't take a definitive stand on which I was—that was a topic for another show.

"Dave didn't show up?" I asked. Lorena shook her head.

"I have to go look for him." I desperately wanted to take a shower first, but I couldn't spare the time. My mouth tasted like sour beer.

"I don't even have a toothbrush." I looked at Mick. "Do you have a spare toothbrush?" Then I realized I needed more than a toothbrush. I needed a place to sleep. "Is it okay if I crash here for a couple of nights?" I added.

Mick shook his head. "Nah. Not for a couple of nights. Stay until we straighten this out or we go..." he motioned with his thumb. "Both of you. All right?"

I grinned and nodded. I wondered if Grandpa was in there realizing that while he'd hurt me by torching everything I owned, he'd also done me a favor. Suddenly I felt less alone. One good thing had come out of this wretched mess—my new friends.

On TV, CNN was covering a mass exorcism at the Believer's Church, one of those mega-churches that looked like an indoor stadium. Eyes clenched shut, the preacher stood with arms spread in front of the standing-room-only crowd, howling at Satan to release them from his unholy grip. On the History channel and TLC all they were showing were programs on possession and exorcism, which was feeding this sort of crap.

I turned to Mick to escape the pull of the television. "So, you talk to your FEMA friend lately?"

"Most every day."

"Do the feds finally understand that it's possession, not mental illness?" I asked.

Mick wobbled his head. "Depends who you talk to. But they all agree that the hitchers aren't bothering anyone besides the people they're inside (unless you count scaring the piss out of people as bothering), and they're not sure how forcefully they should intervene."

"In other words, they're trying to decide whether this is their problem."

"Yeah, that's right," Mick said.

Lorena had her jacket draped across her arm. She tugged me gently toward the door. "Should we get going? I've already been out for two hours."

I shrugged my coat on and followed her out.

"This is so hard," Lorena said as we rode the elevator down. "I want to spend time alone with you. I want to hear everything that's happened to you since I've been gone." The tender sentimentality of her words was rendered so strange by the deep belching roll of her voice.

"I know," I said. "It's so hard, though. I feel like I have to spend every minute trying to get free of Grandpa."

Lorena made a sound in the back of her throat. "That's hard, too. Sometimes I feel like you're trying to kill me, too."

Kill? The word made me squirm inwardly. I wasn't trying to kill anyone. "You know it's not that simple. It's all wrapped together so tightly; it's like we're all different sides of the same coin, and if some come up heads they can't also be tails, even though that's what I want."

We had to pause to climb into the Maserati. When Lorena shut her door, her expression—hurt, angry, empathetic, all at once— made her look remarkably like herself. "That's not exactly a vote of confidence."

"I'm sorry. I don't know how to navigate this." I wanted to add that Lorena was being a little selfish, that it was Summer's body, after all. I didn't have the energy to get into it, though. I was so tired my eyes burned and my head ached.

Lorena opened Summer's purse, rooted around for something. "Oh," she paused, looked at me, "have you called my sister yet?" The hope in her eyes was evident even through the slackness of her face. Here was another conversation I'd been dreading.

"Yeah, I did. Lore, I tried to explain it to her as gently as I could, but—" I struggled for words, then gave up and let it hang.

Lorena studied my face. The hope drained from hers. "She's afraid of me?" she said, her dead croak underscoring the point. Lorena and Fatima had been incredibly close, as close as twins. She squeezed her eyes shut. "I can't believe it. My own sister." She looked at me. "What about my mother?"

I shook my head. Forewarned by Fatima, her mother had hung

up as soon as she recognized my voice.

"Oh, Mom. Not you," she whispered. "They would have died for me. Both of them. Now they won't even talk to me?" Lorena wiped a tear with the back of her sleeve, picked up my phone, which was sitting in the cup holder between the seats. She turned it over and over.

"I can dial for you if you want to try yourself," I said. "Maybe if she heard your voice."

Lorena laughed bitterly. "That's okay. I don't want to—"

Scare her, I thought she meant to say, but couldn't bring herself to.

"Give them time," I said, although I wasn't sure time would heal this rift. I wondered, What would happen if the hitchers did take us over? Would they eventually be accepted back? Would the syndicate allow Grandpa to continue the strip knowing it was being drawn by a dead man? Would people read it?

Lorena shrugged noncommittally at my tepid attempt to console her. She pulled the phone closer to her face and chuckled. "Is that the date? Tomorrow is my birthday."

I did a quick calculation. "Your thirtieth. I've been so preoccupied I lost track of the days." Was it her thirtieth birthday, or did your birthdays stop when you died? So many strange questions arose out of this. If the dead did take over living bodies for good, would they count the age of their bodies, or their souls?

Lorena reached out and squeezed my hand. "Take me out for my birthday? I want to go dancing!" She wriggled her shoulders, tried to snap her fingers but got only a papery sound. Her movements were still stiff and rubbery.

"Sure," I said, trying to sound more enthusiastic than I felt. "If you're here tomorrow night. And I'm here." I sure didn't feel like dancing or celebrating a birthday. What were the odds that we'd both be here, though? I was in control about half the time now, Lorena maybe one third of the time. So, one in six?

I imagined Grandpa suddenly taking control while Lorena and

I were dancing, and it made me a little sick. Not that Grandpa wasn't a fine dancer, as I'd seen. "I should ask Summer if it's okay with her."

Lorena lowered her hands, scowled. "I don't need her permission. I didn't ask to be in this situation any more than she did, and I think I've been very considerate."

It was nice that all we had to do was ask Lorena to do something, rather than wrestle her to the ground and tie her hands. "I know. But—" I was going to say, But it is her body, and thought better of it. "We should all go out of our way to get along."

Lorena's scowl melted. "Fine. As long as I get to go dancing on my birthday."

#

We had no luck finding Dave, or Salamander. Twice I talked to people who said they knew Salamander, that he was "around here somewhere." When the light started fading we gave up and went shopping. I was exhausted by the time I returned to Mick's. It had been forever since I'd slept through the night.

CHAPTER 31

The McMansions along Fairview Road were mostly dark. These were the people who could afford to flee Atlanta for an extended period. When they were packing, I wondered if they had considered the possibility that they might not be allowed to come back.

They weren't calling it a quarantine, which was probably wise. The president called it a "precautionary controlled observation of the situation." As promised, commerce wasn't being interrupted, so we were still able to buy Snickers bars and the new Arcade Fire CD, assuming they could find truck drivers with the guts to drive in and out of the Haunted City (as the press were now calling it), but people weren't able to drive in or out without a good reason.

Rather than risk sounding crazy by talking about the dead rising, or appearing to have his head in his ass by insisting on the post-traumatic identity disorder explanation, the president simply referred to it as "The grave events taking place in the aftermath of the anthrax attack." Using of the word "grave" seemed like a bad call to me, but he went with it. He assured the American people that the problem was contained and would not spread, and that every resource was being brought to bear to help those afflicted.

The federal government had so many resources, so many channels of information, yet they always managed to be a step behind in reacting to any but the most predictable disasters. Their response to an anthrax attack looked like a carefully choreographed dance. Their response to mass possession? More like a drunk stumbling home from a bar, pausing occasionally to vomit in the gutter.

When we hit Little Five Points, with its stretch of cafes, bars, and trendy shops, dark houses gave way to brightly lit streets.

"Wow," Lorena said.

Hitchers were everywhere. It was almost as if they all knew Little Five Points was the place to be.

"How did you know we should come here?" I asked.

"There's a Facebook page for The Returned," Lorena said.

I stifled an ironic laugh. Figured. We were calling them Hitchers, the dead, parasites. They were calling themselves The Returned and twittering each other.

They lurched along the sidewalks on Euclid like extras in a George Romero film, sounding like giant bullfrogs as they greeted each other. We passed a Fox News truck; near it a reporter was interviewing hitchers.

The dead must be eager to go out and live. Most of those still in Atlanta who weren't possessed were probably at home cowering behind bolted doors, watching the news. That's where I would be if my situation were different.

Not all of the unafflicted were hiding, though. A throng of people were standing across the street, watching, shouting things at the hitchers. Some looked scared, some angry. They weren't holding protest signs, but had that sort of air.

We found a parking space three blocks over and walked arm-in-arm to Loca Luna, one of Lorena's favorite hangouts. I wasn't the only person on the street who was not occupying someone else's body, and when I spotted a fellow "living" I smiled at them. I suspected most of them had hitchers that were dormant at the moment.

There was a street preacher on the corner of Moreland. He was discussing Revelations, his lips frothy with emotion, imploring passers-by to let him cast their demons out.

A young woman in a short skirt approached him, sobbing, flat-out begging for his help.

The preacher touched the woman's elbow. "Pray with me." They got down on their knees. Two others joined them on the pavement. The preacher traced the sign of the cross in the air as six or seven others joined the group, causing the flow on the sidewalk to clog as people skirted the group.

"Come on," Lorena said. I couldn't imagine what she was feeling as she watched them there, so desperate to exorcise their "demons." I, on the other hand, couldn't blame them for trying. It wouldn't work, I was sure, but when you have no good options, any option looks appealing. We moved on as more people joined the exorcism.

We passed the crowd of protesters and tried to ignore their angry shouts to go back where we belonged, that we weren't welcome here on Earth. They spat the word "demon" like it was a racial slur, and it felt like one. We picked up our pace, and I felt sweet relief when we passed through the doors into Loca Luna.

Most of the people there were hitchers. Loca Luna was a big turquoise place with high ceilings, recessed lighting, and fake palm trees. The dance floor was packed with people jerking to the Latin beat, their hands shuddering.

I wondered whether Lorena or Summer had picked out her out-fit, a paisley caftan shirt that struck me as vaguely wizard-ish, and a long black velvet skirt. It wasn't Lorena's style, but it was probably the flashiest outfit Summer owned. My guess was Lorena picked it.

"Ooh, I'm getting a t-bone," Lorena said as she put her jacket on the back of her chair. "They do great marinated steaks here." She rubbed her hands together. "It's been forever." Her hands stopped rubbing and her smile became wan. "Hm. That's almost right."

I could see she was desperate for her birthday to seem normal.

She was trying to set aside everything that had happened, set aside the fact that she was dead, that she was in another woman's body, that in all likelihood I would soon be dead. It was a lot to set aside.

"What was it like?" I asked. "Is it bad?"

Lorena shook her head. "Not bad, just so different it turns you inside out." She closed her eyes, took a deep breath, as if mentally returning herself to Deadland. "You feel yourself peeling away, a tiny fraction at a time. Little pieces of your past float off, all of your memories, sounds, smells, thoughts—everything you are, until you start to lose track of yourself." She squeezed her eyes more tightly shut. "Once in a while a piece of someone else would land on me for a moment before floating off again. I would catch a glimpse of that other life. That was nice; I savored those moments. They were my only human contact." She opened her eyes. The vastness reflected in them, the awe and dread, terrified me. "That wind is still blowing through me. I can hear it."

The waitress interrupted. She rattled off the items on the menu that weren't available. I asked her about the limited options, and she said that besides the difficulty finding drivers, suppliers were leery about local businesses' ability to pay their bills going forward. She took our orders and set us up with drinks.

I sipped my drink, leaned back in my seat. "I hadn't realized how much I craved a night like this. It feels good to have a few hours to relax."

Lorena grinned. "Glad I could provide an excuse." She twisted her arm to examine the long tattoo running wrist-to-elbow. "It certainly gets your attention. I'll never understand why people would inject ink under their skin." She switched arms and examined the other, which was a mirror image. "They're very nice arms, besides the tattoos." She ran a quavering finger down Summer's forearm.

"She can see and hear all this, remember," I said.

Lorena put her arm down. "I know. I said she had pretty arms, didn't I?" She laughed as I shook my head. "Didn't I?"

"Yes, you did." Maybe it was inevitable that two people sharing the same body would become antagonistic toward each other.

We fell silent, stared at each other across the table. Lorena let out a big sigh. "What a mess."

"Happy birthday," I said.

Lorena dropped her fork. It clattered on the plate. "Oh, shit." She whined in frustration as the tremor in her hands grew still.

Summer pressed her palms to her temples. "Sorry."

I shrugged. "Not your fault."

Summer surveyed the half-eaten steak on the plate in front of her, then pushed it toward the center of the table. "I meant I was sorry your night was ruined. I wasn't apologizing."

"No. Right," I stammered.

She took the napkin from her lap and set it next to the plate.

"Do you want to finish? Are you still hungry?" I gestured toward her plate. I didn't want to go home. I craved a few hours of normalcy in what had become my extremely abnormal life.

"I'm a vegetarian," Summer said. She rolled her eyes toward the ceiling, shrugged.

"Oh, shit. Right." I stared at the remains of the steak. "And she was eating meat. It never even occurred to me."

"Don't worry about it." She waved off my concern. "Go ahead and finish your meal."

I didn't know why, but I felt terribly uncomfortable, as if I'd done something wrong. "Have a drink, at least." I reached toward Lorena's half-empty glass of wine, realized that even though only Summer's lips had touched it, to her it would seem like someone else had been drinking from it. I looked around for our waitress, trying to remember what she looked like.

"She didn't even get to dance," Summer said, taking a sip from Lorena's untouched water glass. She turned and looked at the dancers on the floor, swaying to a Latin salsa. "Probably a good thing. It's all hips. She'd have trouble dancing like that with my skinny hips."

The music stopped abruptly. We turned to see what was happening. It looked as if the bass player had been taken over by his hitcher, and the hitcher didn't play. After a moment he climbed down from the small stage and the rest of the band soldiered on without him.

"Will you help me do something?" Summer asked, turning back to look at me.

"Sure," I said.

She gave me a look that said I wasn't necessarily going to like what she said. "I want to see my brother."

"The one who died?" Even before she nodded I knew it was. "I thought you said you didn't want to speak to loved ones you lost."

She struggled for words, then said, simply, "I changed my mind."

I waited for her to elaborate. It didn't seem wise for her to mess around in Deadland unless she had good reason. I certainly had no desire to go back. It also seemed a bad idea to use our valuable time running after someone who couldn't help us solve our problem.

"We didn't part on the best of terms," Summer said. "He was bugging the hell out of me and I told him not to call any more." She poked the dinner roll Lorena hadn't eaten, leaving a divot. "The idiot didn't tell me he was dying of cirrhosis."

"How was he bugging you?"

Summer shook her bangs out of her face, looked up at me. "He'd call in the evening, my only time with Rebecca, and repeat the same things he'd said that morning, because he'd already forgotten he called that morning. I had to take him to his doctors' appointments because there was no one else, then he'd get into arguments with the nurses, accuse them of stealing his pills or something." She lifted her glass, drained the last of the water. "I just want things to be right between us, before I—" She trailed off.

"Before you what?"

She stared into her water. "Before I'm gone."

Her tone made me uneasy—Summer seemed like the last of our little trio who would give up. "We don't know you're going anywhere," I said.

"I know. But we don't know I'm not, and I'd like to see my brother while I have the chance. Will you help me?"

"Do you even know if you can get to Deadland?"

Summer tilted her head and flashed her best crooked, wan smile. "Oh yeah." She pointed at a table by the windows. "Someone choked to death right over there."

I couldn't help laughing. "Welcome back to the land of the living! Wow, you just returned from Deadland for the first time, and you're not sobbing or anything. You're Wonder Woman."

"Nah, I knew what to expect." She gestured at me with her glass. "You wandered in blind. I would have wet myself if I'd stumbled into Deadland the way you did."

"Figuratively wet yourself," I said. "You wouldn't have had control of your bladder at the time."

"Sure, figuratively," Summer agreed, nodding, then blew out a laugh between closed lips. She seemed to have a thousand different laughs, from a musical giggle to an inhaled honk.

"And now you want to go right back in." I put my drink down. "Hold on. Your brother died in a hospital, didn't he? In the intensive care unit, I'm guessing?"

Summer nodded. "That's right."

How many people had died in that same room? It had to be hundreds. "That's going to be some scene. Do you think you'd even be able to find him?"

Summer shrugged. "If I can't, I can't. I'd like to try."

I studied her brown eyes for a minute. "If that's what you want, then sure, I'll help."

"Thanks. It means a lot to me. More than I can say."

An up-tempo song came on, causing some of the dancers to hoot. Summer turned to watch them.

"Do you like to dance?" I asked, making conversation.

She shrugged, causing the sprinkle of stars tattooed across her neck and shoulders to crinkle. "I used to. Not many opportunities lately."

She watched the dancers longingly, it seemed to me. I wasn't much of a dancer. Lorena had been the dancer.

"We could dance now," I suggested.

Summer turned. "You really want to?"

"Why not? Let's have a little fun. And if you're dancing, Lorena at least gets to go along for the ride. I would certainly appreciate it if Grandpa would do something marginally interesting once in a while, maybe take in a Braves game. I'm sick of sitting in depressing bars with aging alcoholics."

Without another word she pushed out of her chair. I followed her onto the dance floor.

Summer watched the woman next to her for a moment, trying to get the rhythm, then closed her eyes and let herself go. She didn't dance like the woman next to her, or like Lorena, but she was striking in her own way. She reminded me of a Native American priestess, her hands upturned in supplication, head back, shoulders moving more than her hips. Maybe what was most striking was that she was smiling, really smiling. I was glad.

The song changed, this one even faster, more frenetic. Summer let out a whoop, glanced my way to make sure I was game to stay, and smiled when she saw I was.

After a third song, a slow one came on. Sweating, we went to the bar and got drinks.

"It's been so long since I had fun," Summer said. "You forget. When things are so bad you forget that you still need to kick back once in a while, or you'll lose it."

"You're a terrific dancer," I said.

"I feel like Olive Oyl when I dance." Summer fanned herself with her hand. "That was my nickname in seventh grade. Well, not my nickname; it was what kids called me when they wanted to be mean."

"I can't believe your classmates even knew who Olive Oyl was."

Maybe it was the booze kicking in, but suddenly I was acutely aware of how weird this situation was. We were at a bar filled with dead people. I was dancing with the woman my dead wife was possessing while my dead grandfather looked on.

The slow song ended, replaced by another burner. "Ooh!" Summer grabbed my forearm and pulled. I followed. The hell with it; Summer was right, if I didn't relax and have some fun I was going to have a nervous breakdown.

Some of the dancers were doing this twirling thing, a full 360-degree spin. Summer tried it, laughing, so I gave it a shot. I should have fun like there was no tomorrow. For us, there might not be.

There was an old man dancing on the fringe of the dance floor, his tremulous hands dangling from gyrating hips. Stiff as the movements were, it would have been obvious that a young woman was executing them even if the old man hadn't been wearing a black dress and lipstick.

Another drink, more dancing. In an odd way I felt like I was getting to know the other dancers, linked by the music and the close quarters. Occasionally I would catch someone's eye and smile, like our dancing was a shared secret, a bit of good news amidst all the bad.

A song ended, replaced by another slow ballad. I looked at Summer and she shrugged. We closed the space between us.

It occurred to me that if Grandpa took control at this precise moment it would almost be funny. Not quite, but almost. I'd been in control for nearly six hours. There was no predicting when he'd reappear, but the odds increased with every hour.

"Thanks for this," Summer said. "It's nice to forget for a little while."

"It is," I said into her ear. It felt good to hold her. I wondered if the line between Summer and Lorena was blurring in my mind. I was thrilled when I got to talk to Lorena, but I enjoyed Summer's company almost as much.

Just as much, if I was completely honest. I had done my best to put out of my mind the electric attraction I'd felt for Summer when I'd seen her in the Blue Boy Diner, the day I first met Mick.

Out of curiosity I tried to imagine that the dead had never come back, that Summer was just a woman I was dating. How would I feel about her?

We were dancing with our faces a few inches apart; I could see the little star tattoos on the back of her neck and shoulders.

If Lorena hadn't come back, I would be crazy about Summer. I felt so comfortable with Summer, such a sense of ease. Despite the situation we were in, Summer's fun-loving nature came through. It surprised me that I would be attracted to Summer, because she and Lorena were very different. Had I changed so much over the past two years that I was attracted to a totally different sort of woman? I guess it was possible. So much had happened. It was hard to believe only two years had passed.

I could never let Lorena know what I was feeling. Or Summer, for that matter. But it was stupid to try to hide my feeling from myself.

The song ended, replaced by more Latino bop. I held on to Summer. She stayed in my arms. I expected to feel her gently push away, but she didn't. Without slow music to call it dancing, we spent a long moment in an embrace.

A loud crash startled me. We jerked apart, looked toward the front of the restaurant for the source of the sound. The smoked front window was shattered; there was a big hole in the center with jagged shards and cracks radiating. Someone had thrown a rock or brick through the window.

We moved closer, heard shouts and arguing outside. Through the breach in the window I saw a National Guard troop pushing at people, trying to move them back.

"Satan's army. It's Satan's army! Whose side are you on?" someone shouted. There was a roar of agreement from the crowd.

"Come on," Summer said, tugging my sleeve, drawing me toward the back of the restaurant. "Let's get out of here."

She pushed open the kitchen door, turned to the first person we saw, a terrified kid carrying a tray of dirty dishes. "Is there a back door?"

The sweaty bus boy motioned with his head. "Straight back and to the left."

We spilled out in an alley filled with dumpsters; the angry commotion, now muffled, reached us over the building.

"Whew, I'm a little toasted," Summer said, pressing a hand against the brick to steady herself. I was feeling a little toasted myself. The thud of music from a nearby club seemed to be bypassing my ears and hitting me straight in the chest.

We passed out of the alley, to be greeted by another angry mob. Some of them pointed at us.

"We know what you are," a tall bald guy shouted.

As we rushed past, heads down, a pimply teenager stepped in front of me. When I looked up at him he spit in my face. I glared at the little bastard in impotent fury as I wiped off the spit. Summer tugged my jacket, pulling me into the street and around the crowd.

"No one believes this is a disease," Summer said, glancing over her shoulder.

"Are any of them following us?" I asked.

"No."

The knot of muscle between my shoulders relaxed a little.

"Are you sure the car is this way?" Summer asked.

"We're going to hang a right at the next corner. I parked over on—"

We both stopped at the sound of a scream. It was brief, clipped. It seemed to be coming from the next street over.

"What was that?" Summer asked.

We doubled our pace. "I don't know."

Now that we were paying attention I could just barely hear a voice. It sounded panicked, high-pitched. The bald fear in the tone made my guts twist.

We broke into a run.

"Maybe we should go back to the news vans, get someone to call the police," I suggested.

We passed a shallow alley. A kid who'd been facing a loading dock spun around. I heard Summer peep in surprise as the kid grabbed my passing shoulder and jammed a pistol into my neck.

"Don't move," he said. He turned and, keeping his voice down, called over his shoulder. "I got two more." He was wearing a Braves cap and camo pants, sixteen or seventeen years old.

Another man appeared out the darkness of the alley.

"Hold on," I said, trying to keep the breathless panic out of my voice. "We're just going home."

"No you ain't," said an older, heavy-set guy with big jowls surrounding a tiny chin. "Move. This way." Pointing what looked like a small assault rifle at us, he led us past green dumpsters and stacks of wooden palettes to a lowered fire escape ladder.

"Climb," he said.

"Hang on, hang on" I said, raising my hands in supplication. I could hear voices above us, on the roof.

The big man shoved me, knocking my forehead against the steel ladder. "Hang on nothing. Move."

I climbed, with Summer right behind, followed by the man with the gun. We hit the landing ten feet up, where narrow steps angled up the five- or six-story building. I couldn't see into the small, grimy windows. Everything inside was dark; the building was some sort of industrial place.

"Keep on going," the big man ordered.

"What is this about?" Summer asked. "We don't understand what's happening. We were just going to our car."

The man didn't answer. As we climbed we kept asking, kept explaining that we weren't any part of this, but the man didn't respond.

Panicked voices rang out from below. The kid who'd grabbed me from the alley was bringing two more people up behind us.

One story from the top we heard another scream from above. I didn't want to go up there, didn't want to see what was causing people to scream like that. I considered diving through one of the windows we passed, hoping Summer would follow me, but the man with the gun was right behind us. He'd be on us before we could even get up to run. With my legs shaking so badly I could barely find the steps, I climbed the last flight, onto the roof.

There were eight or nine people on the roof, gathered at the far end. Most of them had guns. One jogged over and took control of us, nodding once to the big man, who turned and headed back down. We were hustled toward the group.

"What is he doing?" Summer said, staring toward the people gathered on the roof.

A man in camo was clutching a woman by the upper arm, dragging her along. The woman screeched and pleaded, dug in her heels, trying to pry the man's fingers from her arm. Another man grabbed her other arm with his free hand. They dragged her toward the edge of the roof.

"No. Stop," Summer said, her hands pressed to her cheeks.

They lifted the woman, who was bucking and bicycling her feet, over the low wall until she was sitting on it. She was blubbering, pleading, gripping the edge of the wall for all she was worth as she tried to twist around.

The men pried her fingers loose and pushed. She fell, screaming.

"Jesus, what are you doing?" I asked.

"Sending you back where you came from," said the man with us. He had a goatee, was maybe thirty.

"We're not," Summer said. "Look. Look at our hands." She held out both hands for the man to examine, glanced at me, said, "Show him yours."

I held out my hands.

"We're not stupid. We know the demons hide," the man said. "Let's go." He raised his gun so casually, like it was a beer and he was about to take a swig.

"You're making a mistake—we don't have any demons," Summer said.

"Yeah," the kid leading the group behind us said. "Then what were you doing in Little Five Points? Partying with the rest of Satan's army, that's what."

"I was walking her home," I said. "It's not safe for her to be out here alone with all of the dead walking around. She was delivering food to her eighty-year-old mother who lives on McClendon." The two men were listening, maybe even looking uncertain, so I kept talking. "This is Summer—"

"I live on Highland," Summer interjected. "Finn is my neighbor. He wouldn't let me go alone."

The guy with the goatee stared at us. "Get over there."

It hit me suddenly, why they were throwing people off the roof when they could simply shoot them. You could only hear screams for a block or two, and there weren't many residences in this area. Gunshots you could hear for half a mile. That would alert police and National Guard troops.

"This is nuts," I said. "We're on your side. You can't just throw us off a roof."

"We're at war with Satan," he said. "Innocent people die in war, especially when the stakes are five billion souls. If you're innocent, it's too bad you were in the wrong place."

"You can't just call something a war and murder people," Summer said. She gestured toward the other end of the roof. "You have to stop them." They were dragging a young guy toward the edge now; it was taking three of them.

The guy's taut expression didn't change. "I'm not gonna say it again. Move." He raised the gun, tensed his finger.

I held my ground; so did Summer. "You won't shoot us unless you absolutely have to," I said. "You don't want the police to hear."

He turned his head, called, "Pete. Need some help here." A man with a rifle trotted over. This guy was tall, with big muscular arms. He strode right up to me and, without a word, belted me in the side of the head with his rifle.

The roof spun; a hard, dull pain spread from one temple to the other. Somehow I stayed on my feet. An arm wrapped around my neck, putting me in a headlock, twisting me off my feet and dragging me. Dragging me toward the edge, I knew. Panicked, I reached up, trying to dislodge the arm. Vaguely I heard Summer screaming.

"Soldiers!" someone called. "Soldiers. Let's move."

The arm around my neck was suddenly gone. I fell to the ground, struggled to my hands and knees as Summer reached to help me.

A gunshot cracked nearby. Then shouts, the thump of boots, and more gunshots.

I lifted my head to look around, but saw only black static dots. My head was killing me. "What's happening?"

"They're running. Someone must have called the police." Summer sank to the roof next to me, started to cry.

A siren rose in the distance, drawing closer.

CHAPTER 32

There were no joggers in Pitman Park, no Frisbee tossers or skateboarders. Since the hammer had fallen on Atlanta, people didn't recreate. Maybe they rode treadmills and pumped weights in gyms, but those were serious things that allowed you to retain a tight-lipped expression. The only type of smile that was appropriate in Atlanta now was a gallows smile, the sort of smile that didn't reach your eyes, and told people you could take a swift kick in the crotch, or the end of the world, in stride.

The only people in the park were hurrying through on their way to somewhere else, and those with nowhere else to go, yet I flinched whenever I caught movement out of the corner of my eye. This place didn't feel safe to me. Nowhere felt safe to me now, except Mick's place. Every time I closed my eyes I was back on that roof; when I did manage to sleep it was all nightmares, all night now.

At the Sally (that's what those who used it called the Salvation Army) I'd been told Salamander might be found here, and what he might be wearing.

He was sitting on a park bench next to a steaming Styrofoam cup

217

of coffee, his dog-eared sneakers crossed, his face hidden inside the hood of a filthy parka save for glints of a thick grey beard. I hurried over to him.

"Excuse me, are you Salamander?"

He pressed his hands on either side of the bench, looked up at me. "Well, I guess I am. My name is actually Sal Mandel, but it kind of drifted, you know?" He chuckled.

I smiled. I'd found Dave, I couldn't believe it. As soon as I'd walked up Dave's heart must have leapt. "Man, I've been looking all over for you."

He jerked his thumb over his shoulder. "A couple of guys told me someone was looking for me." He lifted his cup, took a swig. "So now you found me. What can I do you for?"

"My name is Finn—"

He jumped to his feet, sloshing his coffee, and pointed at me. "You're the one he called."

"That's right! Dave called me. He was my friend. He was looking for his wife." I'd found him, I'd definitely found him.

Sal nodded emphatically. "I thought I was losing my frickin' mind. He took hold of me, made me walk where he wanted, blink when he wanted."

"I know, we're all losing our minds lately."

He pointed at my chest. "You got a hitcher too?"

"I do, yeah. But listen, I need to talk to Dave—"

Sal shook his head. "He's gone."

"I know, but when he comes back—"

Sal kept on shaking his head. "No, I mean he's gone. For good." He grinned, waggled his eyebrows joyfully. "I'm a free man again, master of my own domain."

I frowned. "How do you know that?"

Sal stuck out his bottom lip, raised his shoulders. "I just do. I felt it. When he slid out of me it was like the best b.m. I ever had."

I searched his face for some sign that he was kidding, or lying, that it was wishful thinking. He met my gaze, nodded once. He seemed so certain I half believed him.

"Why would he leave you, when all the rest of them are hanging on tight?" I asked.

He turned his eyes up, thinking. A woman rode by on a bicycle, her tires crunching pebbles and fallen twigs.

"You know," Sal said, "I couldn't tell you. It happened right after that second call he made to you, though, when your lady friend answered. If it was anything she said, I sure do appreciate it."

What had Summer said? She told Dave to meet us at Mick's place. Dave had asked if there was any word from Karen, and Summer had said...

Hope stirred in me like green buds on dead winter branches. Summer had ripped Dave's heart out of his chest. She'd taken away Dave's will to come back. If it was true that the dead who were back were the ones burning to be back, what happened if that fire was snuffed out?

I pulled out my wallet, fished out one of my business cards and all of my cash, maybe three hundred dollars. I held it out to Sal. "I need you to do something for me. It's extremely important."

Sal looked at the money, then at me, waiting.

"Will you promise to call me once a day, and tell me whether Dave is still gone?"

"That's it?"

I nodded.

Sal took the card and the money. "Hell yes. What time?"

"I don't know. How about noon?"

Sal nodded. "High noon every day. I can handle that." He looked at the stack of twenties. "You pay handsomely."

"It's life and death. In fact, I'll give you another thousand two weeks from now if you call me every day."

Sal held out his hand, and I shook it. "You got a deal."

If this is true... I kept thinking on the way back to Mick's place. I didn't want to wish Dave gone, but if he was...

Lorena had insinuated that it wasn't a matter of choice, that she would leave Summer if she could. But that would be like willing yourself to not like chocolate, or to not love someone. You can't not feel what you feel. What if you stop feeling it, though?

The trick was coming up with some way to make Grandpa lose his will to stay. Try as I might, though, I couldn't think of anything. Killing Toy Shop might do it. I could discontinue it, but as I demonstrated after Grandpa was gone, you can always start a strip up again. What could I do—cut off my hands and burn out my eyes? The stony bastard would hold the pencil in his mouth if he had to.

Maybe Sal's revelation could help Mick and Summer, though. Especially Mick. Gilly seemed to be back for one reason, and one reason only: finish the album and get Mick to record it. Beyond that he didn't have much of a life to return to. If Mick pitched in and helped him finish, he might just drift away. In fact finishing the album would also mean Gilly had patched things up with Mick, working alongside him (metaphorically speaking) just like in the good old days, and that seemed to be the crux of Gilly's drive to be back in the world of the living.

We'd been focused on finding a solution that would free all three of us, a one-size-fits-all hitcher-exterminating process. A silver bullet; a wooden stake. But these weren't monsters, they were people, and each had their own reasons for being here. It made sense that each might require a different rite of exorcism. For some, there might be none at all.

CHAPTER 33

As the news droned in the background I paced Mick's apartment, nervous about the trip to the hospital, eager to get started if we were going to do this. There was no point in moving until Lorena showed, and that could be in one hour, or thirty. Once she showed we'd have to move quickly, and hope we didn't draw the attention of any God's Hammer nut jobs.

I brushed past Gilly, who was sitting in a leather chair beside one of the big windows, completely absorbed in his composition, his eyes clenched shut, his lips moving silently.

"How's it coming?" I asked.

Gilly opened his eyes. "It's coming. I wish Mick would try out a few of the songs I finished."

Mick glowered when anyone suggested he do this. He didn't buy my logic. The way he figured it, the more attached Gilly got to his songs, the harder it would be to send him back where he belonged. At least, that's what he muttered when I told him my plan. I didn't think he was being completely honest with me, though. He'd seemed evasive, almost angry when I suggested he help Gilly finish the album.

"How many hours has it been?" Summer asked. Her hair was down today; it was dark and silky, perfectly straight. Not quite long enough to touch her shoulders. She flipped through channels, stopping on a football game. The Bears versus the Colts. "Ooh. Anyone else here a football fan?"

"Eighteen hours and counting. I'm a Bears fan, since I was about nine," I offered.

"Really?" Summer's eyes lit up. She held up her hand for a high-five without leaving the couch; I adjusted my pacing route, slapped it, then joined her on the couch.

"My grandfather was from Chicago. I've been a Bears fan since I was three." Summer dropped the remote and propped her feet on the coffee table. The Bears were down 7-3. While Gilly worked, and the National Guard reinforced the barricades set up around the Route 285 loop to repel a horde that was growing larger and angrier by the day, we watched football. I'd already posted what I'd learned from Salamander on the relevant websites, but still, we should have been scouring the Internet for clues on how to shake our hitchers. Time was not on our side.

I glanced over at Summer, who was staring up at the massive TV screen sporting a half-smile, hugging one knee.

She saw me looking, looked at me. "Mmm, smell that?" The aroma of onions and peppers wafted through the open windows, from Queenies.

"Nice," I said.

"Do you like to cook?"

"No. Lorena was the cook."

"I can't cook either. Opening the refrigerator is a humbling and confusing experience for me. I eat fast to dispose of the evidence."

I laughed; I could definitely relate.

Jay Cutler completed a twenty-yard pass on third and ten. Summer raised her fist in the air.

"Nervous?" I asked.

"Plenty."

"Just be careful not to fall out and you'll be fine."

She shifted position, pulling one foot underneath her. "I'm more afraid of seeing my brother than anything else."

Across the room, Gilly dropped his pencil. "Okay. Hey, Mick." The way he said it reminded me of Dustin Hoffman in Rain Man (only dead); I wondered if Gilly might be slightly autistic. In some ways that fit him, but in others it didn't.

Mick brushed the knees of his jeans, stood and stretched. "All right, Finn? Summer?"

"Good to see you, Mick," I said.

Mick went to the window, stared down at the sparse traffic below. "Good to be me."

Summer jumped up, tugged my sleeve once, and headed for the door. "Let's go." Correction—it was Lorena now. I hadn't even noticed the transformation.

It was remarkable, how different a body looked depending on who was controlling it. Summer's gentle, slightly pigeon-toed gait, her tendency to clasp her hands behind her back, was replaced by Lorena's assertive stride, the flex-relax, flex-relax of her thighs, the loose swing of her wrists. Summer's squiggly smirks, which would have been right at home in a Peanuts strip, would be replaced by Lorena's wide smiles. Although Lorena wasn't smiling just now. She snatched up Summer's coat and purse from beside the door, turned to wait for us. "If we're going to do this, let's go." Her tone was tight, impatient.

We threw on our coats, hurried to join her.

"You don't mind?" I asked, touching her elbow.

Lorena shrugged, looked at the door. "Sitting in a hospital room isn't how I'd like to spend the few hours I get before I'm banished again, but you've all decided already, so let's get it over with."

"I'm sorry," I said. "I wish we had more time to spend together. This is so important to Summer, though."

"Fine. I'm not arguing."

Mick slid past us and out the door without a word.

"Are you all right?" I asked Lorena.

She looked at me for the first time. "You know, in case you forgot, I was there while you and Summer were finishing our date." She spit the word "date" like it was a pit. "I could see how you were looking at her. You looked at her that same way when she was our waitress at the Blue Boy."

I tried to say something, but Lorena cut me off.

"I may have to share a body with her, but that doesn't mean I'm going to share my husband." She folded her arms. "How could you dance with her like that?"

I could feel my ears getting red. "Lorena, you're inside her. When I'm dancing with her I'm also dancing with you. That's always in my mind." That sounded lame even to me. "Besides, I wanted Summer to enjoy herself, too." That was closer to the truth.

Lorena grunted, rolled her eyes.

"You know, she doesn't have to hang around. She could go home, or to Montana, and every time you came out it would take time for us to meet up again."

Lorena's eyes narrowed. "She couldn't afford to go to Montana—"

"Let's just talk about this later," I said, cutting her off. The last thing I wanted was for Summer and Lorena to have any more reason to hate each other.

Lorena spun, breezed through the door. "Fine."

#

Mick drove. The security guard tipped us off that the press were waiting for Mick at the exit from the parking lot, and sent us out the delivery entrance.

As we sped through town I looked out the window, feeling ashamed. For two years I'd mourned Lorena, wondering if I'd ever be able to love someone else. Now, miraculously, Lorena had returned, and I was struggling with feelings for another woman. Maybe it was understandable; wouldn't it make sense that my feelings might blur and become confused when my wife was sharing a body with another woman?

But I'd been attracted to Summer at the diner, before I knew Lorena was inside her. Lorena seemed to think it went back even further. Was I attracted to Summer even when Lorena was alive? I didn't remember that at all. I'd been madly in love with Lorena.

I pressed my forehead to the window. This was a stupid thing to be worried about. The way things were going it wasn't going to matter. It was pretty clear both Lorena and Summer were not going to survive this. There was serious doubt I would survive this. On top of all that, I had no idea how Summer felt about me. I'd left my wife to be electrocuted in a rowboat, and goaded my twin sister into jumping to her death. I wasn't exactly a prize.

"I'm sorry," Lorena said, her voice low.

I looked at her. "What?"

"I'm sorry. Don't worry about it."

I nodded. She took my hand and squeezed; I squeezed back and went back to watching out the window.

There were National Guard troops at most of the intersections, people in olive fatigues who looked like they wanted to go home. The military always wanted a clearly defined mission; this assignment must make them crazy.

"What do you hear from your friend at FEMA?" I asked Mick.

Mick shook his head in disgust. "They're mostly taking a wait and see attitude. I pointed him toward your posting about what happened to your mate Dave, and he said they'd come across a similar case, but didn't see how to capitalize on it on a larger scale. So they're waiting."

So much for the cavalry riding in to rescue us at the last minute.

It occurred to me that that would make a good Toy Shop strip. The National Guard gallop into the toy shop on horseback to help Tina get free of Little Joe's ghost, and stand around doing nothing, asking if anyone has any hay.

#

It was a strange sight, the three of us and a bodyguard Mick had hired, hanging out in a hospital room. Mick was right about the fame thing—he could have asked them to vacate an entire wing of the hospital for a couple of hours and they would have obliged.

"How long do you think she'll be?" Lorena asked.

The muscular man with the black-rimmed glasses glanced at Lorena, then back out the window. Grandpa wasn't going to get another chance to take a swing at Mick, or anyone else.

"It's got to be a nightmare in there. I'm not convinced she'll even be able to locate him," I said.

"Am I part of the nightmare?" Lorena asked.

I turned, surprised. "What?"

"Whenever you talk about The Returned there's this tone of dread and disgust in your voice. The prospect of a lot of dead people in one place constitutes a nightmare. I'm one of them, you know." As if I could forget that, with her voice the way it was, her quavering hands.

"Sorry," I said. "Somehow I never connected you to the rest of them. It's like, I don't know, like you were there by mistake."

Lorena rested her chin on her fist, stared at her feet. "No one gets there by mistake."

The squirming in my muscles started up. Grandpa's turn again. "He's coming," I managed to say to the bodyguard, then I gritted my teeth until I no longer had teeth.

Grandpa eyed the bodyguard and grunted. "If I was in me own body, in me prime, I might have a go at you." He stayed in his chair.

I wasted no time turning toward Deadland. If Summer had managed to make the trip she might be grateful to hear a friendly voice. I braced myself, not sure what to expect.

As soon as the room came into view, I felt myself slipping, like I was sitting on a greased slide. I had to sort of puff out to keep from falling out of my body; it wasn't quite like stretching out my arms and legs, not exactly inhaling deeply to expand my chest. It was something in-between that I did instinctively without knowing quite what I was doing.

Once I felt secured it took a moment to understand what I was seeing. The room seemed larger—more the size of a high school gym than a hospital room. It needed to be, to fit all the bodies. Where the bed should have been was a heap of muttering souls, a giant pudding of entwined bodies. Others were scattered across the floor, some lying, others sitting, a few standing. Yet more were stuck to the walls and ceiling.

Then I saw Summer. I should not have been able to see her, because she should still be in her body, looking at Deadland but not in it. Instead, she was in it. There was someone on top of her, and she was screaming at him to get off.

"Summer," I called.

"Finn?" She turned and looked for me. Her voice was flat, toneless, the distress washed out of it by this world.

The man lying across her was huge. He had his face pressed to her thigh; he was shushing, the way you'd comfort a small child. "Hold still now, Andrew's here to help you along." Then he pressed his mouth to her thigh, worked his jaw, scraping her leg with his teeth.

"Get off of her," I shouted. Soul eater. The words leapt to mind instantly. This was what Krishnapuma had written about, a soul that doesn't want to blow away, so it replenishes itself.

He raised his head, looked in my direction. He moved easily, fluidly, immune to the high-G torpor of the world of the dead. "Who said that?"

"You can't see me because I'm not dead. But I can see you. Leave her alone." I had to speak up to be heard over the constant low rumble of the dead, going through their mindless recital of the things they'd said in life. It was like trying to have a conversation at a crowded party.

The soul eater looked at Summer, then back in my direction. It looked like there were crumbs, or sawdust, on his chin. "Liar. If you're here, you're dead. So why can't I see you?"

"I'm not dead. Summer's not dead either." There seemed to be a lot more flecks blowing off of the soul eater than the rest of the dead.

The man looked at Summer and laughed, his laugh flat, almost mechanical. "Yeah. She's just full of life. Ready to frolic in some sunflowers."

"He's telling you the truth, I'm not dead," Summer said. She struggled to push up onto her elbows but was barely able to get her shoulders off the floor. "Get off of me!"

"What happened?" I asked Summer.

"I just slipped out. I guess I leaned a little, and the next thing I knew I was on the floor."

The soul eater had gone back to work. Now he lifted his head. "You're not fooling me for a minute."

If I could get Lorena to move backward a few feet, Summer might be able to pull herself back up and into her body. That was assuming the soul eater couldn't hold her back, and that I could regain control of my body soon enough to get to Lorena before this thing consumed Summer.

I racked my brain for some other way to help her. I could pop out of my own body, but I wasn't close enough to reach her and pull her. Plus I wouldn't be able to get back into my body.

The soul eater could push her, if he was willing. The problem was he didn't seem particularly inclined to help us.

"Hey, what's your name?" I asked.

A bit of light entered his flat, grey eyes. "Andy Kozlowski. You recognize it?"

"Sure I do." I did, but I couldn't place it. He'd been some sort of celebrity, years ago.

He seemed pleased. "When were you born?"

"Nineteen eighty."

"Way too young to have seen my show. So people still remember me?"

That was enough to jog my memory. He'd been the host of a kid's show back in the dark ages—the sixties or maybe even the fifties. Once in a while you saw a clip on one of those specials about the golden age of television. His name conjured up vague images of marionettes and a cardboard set. "Sure they do. Absolutely."

He made a satisfied humph. "Sometimes when I find a fresh one who's still talking, I ask. Most say they never heard of me, but I suspect they're lying to get back at me." He looked at Summer. "How about you, when were you born?"

"Nineteen eighty-two."

"You ever heard of me?"

"Sure." She mustered a little "Are you kidding me?" laugh. "Of course." I was betting she'd never heard of the guy. Only a pop culture fiend like me would remember a name as obscure as his.

"Look, help me out, will you?" Summer said. "I'm not dead. Really. My body is waiting for me, alive and well, just a few feet away. You can save my life, and at the same time it'll prove I'm not dead."

"Hey, if you're lying here, you're dead, and if you're dead you're fair game." He sounded offended. "Look, why don't the three of us have a nice conversation? Otherwise I'm gonna go ahead and eat your face first so you stop aggravating me."

If our theory was right, and the hitchers were the ones who didn't want to be dead, why was this guy still here? He was hanging on tighter than Grandpa, Lorena, Gilly—anyone. This was the type of guy who sawed his own arm off with a butter knife if he got trapped under a fallen tree in the wilderness. Hell, he was eating people to stay together.

One ghost to a customer. Maybe that was it. He wasn't strictly one person any longer, even if he seemed to be one person and thought he was one person. He clearly had a strong need to be affirmed. Maybe we could use that to our advantage.

"Hey, maybe we can make a deal," I said.

Andy chuckled. "What, you going to give me a thousand dollars? A new car?"

"How about information? We can catch you up on what's happening in the world," Summer said, taking the words right out of my mouth. I marveled at her guts—she was keeping it together remarkably well.

He huffed impatiently. "It's twenty twelve. Barack Obama is president. He's Black. Michael Jackson and Farrah Fawcett died three years ago." He held up a finger. "And I died in nineteen seventy-six, so I never even heard Michael Jackson sing." He seemed to draw satisfaction from our stunned silence. "I keep up. I could eat the heads first, but I enjoy the company. They make better company if you save the head for last."

"Why are you bothering her when there's an entire room of people you could take?" I asked.

He made a face. "They're no good. You have to get the fighters or it's just a waste of time."

The fighters? "Who are the fighters?"

He frowned like he was speaking to a complete idiot. "The fighters. The ones who really, really don't want to be dead. Like your friend here." He ran his bottom lip and teeth up Summer's thigh.

"Don't do that," I cried, almost in perfect unison with Summer.

"What?" Andy said, lifting his head. "You're just gonna blow away anyway. I'm just speeding up the process."

I didn't know if that was true, or if being eaten kept you stuck there as well. There were so many things I didn't understand about this place. At this point it didn't matter—I didn't want Summer to be eaten or blow away.

A part of me stepped back then, wondering at how panicked I was. If Summer couldn't get back, then Lorena would get a second chance at life. It would be unconscionable to purposely strand Summer here, to not do everything I could to help her, but if there was no way to save her, wasn't that a good thing?

It didn't feel like a good thing. In fact it felt like a remarkably, unequivocally bad thing. I couldn't stand the thought of going back to a world that didn't include Summer.

I tried to set my emotions aside and think. Wasn't there anything I could offer him that he might want?

I could offer him me, but that wasn't a particularly appealing solution. What else? It was hard to think while he scraped away at Summer. There was a pronounced divot in her leg now. I shuddered at the thought of seeing her devoured until she was nothing but a head, then nothing at all.

The only difference between me and the (Hundreds? Thousands?) of souls he'd eaten was that I could return to the world of the living. He had all the information he needed, but I could send information both ways.

"Is there anyone you'd like to send a message to on the other side?" I tried. "A son or daughter, maybe?"

Andrew froze. For a long moment we listened to the mutters and cries of the dead. "If you were alive you could do that, couldn't you?"

"I am, and I can."

Andrew rose halfway, swung his head from side to side, straining to see me. "How do I know you're really alive?"

Try as I might, I couldn't think of anything convincing I could say or do. "Hell, Andrew, what do you want me to do? I am. A couple of days ago I watched the Bears beat the Colts. I had a turkey sandwich for lunch."

"Mayo or mustard?" Andrew asked.

"What?"

"Did you have mayo or mustard on the turkey?"

"Mayo."

"Good choice. I miss eating."

"I can prove we're alive," Summer interrupted.

"How?" Andrew asked.

"If you do what we ask, I'm going to disappear back to the other side. If we're lying, I won't. You really have nothing to lose."

Andrew studied her, his hands still gripping her leg in a manner usually reserved for lovers, or for people clutching drumsticks on Thanksgiving.

He looked in my direction. "First you deliver a message to my daughter, and come back and tell me what she said. Then I'll do it. That's the deal."

"No, no, that won't work," I said, panicking. "You have to free her first." There was no telling where this daughter was, if she was still alive thirty-something years later.

"Why is that?"

I stammered, trying to come up with a reason. "You'll just have to trust me. Look, I can do this, and I promise you, it's the only chance you're ever going to get. But it has to be our way."

He stood, came toward me, again shifting from side to side trying to catch a glimpse of me. "My daughter's name is Penelope Harbaugh. There shouldn't be many of those in the phone book. Last I knew she was living in Terre Haute. Here's what I want you to tell her: Even though I've been dead for thirty-five years, I still don't forgive you, and I never will. You got that? Repeat it back to me."

I did. I don't know what I was expecting from a soul eater. Somehow I thought anyone in this place would be eager to make something right, to send a little light back into the world.

"Swear. Swear on her life," he pointed at Summer, "that you'll deliver the message, then come back and tell me what my daughter said."

"I swear it." They were only words. I would have sworn anything to get Summer out of there and away from him.

He nodded, satisfied. "Now, what do I do?"

"Push me," Summer said. "Finn—is she still sitting in the chair?"

"Yes."

"Push me toward that chair." She motioned with her eyes.

The soul eater grabbed Summer by her ankles and dragged her.

"You'll feel a pull," I said. "Go with it. Reach for it."

She was gone before I finished the sentence. I wondered if she even got to speak to her brother. Not likely.

"Well I'll be damned," the soul eater said, staring at the spot where Summer had been. "You still there, Mister Finn?"

"I'm here. Do you believe us now?"

"Don't forget your promise."

"I won't." I would never forget it. That didn't mean I would fulfill it. "Before I go, can I ask you something? How long do you plan to stay here?"

"As long as I can," he said. "Forever, if possible. Who wants to blow away?"

⸸

There was no way to signal Mick that we were done, that we wanted to go home now, so Mick, Lorena, and Grandpa sat in the hospital room watching the news.

I had a hunch that Summer would be the one to signal we could leave, that I would remain imprisoned behind Grandpa's eyes for a good while longer. The pattern of progression made it likely I'd be lost for somewhere between twelve and twenty-four hours.

That sensation of being loose, that I might slip out of my body into Deadland, had not vanished when I turned to face front. It was vaguer, less pressing, but it terrified me that it was there at all.

CHAPTER 34

When I finally regained control of my body two days later I was shaving in a room at the Hilton, and I had a raging hangover. I put the razor down and toweled off my face. Grandpa hadn't finished, so parts of my face would be whiskery, other parts smooth, but finishing was a waste of my precious time. I grabbed my phone and keys, and ran. Running made my head pound even worse.

When I had watched that Bears game, when I had chatted with Grandma about the weather, I hadn't understood just how little time I had, just how precious every minute was, how I should make every one count. Now that I was aware, I wondered how I should spend my precious moments.

I was no closer to shaking Grandpa than I'd been the first time he took possession of me. There was nothing in Deadland to help me. During my latest internment I'd considered one crazy plot after another: drag another soul in with me to oust Grandpa (only one ghost to a customer, after all), or lure a soul eater who would somehow eat Grandpa instead of me. Fantasy. Pure fantasy. There was only one way to exorcize the dead, and that was to take away their drive to return. With Grandpa that wasn't possible.

Maybe I could save Mick, or Summer, though. I could think of no better use of the precious moments I had left than to help my friends.

Friends. Was Summer just my friend? If so, why was the worst part of this the thought of never seeing her again?

I had loved Lorena, had lost her and mourned her and finally let her go and moved on. The memory of love is not the same as love. Summer had been right all those weeks ago: we weren't meant to speak to our loved ones again once they leave this world.

I dialed Summer's number as I cast about in the parking lot under the Hilton, trying to remember where Grandpa had parked.

"Where are you?" It was Lorena.

"Just leaving the Hilton." I tried to mask the disappointment in my voice. "What's going on there?"

"Gilly is working. I've been trying to find you, waiting by the phone, worrying."

"How long has Mick been gone?"

"I haven't been keeping track, but almost as long as you."

"How is Gilly doing on the album?" I finally spotted the Maserati, tucked behind a minivan. I dragged the key along the side of it, really grinding it, before getting in.

I caught pieces of her muffled conversation with Gilly before Lorena came back on the line. "Gilly says he's about halfway through 'Love Two Sizes Too Small,' then he's got 'The Winds of Change.' But he's stuck, because he feels rushed to finish before Mick disappears and there's no longer any point in working on it, and he doesn't work well under pressure."

The Maserati's tires squealed as I backed out of the space. "Well that's just terrific. Can't he just cut the last song? It's a double-CD, for God's sake. What difference does one song make?"

Another pause and muffled conversation.

"It's a themed composition. It all links together, and the final song is crucial."

I muttered curses under my breath. "If Mick comes out, don't let him go anywhere," I said. "I'm on my way. I'll see you in a couple of minutes." God dammit, Mick needed to help him. I had to find some way to make that happen.

As I sped to Mick's I tuned to the news on the radio. It made me crazy that Grandpa had no interest in knowing what was going on in the rest of the city. Maybe he was afraid they would discover a way to exorcise hitchers and didn't want me to hear it.

More people were massing outside the perimeter, and a lot of them were armed. NPR reported it as a loosely organized group; at least three people claimed to be leading it. More people were arriving every hour; the National Guard was getting uneasy.

When I got to Mick's I brought Gilly some iced tea from the fridge and made him a sandwich, gave him a pat of encouragement, and left him alone to work.

Lorena and I talked quietly on the couch until we heard Mick curse softly and rise.

"All right, Mick?" I said.

"Yeh," Mick said noncommittally as he pulled a beer from the fridge. The top popped with an angry hiss as Mick went out of his way to avoid going near Gilly's work.

I didn't understand him. He was acting like Gilly's project was radioactive. "Come on, Mick, you've got to help him finish." I went over and checked Gilly's compositions. It didn't look like he'd made any further progress. I swept up the pages from the table and held them up to Mick. "He's down to two damned songs! One and a half, really."

Mick shook his head slowly. He looked awful, his eyes half-closed and ringed with red, his skin grey.

I didn't know what else to do, so I shoved him in the chest. Beer splashed over his wrist as he was jolted backward.

"Hey, piss off!" Mick flung his bottle sidearmed, sending it spinning over my head spitting beer in a wide arc. "I already told you, but it didn't get through your thick skull." He poked savagely at his own temple. "I can't write any more. My brain is a bleeding fried egg. Gilly had to write ninety-nine percent of my last album, and that was twenty bloody years ago. I'm done. Washed up."

That's what all his foot-dragging was about? I put my hands on my head, shook it in disbelief. "Can't you at least try? I think you've got a fighting chance to get out of this alive." I put Gilly's work back on the table. "That's more than I can say for myself. I wish I had a chance. I'd do anything, if someone would just tell me what I needed to do."

Mick just stared at his feet.

"Why can't you at least try?"

Slowly, he raised his head to look at me. "Because it's fucking brilliant, that's why." He lowered his voice. "Can't you see that? It's—" His eyes teared up; he shook his head, not able to find the words. "It's fucking genius. It's Sgt. Pepper. Anything I add will spoil it."

Summer was back. She'd been standing quietly by the couch; now she spoke up, her voice gentle. "But it's meant for you. He's writing this for you, as much a gesture of friendship as anything. If you're gone, and you don't perform it, everyone loses. You heard him—he's freezing up."

Mick picked up a guitar leaning against the dining table, studied it as if he'd never seen one before. "If he finishes in time, I'll sing it." He plucked a string. "If not, tell Gilly he's got my vocal cords now; he can bloody well learn to use them." He looked at me. "Whatever you do, don't let him overeat and turn me into a bloody Elvis. Make him take me a few laps on a stationary bike once in a while. He can go out on tour as me. My big comeback." Silent, Mick replaced the guitar, stared down at Gilly's work. He shook his head in disbelief, marveling. "Fucking brilliant."

As if on cue, Summer and I approached from either side until we were at his shoulders, as if corralling a skittish mustang. Summer put a hand on Mick's shoulder; as gently as I could I pulled out the chair Gilly had been using.

"He can always erase it," I said, offering Mick a pencil. "If it sucks I'll make sure Gilly chucks it. I swear."

Mick appraised me, then looked at Summer. He pulled one side of his mouth into a dry half-smile, reached and plucked the pencil out of my hand. "Fine. You want to see how washed up I am? What an empty shell I am? I'll write some bloody music. I'll take a dump on Gilly's bloody Mona Lisa."

As he pulled up the chair and retrieved the pair of reading glasses from his shirt pocket, Summer and I retreated. We grabbed our jackets and kept going right out the front door.

We tried to step through the narrow door into the elevator at the same time, bumped and stumbled in like a couple of stooges.

Laughing, Summer nudged me with her shoulder. "Klutz."

I laughed, put my arm across her shoulders for a minute, drinking in the electricity of that touch. I wanted to wrap my arms around her. Maybe I would have, if Grandpa hadn't taken over at that moment.

CHAPTER 35

Grandpa collected all of my sketching pencils out of the case of drafting materials he'd pilfered from Mick's place and hurled them into the trash. "Crap. Fancy crap." He sat at his table, in his house, plucked a plain number two pencil out of the case, slid a fresh piece of Bristol paper from the stack.

It was hard to pay attention to what he was doing, because most of my energies were directed at not slipping out. It was like holding two buckets of water in my outstretched arms while balancing on a beam, or waiting outside a restroom door with a raging case of diarrhea. For hours. Every few seconds I lunged to gain a better psychic grip.

Slowly, inexorably, it was getting worse. I could hang on for now, but what about tomorrow, and the next day? As Krishnapuma had observed, consciousness is osmotic. A water droplet can't resist being pushed through a membrane.

The pencil Grandpa was clutching wobbled wildly over the paper. He held it there, willing my hand to hold still.

It wouldn't.

Frustrated, he dropped the pencil. "God dammit." He couldn't wait to get started. If his hand would stop shaking I was sure he'd do a couple of Toy Shop strips in the old style, without Wolfie, Little Joe miraculously back without explanation, and ship them off before I could intercept them. He probably suspected I wasn't going to waste what time I had left making calls to try to stop them from being published, and he was right.

Pushing out of his chair, Grandpa went to the kitchen cabinet he'd stocked with whiskey. He poured a generous shot of Jack, spilling twice as much on the counter. He carried his glass into the studio and stood at the window, surveying the treeless stretch of lawn.

It seemed so frivolous, to simply stand there gazing out the window. Grandpa had all the time in the world, though; I was the one in a hurry. I desperately wanted to get back to Mick's, to see how the album was progressing, to see my friends, if only one last time.

Grandpa noticed the old Toy Shop originals stacked at his feet, some of the special ones we'd kept when I sold off the bulk of them. He picked up a few.

"Hm," he said, thumbing through them, breathing heavily through my nose. He retrieved another handful, riffled through them, then grabbed all of them and took them to his desk.

He found a boxcutter in the drawer, and proceeded to slice up half a dozen strips, cutting circles around characters, toys, backgrounds, and separating them into piles. I watched, trying to understand what he was up to.

"Even while I was dead, the ideas kept coming," he said as he selected a Little Joe and a Tina from his stack and set them in the first empty panel of the blank strip.

He cobbled together a "new" strip like this, pasting old images into the panels, typing out the dialogue on my computer and then pasting that over old bubbles of dialogue. It was a painstaking process, but even with his shaking hands it was still faster than I could draw a strip from scratch.

I wondered how Summer was doing. I would have given anything to have a few minutes alone with her—completely alone—to tell her how I felt, to see if she felt the same. Sometimes there was something in her eyes, something that might be veiled feelings for me. Or maybe that was wishful thinking.

When the strip was finished Grandpa packed it up, addressed it to the syndicate with a note insisting they print it immediately, that I'd had a change of heart about my new direction and wanted to get back to the basics of good writing and solid craftsmanship. More would follow soon, he promised.

Whistling tonelessly, he took the package to the post office in his Maserati and overnighted it.

In some ways losing to him was the most painful part of this. It wasn't right, wasn't just that the fight was fixed and this cold, arrogant bastard got to win.

"You had thirty-odd good years," he said, as if reading my thoughts. The asshole didn't even know how old I was. "You had use of your legs." He took one hand off the wheel, turned it up in supplication. "I am sorry it's got to end this way."

Yeah, he was all torn up inside; that's why he was whistling.

CHAPTER 36

I felt my fingers begin to tingle while Grandpa was pouring himself another drink. Grandpa dropped the bottle; amber whiskey chugged onto the linoleum, spreading toward the refrigerator.

Gasping with relief, my hands still trembling, I called Summer's number.

"Hey. It's Summer." She was whispering.

I was expecting Lorena, and felt a fluttering in my stomach on hearing Summer's voice.

"Where are you?" I asked.

"The High."

"French Impressionists exhibit?"

"Where else?"

"How is Gilly's album coming?"

"That's why I'm here. Gilly's working frantically. He needed solitude. He'll call when it's finished. And Finn? Gilly said Mick did good. Really good."

I gulped back tears. "That's great. Can I meet you at the High? I'd like to see you."

"Yeah. Hurry."

I hung up without saying goodbye. We kept our conversations short now; precious moments shouldn't be wasted on hello, good-bye, participles or adverbs.

It occurred to me that, assuming I made it to the High Museum before Lorena or Grandpa took over again, this might actually be goodbye.

As the Atlanta skyline rose into view through my windshield, I wondered how many more times would I get to see it. Maybe this was the last.

Maybe I should plan to slip out of my body with the skyline stretched out before me, then I could watch it while I blew away. That wouldn't be the real skyline, though, just a reflection of a shadow of a memory of the real one.

"Maybe we can make this work, find a way to share one body," I said. How transparent that must be to him—I was suddenly will-ing to negotiate because I was losing. Wasn't bargaining one of the stages of coming to grips with your own imminent death? First there was denial, then anger, then bargaining.

I was dying, wasn't I? Not in the usual sense, not because my body was going to cease functioning. I was dying in a completely new and novel way, by having my body stolen from me. Maybe this would be-come the twenty-first-century version of AIDS or the bubonic plague. Maybe every time there was a mass murder now, the hole would open up and souls would flee back to the world of the living. Maybe if I could hold on, keep too much of myself from blowing away, I would get my own chance. I wouldn't want it though; I wouldn't want to put someone through what I was going through. Unless it was Grandpa.

In the stages of dying, depression came after bargaining, then acceptance. I didn't want to go through those last two; I wanted to go back to anger.

I splurged for valet parking, raced up the concrete stairwell, through the folk art exhibit, past urns and mirrors, into the French Impressionism room.

Summer was sitting with her legs crossed, chin on her fist, staring through Reflections of Clouds on the Water-Lily Pond. I sat beside her silently, looked up at the painting.

Summer was right; I felt better.

"When I took an art history class, the instructor went to great pains to make it clear that French Impressionism was overrated by the unenlightened masses," Summer murmured, her chin still on her hand. "He likened it to how children are attracted to bright, primary colors."

"He was full of shit," I said.

"I know."

I rotated 180 degrees to look at a Manet. Summer followed, her slim legs vaulting the bench.

A gondola driver was navigating among blue and white poles jutting from a canal in Venice. The driver looked as if he didn't have a care in the world, had no place to go, could enjoy the cool breeze and rippling periwinkle water all afternoon. I remembered having afternoons like that, but they were so far removed from my present that I doubted my memory. In fact all of my memories from before the day I drowned in that reservoir seemed ancient and unlikely, as if I'd been born in that water, and everything prior had been implanted.

"It's getting harder to hang on in there," I said.

Summer drew her feet up and crossed her legs on the bench. "I felt it for the first time. The pull you told me about."

A hitcher wandered through. He was a big guy—both tall and fat—with a red baby face and long black hair, although that told me nothing about the hitcher him- or herself.

"I never believed it would come to this," I said. "I thought we'd figure it out. I really did."

"Me too. Maybe we still will, and not just for Mick."

"Maybe." I didn't see how, though. "But just in case—"

"There's Gilly," Summer said, pulling her vibrating phone from her pocket.

＃

Mick met us at the door. We looked at him expectantly, but he just shrugged.

"If I'm supposed to feel different, then Gilly's not gone. I don't feel any different." He held up a sheaf of papers. "Here it is, every bloody note in place, and he's still here."

"What did we miss?" I asked, looking from Mick to Summer.

Mick turned and headed inside. "It was a long-shot from the start." He dropped the composition on the coffee table. "It's finished, though. That's something."

Summer looked at me. "It's got to work. Something's keeping Gilly here."

I tried to put myself inside Gilly's head. His masterwork was complete; no more music running through his head. Fences were mended between him and Mick. But he was still watching through Mick's eyes, hanging on despite himself. For what? If I was Gilly, what would I want? I closed my eyes, imagined I had just finished what Mick called one of the greatest rock albums of all time.

I'd want to hear it, or course. I'd want to see other people hearing it. We didn't have time to organize a concert, though. I put my hands on my head, trying to think, staring at the wall.

The answer was right there, on the wall. The framed poster of The Beatles' movie, Let It Be.

"Oh, shit. Mick?" I shouted.

Mick turned at the urgency in my voice.

"Do you have an amplifier here? And a microphone? You'll need a microphone."

He canted his head, trying to read me. "Yeah. What do you have in mind?"

"Help me get everything to the roof." I spun around. "Summer, get on the phone and call every news agency you can think of." I gestured out the window. "All the networks that own those helicopters buzzing around out there. Give them this address. Tell them

Mick Mercury is going to give a concert. Tell them he's going to perform a new album recently co-written with his dead ex-collaborator Gilly Hansen. On the roof."

Mick burst out laughing. "Brilliant."

"I hope Gilly thinks so. God bless The Beatles."

CHAPTER 37

Half a dozen helicopters buzzed overhead as Mick made his entrance to wild applause (wild applause from Summer and me; the dozen or so press reps who were present clapped politely). Mick was dressed in black leather pants and a plain white t-shirt with the sleeves torn off, or maybe chewed off from the look of them. He waved to the helicopters as he approached the mike, raised his arms and shouted, "Hello, Atlanta!"

We'd stacked every amplifier in Mick's apartment along the edge of the roof, and the sound was impressive. I'd had no doubt the press would flock to cover this—it had everything they craved—drama, celebrity, a feud, hitchers.

The helicopters descended, jockeyed for the best vantage point as Mick launched into the first song.

I'd heard bits and pieces of songs, croaked by Gilly, mostly under his breath. I'd had no idea.

By the third song tears were streaming down both Summer's and my face. We kept exchanging astonished glances. Are you hearing this? the glances said. We knew something important was happening. This music was alive; it was breathing. It had undertones of New Wave and Punk, but it was neither. It soared to breathless heights, plummeted to low, dark places that chilled me, because I knew Gilly had composed them in Deadland.

The dead had returned to Atlanta, and they had brought something new.

Though Mick didn't know the songs by heart (we had to tape the pages to the back of a hutch hauled up in the elevator), he sang as if the music was being pulled right up from his soul.

People hearing the music from the streets filtered onto the roof, slowly forming an audience, and Mick fed off their energy. There was a nip in the air, but he was pouring sweat. On the street below more people congregated, craning their necks toward the sound. Others gathered on nearby rooftops, or watched out apartment windows. The applause grew louder with each song, until it sounded like we were at a rock concert in Mick's prime. Twenty years melted off Mick as he performed.

When the last note fell silent, a deafening roar filled the air, blocking out even the drone of the helicopters. The press rushed forward wielding microphones, but Mick pushed through them to reach Summer and me. The three of us came together in a hug.

Mick ruffled my hair; I could just hear him over the crowd. "You did it. He's gone."

I threw my fist in the air and hooted. For a few hours I'd been able to forget my own impending end, and, I thought, as I stood there with my fist in the air and remembered, it had been time well-spent.

CHAPTER 38

An hour later, Grandpa took over. I was grateful to the cosmos that I'd gotten a good four hours, enough to see Mick's glorious concert to the end. Now I returned to my own struggle, clinging to my body as Grandpa went about planning his new life.

I, on the other hand, went about planning my death.

If I was going to die, I decided I would at least choose the time and place. It wasn't an idle decision; I knew I would spend decades wherever I slipped out.

The idea of that, the hard truth of it, rattled me to the bones. My time was almost up.

I tried to calm myself so I could think, but all I could think about was that place where all of the color drains out of your eyes. I dragged my thoughts back to the matter at hand. Where did I want to be?

Gilly had been lucky, slipping back into Deadland on the roof, where his life's ambition had been realized.

It would be nice to have company. Maybe I could end up near Summer. It would be comforting to have Summer with me. I was further gone than her, though, so unless she made a point of dying in the same place as me, I couldn't make it work.

I'd much rather be outdoors. The thought of spending decades in an apartment, like Annie, depressed the hell out of me. Better to see trees, water.

Maybe the ocean.

It came to me with a clarity bordering on prescience. I should die beside Kayleigh, on that pier overlooking the ocean. It was perfect—twins reunited, the timeless ocean. There couldn't be much of Kayleigh left, but maybe there was something. We could mix and blow away together.

I pushed the image away. Thinking about it was like falling into a damp, dark well. That's what disturbed me most—being swept off a crumb at a time. I would be far more comfortable with an afterlife that involved staying whole.

I wasn't sure if this plan was even possible; Tybee Beach was a three-hour drive, if I drove like mad. I was getting three or four hours tops, and less each time.

If I was going to do it, I had to do it the next time I was in control. As Grandpa drank, cut-and-pasted strips, and began getting back in touch with a few of his old friends, I made a mental to-do list so when I next took control I could spring into action.

CHAPTER 39

I came back to myself, probably for the very last time. I was a little drunk. That was a good thing; it took the edge off the terror I felt, contemplating this as my last day on Earth. There was no turning back, though. I had decided. I grabbed a bottle of water and headed to the Maserati, praying I could make it to Tybee in time.

As I drove I had to keep wrapping my mind around what was transpiring. It was over. I couldn't believe it.

What would Grandpa do now? Would he live out his life claiming to be me, or insisting he was himself? Would he marry and father children? If he did father children, would I be the biological father, or would he? Imagining my body carrying on in the world without me was like trying to picture two objects occupying the same space. I was dying, and I was not.

Fifteen minutes into the trip I realized I had overlooked a painfully obvious detail. The quarantine. I rolled to a stop in front of a roadblock on I-75. A National Guardsman around my age, a pistol strapped at his waist, squatted as I lowered the electric window.

"Do you have transmittal papers?" he asked. Then his eyes brightened. "Hey, you're the Toy Shop guy."

I offered my hand through the window. "Finn Darby."

He turned as he shook, called, "Hey, it's the Toy Shop guy."

Another uniform-clad guard came over, a chubby woman in her twenties, carrying a rifle. "You draw Toy Shop?" she asked.

"I do, yeah," I said. "Listen." I propped an arm on the steering wheel and leaned out the window, trying to channel my inner Mick. "Can you help me out? I've got business I need to get to, but I don't have any papers." I held out my empty hands.

They looked at each other; the woman shrugged. Grinning, the guy said, "Will you draw a couple of Wolfies first?"

I sketched my last two Wolfies, asked my new friends their names, inscribed the drawings to them, and I was on my way.

Fame. It didn't suck. If only I was going to be around to enjoy it.

Ten minutes later I thought of something else that hadn't occurred to me while I was planning my swan song. Grandpa would turn right around and head back to the city as soon as he took control. He wasn't going to hang around the pier on Tybee for even a second to wait for me to exit. Even if I threw my car keys and wallet off the pier, it would make it harder for him to get home, but it wouldn't keep him on the pier.

For the thousandth time I silently cursed my son of a bitch grandfather. Then, on second thought, I cursed him out loud so he could hear me.

I needed to lock myself to a bench or something. Handcuffs would be perfect, but I didn't know where to buy them. I tried to picture the pier—were there benches? If not, the railing might work. Had it been made of metal or wood? If it was wood Grandpa might be able to knock the rail out where it was joined. The surest thing would be to lash myself to a piling under the pier, but then I'd be in the water…

An idea occurred to me. A sneaky idea. Heart hammering, I ran it over and over in my mind, examining it for flaws. When I couldn't find any I went over it again, deciding if I really wanted to do it, and if I had the guts.

Yes, and yes, I decided.

I called information and got the tide line for Tybee. High tide would be in six hours. Perfect.

There was a Home Depot near the exit to Forest Park. Tires squealing, I flew into the parking lot. Inside I jogged up the lock aisle and grabbed a twenty-foot-length of chain and their best padlock.

Back on the road, I brought up Summer's number, wondering if it would be Summer or Lorena who answered. I punched the number. The rings built one on top of another, then the familiar click as I was transferred to voicemail. I chuckled at the irony.

"Hi," I said after the beep. "Hi Lorena and Summer. I'm about out of time. I don't want to wonder each time I get a few hours if it will be my last, so I've decided to take matters into my own hands. I'm going to the spot where my sister died, and—" And what? Kill myself? That wasn't right. "I'm going to stay with Kayleigh. Summer—" I hesitated again, I didn't want Lorena to hear what I wanted to say. I decided it was too important to leave unsaid. "In a couple of weeks, if you find yourself in the same situation, maybe you'll decide to join me. I'm guessing Kayleigh won't be very good company by now. It would be nice to have a friend. My mother can show you where I am, if you decide to come." I choked up, as the weight of what I was doing hit me afresh. I would never see my mother again. "I love you, Lorena. I love you, Summer." The tears came in a flood. "Goodbye," I managed to choke before disconnecting.

I took a few deep breaths, wiped my eyes with the back of my wrist. I had more calls to make.

When I'd pulled myself together sufficiently I called Mick's land line. He answered on the second ring.

"Hey. I'm in the car."

"Where you headed?" Mick asked.

"Savannah. Tybee Island. I'm going to be with my sister."

He didn't say anything for a long time. Then, finally, in a strangled voice he said, "I'm sorry, mate. I'd trade places with you if I could. I swear I would."

"I know you would. Hey, my last months were so much better for knowing you. Thanks."

Mick took a minute to compose himself. "Same here." He sniffed. "Ah, Christ this is not fair."

"I know. I don't want to blow away and forget myself."

"I won't forget you, if that's any comfort."

"It is. Thanks." But I was way beyond comforting.

I told Mick I needed to call my mom. We said our final goodbye, and the phone went dead. I called Mom.

"Where are you?" she asked.

"Just taking a drive. Clearing my head." She'd understand why I didn't tell her the truth, once she got over the shock and grief. There was simply no way to spare her that grief, but I could delay it for a few hours.

"How are you doing?" she asked.

"Not so good, Mom. I don't think I can hang on much longer."

Mom sniffled into the phone. "I know you're trying, sweetie. Hang on." She took a big, shuddering breath. "He swears he can't help what's happening. Is that really true?"

I was tempted to lie, but if everything went as planned, I'd have the last laugh anyway. "Yes, I think he's telling the truth."

I wondered what it had been like for her, growing up with Tom Darby as her dad. She'd told me stories. Some of them were typical Grandpa, others surprised me. Grandpa used to take her fishing, just the two of them. And he spent money on her behind Grandma's back.

"Come and stay here with me for a while," Mom said.

"Maybe I will. I will, if I'm still here."

The Maserati's engine whined as I leaned on the gas even harder. Ahead there was nothing but grass, trees, and a line of concrete that disappeared in the distance.

Somehow Mom had managed to retain Grandma and Grandpa's

mental toughness without losing her warmth. She was kind of like Summer in that way.

"Mom, can I ask you something?"

"Anything, sweetie."

"Do you think Lorena was the right woman for me? Were we…I don't know, were we meant to be together?"

She blew out another big breath. "It's hard for me to say."

"Mom, just tell me. I want to know what you really think." I passed a big log truck like it was standing still.

"I love you. I love Lorena. You're both wonderful people."

"But."

"But I don't think she was perfect for you. She was the kite, and you held the string. You didn't get to do much of the flying."

Her words surprised me. I'd seen it; it wasn't like I hadn't, but I'd never thought it was a problem. "I'd always thought of myself as a string holder. I felt lucky to have such a fabulous kite."

Mom laughed at the metaphor. "You're not just a string holder, though. Sometimes you're a string holder, sometimes you're a kite. You're a good balance that way."

I wished Mom had met Summer. I wanted to ask if she thought Summer and I would have been a good match. I already knew the answer to that, though.

I wished I could tell Summer.

I didn't want to say goodbye, didn't want to face the empty car hurtling me toward my death, but we'd said what we needed to say. It was time to say goodbye, or raise Mom's suspicions.

When we hung up, the road was deathly quiet, save for the thunk of the tires running over the grooves in the pavement.

"I'll give up Toy Shop. Is that what you want? I'll bring Little Joe back. I'll print an apology and discontinue the strip."

No answer, of course.

I was back to bargaining, the third stage in the dying process. I hadn't realized you could move backward; I thought once you finished a stage that was it. I had been in the depression stage, and thought I'd been moving closer to acceptance with every mile I covered, but here I was bargaining again. Even if Grandpa had some control over what was happening, and all signs suggested he did not, why would he bargain now? He'd won. At least, he thought he'd won. I shut my mouth, resolved to follow this through in silence.

What was it Krishnapuma had written about dying? It had been strangely comforting when I read it.

You're not forgetting yourself, you're remembering. You're just a tiny sliver that has split off and forgotten it's part of something much bigger. This journey is about remembering. It's all part of the dance.

I sobbed. I didn't want to remember yet. In fifty years I might embrace it. Maybe it would be comforting to understand what was happening. But I had a lot of time left, or I was supposed to. Right now I didn't want to take the ultimate journey into the godhead; I wanted the mundane things, the day-to-day. My work. My friends. Summer.

I tried Summer again. Still got her voicemail. I pushed the Maserati harder.

CHAPTER 40

I barely recognized Tybee Beach. The seedy bars had been replaced by upscale surf shops, rooming houses by giant condos on stilts. Heart pounding, I sought familiar landmarks. The street names were no help; I didn't remember which street Grandpa's house had been on, and none of them were familiar.

A cold ocean wind cut through my leather jacket as I trotted up and down the boardwalk clutching a Home Depot bag, past bicycle rental kiosks and custard stands, all shuttered for the winter. Piers jutted over the grey water every tenth of a mile or so, abandoned save for the occasional weekend fisherman. They all looked the same.

I tried to reel myself back to the days when this boardwalk was a second home to Kayleigh and me. We'd fly kites here—triangular black bats with long yellow tails. Once we'd built a fort underneath the wood planks and giggled as people walked by, unaware of us. We lived on French fries and fried dough served on paper plates, salt-water taffy that stuck to the paper wrappers.

Was she still under that pier? Where was that pier? I could see it so clearly in my mind's eye, but I had no idea where along the beach it was. I scanned the boardwalk.

Beyond an ice cream shop, a patch of open space caught my eye. It was a miniature golf course with a pirate theme. The neon sign—Blackbeard Golf—was new, but the course wasn't. Grandpa's rooming house had been on the street directly behind Blackbeard Golf, the pier fifty yards to the left down the boardwalk.

"I bet you recognized it long before I did," I whispered. I slowed, my steps thudding hollowly on the wood planks. The cold ocean wind reminded me of the wind in Deadland, the wind that worked on you like sandpaper.

We had the pier all to ourselves. Green wooden benches lined the low railing on both sides, with ornate lampposts running along the center. The benches were familiar but I was sure the lampposts were a recent addition. The pier stretched out fifty yards or so, the planks thinning to lines.

When I reached the end of the pier I looked into the white water crashing against posts covered in green slime. Anyone passing would have seen a lone man, but there were three of us here. At least. Who could say how many souls had drowned off this pier?

Who could say how many more would follow?

I backtracked off the pier, found stairs leading down to the beach. Hunched against the cold wind, I following the knobby beams, canted this way and that, supporting the pier.

I stopped at the edge of the surf, watched a little white bird race in and out with the waves, plucking unseen things from under the wet sand.

There was no point in putting it off; every minute increased the chance that Grandpa would take over and wreck my plans. I pushed into the foamy white water. It was freezing.

"You want to play, old man? Let's play."

It was my body. I could do what I wanted with it.

A wave rolled in. I turned sideways and set my feet; it crashed into my thigh with numbing force. I surged on, my teeth chattering, exhaling in breathless puffs until I reached the end of the pier. The water was waist-deep.

I pulled out the chain and padlock, allowed the waves to sweep away the plastic bag.

The tug of the surf was so powerful I could barely keep my footing as I pressed my back to a post, fumbled with the chains, wrapping them around and around, lashing myself to the post, my hands throbbing, my toes numb.

"How do you like me now, you old bastard?" I shouted, my throat raw. It wouldn't be murder. No one would blame me. I pulled the chain tight, pushed the padlock through two links and snapped it closed. Clutching the key I tested my work; I squatted, jumped, pulled, squeezed. The chains held tight—there was no way he could break free.

I tossed the key into the water, watched it disappear with a tiny plunk.

It wasn't a perfect plan. Someone might come along the beach and call the police. If I was still in control I would wave them off, tell them it was one of those charity things—that I had to stay chained to the post until my friends donated a thousand dollars for cerebral palsy research. I would tell them who I was. Hey, I'm sort of famous, I'm allowed to do crazy things.

For the first time, though, I was hoping Grandpa would take over sooner rather than later. The plan was for me to be long gone by the time the tide came in and this freezing water filled my lungs. Once Grandpa took over he'd call for help. Hopefully no one would hear him, or they wouldn't be able to cut him loose in time. Then the three of us would blow away together, with me chuckling until my mouth was gone. If not, if he made it out, then bully for him, he would win another fifty years of life.

"Eighty-six years you had. You couldn't let it go at that. You had to take my years, too."

My phone rang. I fished it out of my jacket.

"Where are you?" It was Summer.

"The beach." I left out the part about being waist-deep in the water, chained to a post.

"What beach? What are you doing at the beach?"

"Didn't you get my message?"

"I saw you called, but I didn't listen to the message. I can barely hear you."

"I'm right near the water. I'm at the pier where Kayleigh died." I swallowed a lump in my throat. "I'm going to stay here with her."

There was a long pause. Then I thought I heard sniffing.

"In the phone message I invited you to join me if you ran out of time."

Summer laughed spasmodically through her tears. "That's very thoughtful of you." I heard the blubbering of a nose being blown. "God damn it Finn, don't quit yet. We still have time."

"You do," I said. "I'm out of time. I want to choose where I end up, you know?"

Another long pause. "I'm scared. I don't want to be alone."

"You're not. Lean on Mick. He'll stick by—"

The snakes ran under my skin; pain and cold receded. At the last instant it occurred to me that Grandpa could simply call 911 with the damned phone I was clutching. I strained to open my trembling hand.

The phone plopped into the water.

"You stupid son of a bitch," Grandpa shouted a moment later. He threw one shoulder forward, then the other. "You must have slipped an extra key into your pocket when I wasn't..." He fumbled through the pockets he could reach, although I had no idea how he thought I could sneak something into a pocket without him noticing. "Ah, God, you stupid asshole."

I rotated toward the doorway in the back of my head one last time, and Grandpa's ranting grew dim, then was snuffed out by the sound of the wind as my new home rolled into view. I hadn't had to strain at all this time, as if Deadland was welcoming me with open arms.

I squeezed out of my body like I was greased, dropped into the surf, and stuck there. I'd half-expected the water to wash me toward shore; I'd forgotten how still this world was. The water was a still-life, the whitecaps sculptures made of cottage cheese.

I'd never felt so alone.

I'd have Grandpa for company soon, though. We'd have plenty of time to work through our differences. I was almost looking forward to it.

I rotated to face the horizon, which was beautiful in a stark, grey metal way. The sky flickered like an old-time film of a sky.

Not so bad, Annie had said. Maybe it got better.

There was no sign of Kayleigh. Here and there in the shallows half-submerged dead were visible; a few lay on the beach like sleeping sunbathers. The wind carried snippets of their mutterings to me.

Deal. It's a deal.

She sold sandwiches outside the gate.

I held phantom hands in front of my face, looked closely, saw flecks of myself whisking off.

How long should I hold out hope that Summer might join me? A month, maybe? I would have to keep track of the days so I would know when to abandon hope. Were there days here?

Don't drop the baton. Baton.

Sisyphus.

The mindless words of the dead seemed to be all around me. I would start talking like that soon. It was part of the emptying out. All of the words came out of you. Everything came out of you.

The correct answer was cartel.

Try to be nice.

Finn would know.

I jolted from my stupor. I listened more intently, praying I hadn't misheard, straining to hear one voice amidst dozens.

Get the red one? The red one. Red.

She wanted the red bike, didn't want to get a girl color. It had to be her. My sister was here.

"Kayleigh?" No answer.

Anxiously I studied each of the dead in turn. None was Kayleigh, unless she was one of the unrecognizable lumps.

Can you draw me?

I was locked in on her voice now; the rest had receded into the background.

Too high.

Too high. Yes, it was. I looked up at the underside of the pier, at the worn beams high overhead. She shouldn't have tried it. I shouldn't have either.

"Kayleigh? It's Finn. It's your brother." She was close, I could feel it. I looked all around, leaned forward to peer up beyond the railing. Nothing.

Maybe she was under the water? It didn't seem possible I would hear her so clearly if she was underwater, but who knew what the rules were in this place? I ducked my head under.

There was no resistance, no sense of getting wet. I looked around.

I was nearly standing on what was left of Kayleigh.

She was on her belly, her wrists cradling her chin like a sunbather. So much of her was worn away that she was almost two-dimensional, a wafer-thin slice of Kayleigh. Her eyes, nose, and ears were gone, but her mouth was there, so close to the sandy floor she was almost kissing it.

"It's Finn." I had no trouble speaking.

Kayleigh gave no sign she heard me. After a moment she sighed, said, What are you writing?

Mom used to call her a question machine.

The nubs of her feet were clinging to legs worn to points, the tips of her white Reeboks visible. The feet would drop off soon.

No fatigue or stiffness grew in my joints as I stayed bent over, my head underwater, and listened to Kayleigh, soaking up each utterance, trying to set it in a place and time and context. A lot was from her last days, and each of those was painfully familiar. I'd gone back over those last days so often after she died, combing my memory for important things we might have shared, regretting even the slightest of slights I had made.

Too high Grandpa. Don't want to.

Too high, Grandpa? When would she have said that? Climbing a high slide at a playground or something.

I craned my neck to look up through the cloudy water at the pier, pictured Kayleigh up there, legs dangling over the railing, over the black water. It was hard to picture her out there, all alone in the growing dark, leaping into that booming surf. There would be no witnesses, no one to attest to her fearless leap. If she was going to jump, why not wait until I was there? I imagined coming back from having fried clams with my parents, Kayleigh pushing open the screen door as soon as we pulled up, shouting that she'd done it, she'd done the jump. My twelve-year-old self's first reaction would be, No way; no way you jumped in the dark. Acts of daring demanded a witness.

It's too high, Kayleigh repeated.

I looked up at the pier again.

Too high, Grandpa?

I imagined Grandpa holding the screen door open for Kayleigh, following right behind her, his jaw set but a satisfied smirk just under the surface. The lass did it, I saw her. I'm her witness.

You're not so great—your sister did it too. You're still afraid of the dark, afraid of the spooky road. Nothing but a God damned sissy.

Leave me alone or I'll tell them a thing or two, Grandma had said. And hadn't Grandpa mostly left her alone after that? He knew where she was, but he steered clear.

If my heart had still been in my chest, if I'd still had a chest, it would have been hammering my ribs. All the guilt I'd felt, thinking she'd gone out there and died alone because of me. Had he been there? Had he egged her on? He was always looking for opportunities to teach us to be tough, to suck it up and take our lumps.

Grandpa, Lorena, all the rest of the dead who couldn't stay dead had some gnawing reason to hang on, to hold themselves together in the teeth of this hungry wind. Suddenly I did as well. I wanted to know the truth.

Inching my way right up against the post, I felt the vacuum pull of my body. I reached for it with outstretched arms, imploring my body to take me in one last time. The pull was weak, more like a bathtub drain than a vacuum. I repositioned myself, inched side to side, forward and back.

"Come on. Come on." I splayed my fingers, managed to rise half an inch before dropping back. "Shit." I sensed that the pull was going to weaken as time went by—my best chance was now. I reached again, stretching my phantom arms until they seemed to dislocate from their sockets. I rose and dropped, bump, bump, bump.

I tried for half an hour, but it was no use. The suction wasn't powerful enough. I lowered my arms and listened to the muttering of the dead, trying to think of another way to get back in my body.

Krishnapuma had written that this was not a physical realm but a supernatural one. The dead didn't protect themselves from the wind by hiding behind a wall, they held themselves together because they didn't want to come apart. Maybe I had to want it more.

Why did I want to live?

I wanted to know if Grandpa had been there. If he had, I wanted others to know. I wanted my mother to know.

Partly I wanted this out of spite. If Grandpa had been there when Kayleigh died I wanted him to look my mother in the eye and admit it. If he was going to steal my body I wanted him to stand in front of my mother in it and mumble an apology, nineteen years too late.

My fingers tingled as the pull strengthened.

If I wasn't completely to blame for Kayleigh's death, I wanted to be released from some of the guilt that gnawed at me. If I was due a little peace in death, I wanted it.

My arms stretched like salt water taffy; the rest of me lifted, swung like a bell.

If Kayleigh was not a reckless idiot who'd snuck off in the dark on her own and leapt off a pier, if an adult she trusted had been there, maybe even encouraged her, I sure as hell wanted people to know that.

I flew up suddenly, pulled through an invisible hole.

"—don't have a choice in this?" Grandpa was shouting as I snapped back behind my eyes. "I didn't come here of my own free will. I didn't squeeze my way inside you with a switchblade and a can of WD-40. There are bigger forces at work. Can't you see that?"

"Help!" he called, his voice ragged. His whole body was trembling uncontrollably with the cold.

The water was up to his chest. A wave rushed in; Grandpa turned his face as foamy water slapped his cheek, leaving him gasping.

I would have given anything to have my mouth long enough to ask him: Were you there? Did you goad her into it?

Grandpa threw his weight against the chains, shouted for help again. My shirt was nothing but rags; bloody scrapes crisscrossed my chest and belly. "You have no idea, what I had to go through. Working fourteen-hour days when I was twelve. Crossing over in the bottom of a boat sharing a potato sack for a blanket with the rats. You've no idea what it's like to be down so low the dogs won't have nothing to do with you."

What could I do if I got back into my body that Grandpa wasn't already doing? Could I slide the chains up the post, try to rise above the water? I doubted it—the chains were wound tight.

Someone called my name. I thought it was Kayleigh, beckoning me back. But it had come from the beach.

Grandpa twisted to look toward the beach.

Summer was wading toward us, her arms raised out of the water.

"Help me," Grandpa called. "For God's sake, help me."

Summer paused, lifted a phone to her ear. She was calling 911. When she finished she rushed out the last twenty yards.

"You stupid ass. What did you do?"

"I didn't do anything," Grandpa shouted over the crashing waves.

"It was that idiot Finn."

"I wasn't talking to you," Summer said. She examined the chains pressed to the post, then grasped the lock and tugged at it. "Where's the key?" A wave broke over her shoulders; she clung to the chains to keep from being knocked backward.

Grandpa motioned toward the water with his chin. "He tossed it."

"Oh, that's just great." She swiped wet hair out of her eyes.

The howl of a siren rose in the distance. Summer looked toward the sound. "Hang on. I'll be right back."

The siren grew louder.

"Thank goodness your friend there isn't as stupid as you," Grandpa said. He laughed. "You're not so bright. Next time don't tell your girlfriend where you're going to bury the body before you've even bought the shovel."

Soon Summer was back, leading three fire fighters in big rubber boots. One of them had an ax. Shouting to each other, they waded out.

"You okay?" one of them asked. She was a big woman with acne-scarred cheeks.

Grandpa said he was. The firewoman signaled her buddy with the ax, then took a step back. I heard the ax hit the post, then the chains loosened all at once, sagging around my waist. The fire fighters lifted Grandpa, carried him to the beach where two EMS workers were waiting with a stretcher and blankets.

"I'm fine. Just put me down." Grandpa struggled to rise as the fire fighters set him on the stretcher.

"Look at his hands," one of the EMS guys said, holding the blankets up like a shield and backing away.

"Oh, shit," the lead firewoman said, jerking her hands away as if Grandpa was scalding hot. She looked at Summer. "What the hell is going on?"

"Why the hell are you asking her?" Grandpa asked, sitting upright. "Give me a blanket, will you? I'm freezing to death."

The firewoman kept her eyes on Summer.

"This is Thomas Darby," Summer said, gesturing toward Grandpa. "He's pushing his grandson, Finn Darby, out of his body."

"The cartoonist?" one of the EMS workers interrupted.

"Yes, the cartoonist. Evidently Finn decided if he couldn't keep his body, his grandfather wasn't going to have it either."

Everyone just stared.

"Somebody give me a blanket," Grandpa said.

"For God's sake, give him a blanket. He's not going to bite." Summer yanked the blankets out of the EMS worker's hands, draped one over Grandpa's shoulders, dropped the other across his lap.

Clutching the blanket around his shoulders, Grandpa stood. "Well, I'm going home."

The emergency workers looked at each other, uncertain. Clearly they didn't relish rushing a hitcher to the hospital.

"What's to stop him from going right back out there?" the firewoman asked Summer.

Summer looked at the sand. "I don't think he's in there any more."

"You don't think who is in there?" one of the men asked warily.

"Finn Darby."

From the look on his face, the guy who'd asked the question was still confused.

"You'll make sure this one gets home okay?" the firewoman asked.

Summer nodded. She took Grandpa by the elbow.

CHAPTER 41

The ride home in the Maserati was awkward. Summer and Grandpa didn't have much to talk about. Not that I could concentrate on what they were doing. It took all of my energy just to stay in my body, like trying to hold a long series of numbers in my head while clinging to a windowsill.

Mick had been half an hour behind Summer, who lived further south and hadn't wanted to wait for Mick. He'd turned around when Summer called with the news, and now he was ahead of us.

We were nearly home when Lorena took over. Her hands made for a jerky ride, but she managed.

"This is so messed up," she said. "I died and left you here alone. Now I'm coming back and you're—"

Barely hanging on. It was becoming excruciating. If I could hang on long enough, surely I would eventually get flipped back into the driver's seat.

"Are you even there?" Lorena asked. "I'm so afraid you've already left me."

"Oh, he's still there," Grandpa said.

Lorena glanced over at him. "How would you know that?"

Grandpa opened the glove compartment and retrieved a pack of cigarettes he'd stashed there. He engaged the car lighter, took his time unwrapping the cellophane and peeling back the silver foil. Lorena kept glancing over at him, waiting for an answer.

"When all this is sorted out, you're the one who's going to be around for me to sue," Grandpa finally said.

"How do you know—"

"Because you can feel it," Grandpa interrupted. "I felt him go when we were in the water, and I felt him come back. I know just what it feels like because he did it once before, only then I didn't realize what it was." He lit the cigarette with palsied hands, then muttered, "If I'd known what it was I wouldn't have gone back for a piss, and I'd be done with him." He exhaled a plume of smoke through his nose, pointed through the windshield at the turn up ahead. "Drop me at my house."

"The hell I will. I'm going to Mick's. If you don't want to be there you can walk home."

Grandpa glared at her. "We're in the same situation, you and me. From what I can see the little miss you're crowding out doesn't like it any better than Finn, and I don't have any more choice than you."

"I didn't burn down her apartment. I didn't try to bankrupt her."

"She didn't steal—" Grandpa paused, because the shift back to me had started. I cried out with relief as I came back into my body.

"Get me to Aunt Julia's house," I said to Lorena. "Fast. Like my life depends on it."

CHAPTER 42

Mom answered the door. She held it partway closed, looking ragged and depressed, as I stood in the rain.

"I have to see Grandma," I said.

"Who has to see her?"

I held my hands in front of her face. "It's Finn. If it was Grandpa my hands would be shaking."

"Oh God, Finn, I'm sorry." She let the door swing open and called to Grandma.

For once Grandma didn't even pretend to be happy to see me. She sat on the edge of Aunt Julia's sofa while Mom took the love seat. That left an uncomfortable antique wooden chair for me.

I looked at Grandma; she looked at her hands. "I need to ask you something, and I need you to tell me the truth."

Grandma didn't respond; no nervous laughter, no offer of a cup of tea. Her wrinkled fingers worked furiously, as if she were darning invisible socks.

"I talked to Kayleigh," I said.

Grandma's fingers froze. She lifted her eyes and looked at me as

Mom started to cry.

"God, leave Kayleigh out of this," Mom said.

"She said she wasn't alone on the pier that night," I said, speaking over Mom.

Grandma put her palm over her mouth, shook her head. "I don't know what—"

"She told me to say she was counting on you." I struggled to find words that would burrow into Grandma's conscience. "That she loved you and trusted you. She begged you to tell the truth." I knew I was out on a limb, but if I was wrong, what did I have to lose?

A tear dropped from the corner of Grandma's eye and vanished into the creases in her cheeks. She turned her head away, covered her face like a child playing peek-a-boo.

My heart rate doubled. I wasn't wrong. "It's time, Grandma. You've carried it long enough," I said.

"What are you—" Mom started, but I motioned her to silence. We waited.

Finally, Grandma let her hands drop. Her entire face was quivering. "I was the one who had to tell you about poor Kayleigh. It was the hardest thing I've ever done." She looked at my mom. "I dialed your number and put the phone to his mouth. I told him he had to do it—he had to tell you, but he jerked his head away and whispered, "'I wasn't there. Do you understand me? I wasn't there.'"

Mom was shaking her head slowly, her mouth open. She wasn't following.

"He made me lie, because he was afraid you'd never forgive him."

"Forgive him for what?" Mom asked.

I wanted to jump in and save Grandma from having to say it, but it had to come from her.

"He…" She trailed off, her voice trembling.

In the kitchen, Aunt Julia's cuckoo clock went off. We waited through six utterly incongruous cuckoos.

"He was at the pier that night. With Kayleigh."

Mom leapt to her feet. "What?"

I leaned toward Grandma, my heart thumping. "It was his idea to go. Wasn't it?"

Grandma nodded.

I knew it. I could almost hear him. Come on, get your suit on. We're going back to the pier.

All this time, he let me think it was my fault. I'd spent twenty years carrying his guilt for him.

My heart was racing so fast the corners of my vision went grey; for a moment I thought I was going to pass out. I'd come so close to never knowing.

I came back to myself to find Mom in my face, trembling with rage. "You son of a bitch." She grabbed the front of my shirt and shook me. "Get out here. I want to hear it from you. I want you to look me in the eye and tell me why my daughter is dead." She slapped my face. It felt marvelous, because I knew it was meant for him. "And now you're going to take my son?" Mom lifted my hand, examined it, saw that it wasn't trembling and let it drop. I wanted her to hit me again, wanted her to curl up her fist and punch me in the eye. I didn't care that I was the one who was feeling it; he was in there watching. The lying bastard. Give him one for Kayleigh. Better yet, go get a knife from the kitchen.

A blush of triumph washed through me. You want to play, old man? I'm not twelve any more. I almost wanted him to come out now; I wanted to watch him face the truth. I felt light as a cork bobbing on water. Like an airship that snapped its tethers and was rising into the blue sky. I felt as strong as The Hulk.

Then I realized why.

You can feel it, Grandpa had said. I felt him go when we were in the water, and I felt him come back.

I couldn't be sure, yet somehow I was.

"Jesus, he's gone," I whispered. I looked at my mother.

She studied me for a moment, then nodded, as if Grandpa needed her permission to go. "Good." She sniffed, wiped her eyes on her sleeve.

Then she seemed to fully grasp what it meant. She laughed, and grabbed my head and pulled it to her. I put my arms around her waist and squeezed.

We stayed like that for a long moment. When Mom finally let go, she turned to face Grandma, who lifted her chin, her eyes glassy but free of tears. "What good would it have done to tell you once he was gone? All it would've done is cause more pain."

"That wasn't for you to decide," Mom said. "Jesus, can't you see that?"

Unable to hold eye contact with Mom, Grandma looked toward the TV, which was off. Nothing good on.

We waited for some response from her, but none came. I could understand why Mom was angry at Grandma, but I wasn't sure what I felt. I was too relieved to care. Maybe later I'd hate her for it, or more likely pity her, but suddenly my entire future was stretched in front of me. There was no need to say goodbye to my friends, my family.

Although that wasn't completely true. I went to the window, pulled back the thick curtain and looked at Lorena waiting in the Maserati. Or was it Summer? No, through the blur of the rain-streaked windshield I could see her putting on lipstick, clutching it with two hands to steady the shaking. It was Lorena.

I turned back to Mom. "I have to go. I have to help Summer. And Lorena. I'll call you soon."

Mom hugged me. "I'm sorry," she said in my ear.

I pulled back to look at her. "For what?"

"I always blamed you."

A lump rose in my throat, thinking of what was left of Kayleigh with her wafer-thin sneakers, still talking about her red bike.

"It was still partly my fault," I said

Mom squeezed my arms, shook me slightly. "No, it wasn't. You were just a kid."

It's never that easy, though. That I was a kid wouldn't bring Kayleigh back. There are no do-overs. At least, there aren't supposed to be.

The screen door gave a cheap aluminum screech as it closed behind me. Lorena looked up, smiled hopefully with Summer's mouth.

"What did you find out?"

I found out that hitchers can't leave even if they want to, if in their heart of hearts they want to stay. But if they lose that desire, they slip away like they were buttered.

I thought I knew how to free Summer.

I slid into the driver's seat.

"Well?" Lorena said.

I considered lying. Would it hurt Summer's chances if Lorena knew how I had overcome Grandpa? Would she see that the conversation I was having with her was an attempt to send her back as well?

I'd never lied to Lorena, and my instincts were that now wasn't the time to start. The truth I needed to speak, if I could muster the strength to speak it, was bad enough without preceding it with lies.

"What's the matter with you?" Lorena asked.

I clasped my hands behind my neck, pulled my elbows together. "I'm struggling with something. I don't know how to say it."

Lorena smiled uneasily, her eyebrows knitted. "Okay."

For a moment I was back on that riverbank, holding Lorena's body, her shoes smoking, her eyes open and empty. How could I possibly do this?

I took a deep, shaky breath. "Grandpa is gone."

Lorena inhaled excitedly, leaping forward in her seat. "Oh God, Finn. That's…" She pressed her palms against her face, shook her head. "I can't believe it." She grabbed my hands and squeezed them. "You're sure?"

"I'm positive."

Lorena threw her head back, shook her fists and howled with joy.

I gently grasped one of her wrists. She stopped. "What's the matter? Why aren't you happy?"

Was she imagining we would pick up where we left off on the canoe trip, that I could look into Summer's eyes and see only Lorena, as if Summer had never existed?

"Because it's not just about me." I pointed at her heart. "Summer is in there, hanging on for dear life. She has a daughter. She has dreams, and plans. She's courageous. Kind down to her bones." Lorena was shaking her head, forming her answer. "Summer doesn't deserve what's happening to her."

Lorena pressed a hand to her chest. "I'm not trying to take that away. I can't help—" She stopped. She studied my face. I turned and watched my mother and Grandma through Aunt Julia's window.

"Why didn't I see it before?" Lorena said, studying my profile. "How could I have missed it?" She touched the side of my face. "You're in love with her."

I cupped my hand over my mouth, stared at the grit worked into the creases in the leather steering wheel. I was relieved that she had said it, so I didn't have to. I knew I would never forgive myself for admitting this to Lorena. But if I denied it and Summer was dumped into Deadland, I would also never forgive myself, and Summer would die.

Lorena's voice got low, almost inaudible, like she was talking to herself. "I did see it; of course I did. I just didn't want to admit it. The way you look at her, the lingering eye contact. You used to look at me that way, now I only see it when I'm behind her eyes. When I'm here you're looking everywhere but at me."

I opened my mouth to speak, but couldn't find words.

"Look at me," Lorena croaked.

I swallowed thickly, turned to Lorena. It hurt.

"You're in love with her." Lorena's eyes squeezed closed. "I can't believe it. I've lost you."

I wanted to rush in and fill her with assurances that I still loved her, that I didn't deserve her, that I never deserved her.

"I'm sorry," I whispered.

She took a gasping breath, tried to get hold of herself. "I don't understand. What happened?"

It had only been two years since I last saw Lorena, but when you reach into Deadland, two years becomes two hundred. The memory of love can last a lifetime, but actually loving someone who was dead—who is dead? That's something else entirely.

"You died," I said. "We had our chance, and we blew it. We let you get killed."

She nodded slowly, wiped her cheek, the back of her hand coming away slick. "So are you saying if we can't help what's happening, you don't want to be with me? You want a divorce?"

"We're not married," I said as gently as I could. I put my hand over hers. "You died, Lorena."

She drew her hand away, set it on her lap. "I forget sometimes." The rain got harder, pelting the windshield. I half-expected it to turn to hail. I watched it make tracks down the windshield.

It occurred to me that Summer was hearing all this. I'd momentarily forgotten. I wondered what she was thinking, whether she had feelings for me, and if I'd ever know.

"You always said you weren't good enough for me, always insisted you loved me more than I loved you," Lorena said. "But it wasn't true; I always loved you more than you loved me."

"Loved. Not love. Don't you see? And I did love you, with all my heart."

There was a pink envelope, the kind that held a greeting card, wedged between Lorena's thigh and Summer's purse. I hadn't noticed it before. Now she slid it into the purse.

"What's that?" I asked, though I already knew. Lorena was always giving me I Love You cards—the kind that show couples walking on the beach holding hands.

"Did you really love me once?" Lorena asked, ignoring my question.

Was it a mistake to admit I had? Did I have to pummel Lorena the way Mom and I had pummeled Grandpa before he finally lost his grip?

I imagined Lorena, blowing away in Deadland, alone with her thoughts, without even memories of someone who loved her for comfort.

I started to cry. I'd been doing my best, trying to stay strong, taking deep, slow breaths. But this was too much. This was Lorena, my wife. "Of course I did," I said.

She pondered for a moment. "But then I died. And now you love her."

Was that unfair? At that point I couldn't say.

Eventually I stopped crying, and we sat frozen for a long time, both of us staring through the windshield. Grandma sat stiffly in the living room. Mom was nowhere to be seen. The rain let up, settling into a soft drizzle.

It must have been twenty minutes later when Lorena finally spoke.

"I don't belong here," she whispered. "My sister won't talk to me. My own mother is terrified of me. My husband loves someone else. I'm dead to everyone."

I sat there wishing Grandpa would come back and take my place so I wouldn't have to endure the howling sadness tearing through me.

"I don't belong here," Lorena whispered again.

The trembling in her hands stopped, then started again, then stopped. She covered her ears as if against the boom of some terrific explosion, then turned to me.

"I feel so strange. Like there's a hole inside me."

"Summer?"

She nodded.

"She's gone," I said. "That's what you're feeling."

Summer's face scrunched up and she started to cry. I leaned over to console her; she pressed her face into my shoulder and cried harder. I'd like to think a small part of her crying was sadness for Lorena, but I didn't ask.

CHAPTER 43

What does a four-panel finale to a life's work look like? It was harder than I thought, I realized, as I tapped my sharpened pencil on the desk.

I had gone through half a dozen ideas and discarded them all. Pay tribute to Thomas Darby, the strip's creator? Even now I didn't have it in me to do that. Not sincerely.

A note of explanation to my readers, who would be disappointed? My agent and the syndicate certainly were. Some sort of tribute to those readers? I couldn't think of a way to do it without being wincingly schmaltzy.

The Bill Watterson route, where the characters move on, but on a happy, hopeful note? That in no way reflected the truth behind the strip, the emotional tug-of-war between my grandfather and me, both before his death and after.

I had mixed emotions about the strip. The success I'd found with it would likely always be the high point in my professional life. For better or worse, I would always be remembered for Wolfie, would always be connected to Toy Shop. At the same time, Grandpa had been right: I had no right to take it. I had violated a man's dying wish, and I'd gotten caught. I was probably the first person in history who could honestly say that. But even if Grandpa had stayed dead, I had no right.

Chances were that I wouldn't die in Aunt Julia's living room, in which case I would never have the chance to tell Grandpa that Toy Shop had crossed over into Deadland, if a bit later than he'd wished. Hopefully Grandpa was finding it easier to let go of this world, and would be long gone by the time I crossed over in any case.

Toy Shop was crossing over into Deadland. The thought sparked an idea. What better ending for a strip that was so intimately tied to that world?

It was dark, but it felt right. Some hitchers were here to stay, and we were going to have to learn to live with them. We were also going to have to come to terms with Deadland. While the TV newscasters had been racing around asking the dead a series of disconnected stream-of-consciousness questions, Amy Harmon, a New York Times journalist, had focused on one issue: the nature of Deadland. Her meticulous account, "Where We Go When We Die," had hit the newsstands and Internet yesterday, and caused a worldwide furor. Many were decrying it a pile of lies, but the shrillness and panic in the tone of these naysayers was telling. Even they seemed to understand that there was no stifling this new order. The uncertainty of life after death had always terrorized us, now it was replaced by a new terror—the certainty of it, of what it was.

What better way to cope with fear than to laugh at it?

I put up my materials, grabbed my keys, and headed out to the Maserati. It looked absurdly out of place in the parking lot of Summit Pointe, my new home in Decatur, just east of the city.

The Maserati leapt out of the parking space as soon as I touched the pedal. It occurred to me that Mick would look more natural in this sort of car than I. I would have given it to him, if not for Lorena. There were yellow roses set on the dash. I wasn't sure she could see them—I still wasn't clear how closely things in the real world translated in Deadland—but I hoped she could.

From my new place it was only a ten-minute-drive to Summer's apartment. The Maserati seemed even more absurd in her complex, surrounded by rusting Grand Marquises and trucks propped on blocks.

I rang the bell; inside I heard the pathetic buzzing thunk that reminded me the bell didn't work. I rapped on the door.

Summer was wearing black jeans and a bright tie-dyed t-shirt sporting Elvis's face.

"Hey," she said, pushing the screen door open to let me in.

Suddenly I was nervous. Until now I'd always had a reason for calling.

She sat on the couch, propped one foot on the coffee table. "I've got to go to my new job in a half hour, but I'm glad you stopped by. I was going to call you. How are you?"

"I'm good. Mostly I've spent the past two days on the couch. Being lashed to a piling for four hours can be tiring."

She shook her head, laughed.

"What?"

"I still can't believe you did that. I wish I could have seen the look on Grampie's face in that moment when he first came out."

"Oh, he was pissed."

"I imagine he's still pissed."

I laughed, but it came out as more of a pained grunt. I wasn't sure I could ever go to Aunt Julia's house again, knowing he was right there, probably on Julia's couch, staring at the oil painting of Julia's late, beloved Chihuahua Petey that hung on the opposite wall.

Summer sprung up, headed for the kitchen. "You want anything? I need some water. I'm nervous about this new job."

"You'll be great. Plus Mick will have told everyone about the role you played in saving him, so they'll all love you from the start."

"I guess. How's the rescue effort going?"

"Okay." I waggled my hand. "I thought I'd be spending most of my time trying to help people dump their hitchers, but a lot of the time they've got me coaching other volunteers. I don't know how many we'll be able to save. Time's ticking."

"I feel guilty that I haven't stepped up to volunteer."

"Nah. You put in your time with the dead. You've earned a little respite." It was strange. Summer was acting like she hadn't heard me tell Lorena that I was in love with her. I wasn't sure what I'd been expecting. A passionate embrace in the doorway? Summer and her daughter on my doorstep, suitcases in hand? To me it felt like my confession was a big, honking presence in the room. At the same time, as I sat there, I knew down to my bones that it was true,

I was in love with her. I wanted to know if she felt the same, but didn't know how to ask.

"So, Rebecca's in school?"

"Yeah. It's good to have her back."

I nodded. "I bet." I went on nodding, not sure what to say next.

Summer tilted her head, broke into a crooked smile. "You okay?"

I was tempted to just bring it up, but chickened out. "Yeah, I'm fine." Even to me my voice sounded strained.

"Sooo," Summer rolled her eyes to one side, made a popping sound with her lips. "There's nothing you want to ask me?"

I looked into her eyes, searching for where she was going with this. She smiled, shrugged.

"Um, can you help me out here?" I asked. "There are a lot of things I want to ask you, but I'm having trouble figuring out how to dive in."

Summer's smile grew wider. "Well, I just thought you might have come over to ask me out. You know—dinner, or a movie. Maybe mini golf."

I felt my chest loosen with relief. Yes, that was a fine place to start. "I did indeed come over for just that reason," I said without missing a beat. I cleared my throat. "Would you go to dinner with me? With maybe a quick stop at the French Impressionist room at the High beforehand?"

Summer gave me a big, emphatic nod. "I'd love to. When?"

"Tonight, if that's not too presumptuous?"

"Not at all. Tonight it is." She put her finger to her lips. "No, wait, we're going to Mick's tonight, remember?"

"Right." How could I have forgotten? Only asking Summer out for the first time could have blanked my mind like that. "Can I pick you up? We could go together."

"Absolutely."

She looked at her watch. "Ooh, I need to get going." She held out her hand, soliciting a boost off the couch. "Walk me to my car?"

I took her hand, pulled her forward, holding my ground so we came face to face. I needed to get it out in the open, and this seemed like a good time. "What I said about you to Lorena? Normally I wouldn't blurt out something like that before we'd even been on a date, you know? I feel a little weird."

Summer took my other hand. "It's okay, you don't have to feel weird. I thought maybe you just said it to save me." She shrugged, quickly added, "Which would be fine."

"No, I pretty much meant it."

She gave me a mock-questioning look. "Pretty much?"

"No." I wrapped my arms around her waist. "Delete the 'pretty much' part. Leave the rest."

This seemed like a good time to kiss her, so I did.

#